Dear Reader:

Mail-order bride... intrigued us. What ~~would~~ across the country to marry a man she had never seen before? Did these women find happiness? What were the unexpected consequences? When I asked three authors to create mail-order bride stories, it turned out that the reasons they picked for their women marrying strangers were as individual as the writers themselves.

In HEARTS ARE WILD (April 1993) by Teresa Hart, deLacey Honeycutt is a clever female card sharp who is down on her luck. Desperate to get enough train fare to once again gamble with gentlemen in their private cars, she signs up with a mail-order bride agency only to get a free train ticket. Unfortunately, she runs across the very man she was expected to marry—with unforeseen consequences.

SWEPT AWAY (August 1993) by Jean Anne Caldwell is a delightful story about a girl who can't quite make up her mind whether she wants to go through with a marriage to a stranger . . . so she pretends to be the maid who is hired through the mail, not the bride. Of course she is soon unmasked.

SCOUNDREL (January 1994) by Pamela Litton is the story of a dreamy woman from Boston who has always longed for adventure. She travels west after corresponding with a man who writes proper and respectful letters. But when she arrives, she finds a different, much more compelling man waiting for her. How she turns the town, and her life, upside down will charm you.

All three of these stories start in St. Louis, where the women meet for the first time. Though strangers, the women know that the choices they've made have bonded them as sisters of the heart. I hope you enjoy these romantic stories.

Best wishes,

Carrie Feron
Jove Books

BRIDES OF THE WEST

SCOUNDREL

PAMELA LITTON

JOVE BOOKS, NEW YORK

BRIDES OF THE WEST: SCOUNDREL

A Jove Book / published by arrangement with
the author

PRINTING HISTORY
Jove edition / January 1994

All rights reserved.
Copyright © 1994 by Jove Publications, Inc.
This book may not be reproduced in whole or in part,
by mimeograph or any other means, without permission.
For information address: The Berkley Publishing Group,
200 Madison Avenue, New York, New York 10016.

ISBN: 0-515-11251-8

A JOVE BOOK®
Jove Books are published by The Berkley Publishing Group,
200 Madison Avenue, New York, New York 10016.
JOVE and the "J" design are trademarks belonging
to Jove Publications, Inc.

PRINTED IN THE UNITED STATES OF AMERICA

10 9 8 7 6 5 4 3 2 1

PROLOGUE

"All aboard for Kansas City and points west," the call rang out. "Track three."

"Points west." Lucy Drummond gave her spectacles a nudge up her nose. "That's me."

Unable to suppress her excitement, she turned to the young woman sharing the bench with her and offered her hand. The wariness that added an edge to the woman's pretty face sharpened, then disappeared with the briefest of smiles and a firm handshake.

"Good luck to you," Lucy said.

"Luck?" The woman released Lucy's hand and her smile tilted into a skeptic's slant. "Luck is a fickle lady, totally undependable, as our friend who just left for Denver discovered."

Lucy clutched her faded carpetbag closer and surveyed the crowded St. Louis train station. So many people, all rushing to wherever destiny and a locomotive would take them. The other young woman who had waited for her train with them had indeed learned one couldn't be too careful, a lesson she herself should take a longer look at.

"I never saw the thief who took her bag," Lucy said.

"He was quick, all right," the other woman replied. "Bad fortune always is."

Memories of all she had left behind in Boston tugged a frown between Lucy's brows. "Then we have to be faster."

"And smarter," her benchmate added.

Lucy cast a quick glance over the woman's plain calico dress and ugly slat bonnet, an ensemble that appeared strangely at odds with the golden-haired woman, like a beautiful leopard hiding her spots beneath a dulling layer of dust. Misfortune's consequence or perhaps a disguise?

Lucy knew better than to ask questions. In the West, one didn't ask after another's business or pry into the past. Almost every dime novel said as much. Still, she wondered about this woman as well as the Denver-bound lady with her mountain of luggage, rich silk trappings and vague, unlikely statement of employment waiting at her journey's end.

While they had waited, both ladies had appeared preoccupied and uneasy. Neither had said much, unlike her own nervous prattlings about David's letters and this mail-order marriage endeavor she had embarked upon. She had been talking more to herself than to the other women, trying to inject confidence into her misgivings, even a sprinkling of romance into this long journey to Starlight, New Mexico.

"Last call for Kansas City and points west. Track number three."

Holding her bag close to her, Lucy rose from the bench. She summoned a smile for the woman and a needed boost of optimism for herself.

"Let's hope we've left behind all of our misfortunes," she said.

Lucy detected a shadow of vulnerability in the wise blue eyes lifted to her. Like the dark-haired, wealthy woman's future, this woman's past intrigued her.

"My daddy couldn't have said it better," the woman replied, "but remember what I said earlier. Don't expect too much."

Lucy glanced over her shoulder, searching out a path to track three, then placed her hand on the woman's shoulder. "Don't expect too little."

Rewarded with a startled expression in the woman's wary blue eyes, Lucy turned and wove her way through the crowd toward her train. Too much, too little, she didn't know what to expect in Starlight, but she knew what she had left in Boston. At least Starlight promised her a chance at a new beginning, a risky chance to be sure, but one must move forward or be forever lost in the past.

CHAPTER 1

Please God, let him love me.

Lucy Drummond opened her eyes and stepped from the train onto a long, wooden platform. The powerful locomotive vibrated the boards beneath her feet, shaking her unsteady knees. Forgetting not to squint, she peered into the distance. Something appeared in the gray uncertainty of the train's vaporous breaths. Something vague and dark. Her future.

The man dressed in black stepped off a loading dock next to the train depot and crossed the road separating the two buildings. His stride was long and purposeful, yet unhurried. Without her spectacles, Lucy couldn't distinguish his features, but he moved as if he owned the street. No one else waited on the platform and no other men approached her.

The man walking toward her must be David McQuaid, the man she had traveled half a continent to meet, the man she planned to marry. Love had nothing to do with this match, but one could hope, even pray. Maybe she was a dreamer, just as Aunt Ada claimed, but dreams were all she had left and a prayer all she had to give.

Steam spewed from the train engine, clouding her view, masking her long, deep sigh. All the speeches she had rehearsed flew out of her head. What did one say to a stranger one had arranged to marry? Nice to meet you. When's the wedding?

She had suggested a get-acquainted period in her last letter. The idea appealed to her more and more as the man in black strode through the wispy curtain of steam and drew closer to her strained inspection.

Something about him disturbed her. Nothing tangible, nothing she could put into words. Simply an uneasiness, an odd sense of . . . foreboding? No. It was a sensation she had never experienced and couldn't name, a confusion of emotions that waited in the back of her mind, alien and adrift, just as she waited at this lonely train station high in the Black Range of New Mexico.

The man climbed the stairs at the end of the depot's platform; his boots clipped out each unhurried step. She saw that he was tall and his hair was dark beneath the Western-style hat, just as David McQuaid had described himself. But somehow she had never pictured him dressed in a black frock coat and brocade vest, a black leather gunbelt strapped to his hips.

The strange uneasiness grew stronger with each step he took. Lucy reached for the wire frames usually resting on her nose and, instead, tapped the soft skin between her brows. She dropped her hand self-consciously and focused on the dark-clad man, willing him to match the respectable husband she had conjured from his letters back in Boston.

Her gaze dropped to a gold watch fob swinging gently against the satiny cloth of his vest, then lower to his gunbelt and its row of leather loops filled with brass cartridges. Lucy shifted her weight and stole a glance at the waiting train. She looked anxiously around the empty depot, then back to the man in black.

With his measured, steady pace, he advanced toward her, his gaze direct from beneath the wide brim of his hat, his hands relaxed by his sides. He looked like one of those pistol duelists on a cover of *Beadle's Half-Dime Library*— particularly, the issue about Tombstone.

Ridiculous! She was allowing her imagination to run away with her good sense. Mr. David McQuaid was a very sweet and sincere man. Only such a man could write the earnest letters that had convinced her to head out west in hopes of a promising marriage. She was sure once his features became clear, her silly imaginings would be forgotten.

She focused on this optimistic view as she watched and waited for David McQuaid. Slowly, his face came into focus and her hard-fought reassurances crumbled. His mouth had a hard line to it, almost grim, despite the fullness of the lower lip. A broad, sharp-angled jaw matched the stern resolution of his mouth. Only the slight cleft indenting his chin gave a light and boyish charm to the otherwise unwelcoming face. She looked for more clues to this man who had courted her so eloquently with pen and ink, but his eyes remained a mystery, shadowed by the flat-crowned hat he wore low on his forehead.

Lucy watched for a smile, longed for a mere hint of the humor so apparent in David's letters to appear on that tight-lipped mouth. Judging from his dark expression, removing her spectacles hadn't helped in making a good first impression after all.

Lucy struggled with her growing uneasiness and confusion. This dark stranger couldn't be the author of those warm, friendly letters to her, or if he was, then he was very displeased with what he saw—her. Distressed with either conclusion, Lucy gripped the copy of *Ivanhoe* she carried and pressed the leather-bound volume against her unsettled stomach.

Turning slightly, unable to witness his dissatisfaction, she gave her full attention to the train and covered her disappointment with an uncertain expression she hoped was as unreadable as his. Had she made a huge mistake? She picked up her bag.

The locomotive sighed and grumbled its impatience to continue its race westward, then strained and let off more steam.

"All aboard," the conductor called.

Lucy took a step, then hesitated. She had come all this way for a chance, a slim chance to be sure, but the only avenue that had opened for her and her mother. The letters couldn't be a complete lie. Her fingers fanned around the handle on her valise, firming her grip to a white-knuckled fist. They couldn't.

"All aboard."

Aunt Ada's warnings loomed before her as large and powerful as the train. The letters were all a trick to lure young women to ruin, her aunt had said. Anything that sounded too good to be true usually was, she had told Lucy over and over in her thick Irish brogue.

Lucy hated the thought of going back home, retreating, giving up, telling her mother her plan had failed, admitting to her aunt and smirking cousins they had been right. Still, who was this tall, unsmiling man dressed in black? Surely not David. Certainly not anyone she wanted to marry.

The train creaked into motion. Blood pounded through Lucy's head. She wasn't ready to run, not yet, not until she knew for certain she had been played falsely. Too much was at stake.

Lucy watched splashes of crimson sunset slide from one

window to the next and listened to the boots cross the
wooden platform, coming closer and closer, while the clank
of the steel wheels slowly picked up speed. The footsteps
stopped. She didn't turn to the man who stood next to her
but watched the train slip out of the station.

"I see that's *Ivanhoe* you've got there," the man said.
"You must be Miss Lucilla Drummond."

Disappointment crept into Lucy's throat in a painful lump
that might prove dangerous. Tears would be disastrous. She
held no doubts now that the man was David McQuaid. She
had written to him before she had left Boston agreeing to his
suggestion that she carry *Ivanhoe*, a favorite they both
shared.

The weariness of the long journey settled over her
shoulders like a wet wool blanket. His gesture had fit so
wonderfully into her romantic notions, her certainty that the
man who had written those letters, who had admired a story
of knightly chivalry, would agree to send for her mother.

"Miss Drummond?" The deep-voiced question held the
sharpness of a command.

Squaring her shoulders, Lucy prepared to meet the man
who had enticed her with his obviously misleading letters to
traipse across the country on a fool's errand. She cleared her
throat. "Yes, I'm Lucy Drummond."

She turned to say more but found her thoughts scattered
by the intense blue eyes fixed on her. She didn't need her
spectacles to see the calm disinterest expressed in blue eyes
that possessed a worn, hardened look as if they had seen too
much, like hands that had worked too hard. Her disappointment grew to a quiet panic.

"I'm Sam McQuaid, Miss Drummond." He touched the
brim of his hat. "We have something to discuss and—"

Lucy dropped her bag. "Sam McQuaid . . . not David?"
She couldn't disguise the relief in her voice. Her future

didn't depend on this dark-visaged man. David had sent his
brother to meet her. She paused, her relief short-lived.

But why?

She clutched the book hard against her pounding heart,
holding on to her hopes just as tightly. "What's happened to
David?"

Sam tipped back his hat, his coat parting slightly to reveal
a dull tin star pinned to his vest, and lifted his gaze past her
shoulder. "Nothing a good horsewhipping wouldn't cure,"
he muttered.

"I'm afraid I don't understand." She ventured a look at
the five-pointed star that read: TOWN MARSHAL, STARLIGHT, N.M.
TERR.

"I can't say I do, either, Miss Drummond, but he left you
a letter." Reaching into his coat, Sam pulled a white
envelope from an inside pocket and presented it to her.
"This should explain the situation."

Her heart sinking, Lucy shoved her book between her arm
and side, then accepted the letter David had left for her. She
slipped a finger beneath the edge of the flap, not wanting to
know what disaster the familiar broad strokes of black ink
spelled out for her but bracing herself for the worst. She was
good at that. She had had a great deal of practice in the last
six years.

Sam saw all the signs as he watched Lucy work the
envelope open: the slow droop of her shoulders, the ease
with which the corners of her pretty mouth settled into a
frown, the little sigh. Like many of the gamblers he sat
across the table from nightly, this woman drew more losing
hands than winning ones.

He could never understand those gambling men, why
they continued to play, continued to believe the next hand
would be a winner. He didn't know what Miss Drummond
had expected either by registering with an agency to find a

husband, but he regretted not taking her someplace private to read David's message.

"Maybe you'd like to read that over at my office?" Sam said.

Lucy's hands stilled, though she didn't look up. "I know what it must say, Marshal McQuaid," she said quietly, and lifted the single folded paper from the envelope. "The particulars won't be a shock."

"Miss Drummond, I think you might be more comfortable . . ."

Too late, he thought. She had begun to read the damned thing. His lips forming a silent curse, Sam turned his shoulder to Lucy, giving her what privacy he could. He'd like to choke his brother.

Lucy held the corners of the paper against a sudden breeze that tugged at her skirts, fluttering wisps of hair about her face. She held back the worrisome tendrils and began to read.

Dear Lucy,

I suppose by now you realize our marriage is not to be. I have wed another, a woman I thought lost to me forever. There is little else to add, except I regret I had no time to telegraph you before your departure from Boston. My brother, Sam McQuaid, will see to your needs while in Starlight and assist you in returning to your home.
With sincere regrets,
David McQuaid

Lucy scanned the note again, as if a second reading would reveal something more, some slight consideration for her feelings. But the message remained the same and was quite clear. She was to be returned to Boston like a package marked "RECEIPT REFUSED." Warmth crept past the tight knot in her throat, spreading to her cheeks in a hot blush as she refolded the page and prepared to face the man in black once more, the man charged with sending his brother's unwanted bride-to-be packing.

Lucy strove for composure, and though her hands shook, she was able to fit the paper back into its envelope. She knew she shouldn't feel such crushing humiliation, but she did. This marriage plan had meant so much to her, yet nothing to David . . . even less to this forbidding lawman. She wouldn't cry. Not now. Not while Marshal McQuaid stood over her with his measuring looks.

Sam caught the soft sound of rustling paper and cast a glance toward Lucy. Her head was bowed, and the straw hat she wore guarded her face from his view. A nosegay of faded paper violets decorating the hat quivered slightly, whether with the breeze or with reaction, he couldn't be certain. Quick, jerky movements dispatched the note to its envelope. She fumbled to loosen the strings of her reticule while she held the book clamped to her side. Obviously, Miss Drummond was stalling for time. He would give her what he could.

His attention wandered to the golden wisps of hair that danced around her face, catching glints of dying sunlight. David's letter to him hadn't mentioned she was blond, just to meet a woman carrying a volume of *Ivanhoe* at the station and a brief explanation telling him why. A mail-order bride, of all the crazy notions. A hell of a thing for David to spring on his big brother the day the rascal had run off with the mayor's daughter.

Stuffing his brother's letter away in her bag, the Boston woman jerked the reticule's cords, then lifted her gaze to him. Sam saw trouble. Gold and green and gray trouble. Eyes like hers caught a man's attention. In a boomtown full of half-wild cowboys and lonesome miners that meant trouble. And she was his trouble now.

With a sharp sigh that didn't come close to venting his disgust with his younger brother, Sam jerked his thumb toward the ticket window behind them. "Morning train east leaves at nine o'clock in the morning, Miss Drummond. I'll purchase your ticket now, then I'll take you to the hotel."

Lucy cocked her chin a notch higher. "Don't bother, Marshal." She swallowed hard before she spoke again, but she was no unwanted package to be dumped in the return mail. "I . . . I don't require your assistance," she finished. The words felt good slipping off her tongue, even if it wasn't quite the truth.

Lucy met his cool inspection, knowing her mother's outdated black traveling suit didn't fit her own trim figure, knowing the carpetbag at her feet was faded and worn, knowing pride was too expensive for her meager purse. His blue eyes met hers, tired and solemn. He knew it, too.

"My brother brought you out here, Miss Drummond," he said. "While you're in my town, you're my responsibility." His eyes flicked over her once more, his mouth pulling as flat as his tone. Presenting his back to her, he walked toward the ticket window.

Lucy took a step, raising a hand. "Marshal . . ." Her arm dropped to her side. She could see that protesting was useless. What a tangle! Lucy twisted around, unable to witness the consequence of her foolish trust in well-written promises and her own blind optimism.

Along the other side of the tracks were empty cattle pens and behind them, low dusty hills crouched one after another until sparsely pined slopes disappeared into a darkening sky. Low murmurings from the ticket window mixed with the evening breeze, and it wasn't difficult for Lucy to imagine the whispers waiting for her at home. "I told you so," her cousins would say. "I told you so."

Miss High and Mighty, they called her. Too good to work at the mills or go into service. Forget your papa was once a big shot in the neighborhood, her Aunt Ada advised. Powerful men made powerful enemies.

Lucy closed her eyes. She couldn't forget. She'd never forget how much she hated Boston or how her mother, after selling off bits and pieces of her life after Papa's death, was penniless and ill and forced to move the two of them in with her brother's family. Lucy had promised to seek a better life for them; she couldn't give up now that she was so close.

"Here's your ticket, Miss Drummond."

Lucy's eyes flew open and her spine stiffened. "I can't—" —*go back*. This man wasn't interested in her problems. Furiously thinking of something else to say, she turned and faced the marshal once more. "I can't accept—"

He took her free hand and pressed the ticket into her palm. "We've discussed that, Miss Drummond."

Lucy wanted to escape the firm grip of his large, warm hand, but instead, an unexpected loss of breath stole away her voice.

His grip tightened and he captured her attention with the compelling intensity of gun-metal eyes. "Don't make this situation more difficult than it already is."

Releasing her hand, he bent and caught up her bag, then started for the corner of the depot. "I'll take you to the hotel now, Miss Drummond. Then I have rounds to make."

Lucy clutched the ticket so tightly, the stiff paper dug into her palm. She watched the marshal carry away all she owned and realized she had no choice but to do as he asked no matter her bruised pride or the injustice of it all. Justice wasn't for people like her, with their small hopes and even smaller dreams. She supposed she should be thankful Sam

McQuaid took his obligations more seriously than his brother. Despite her brave words, ten dollars wouldn't have taken her far.

Disappointment dragging at one foot and frustration shackling the other, Lucy forced herself to obey the impatient wave of the marshal's arm. She started for the corner of the depot where he waited.

Crossing the platform, her heels hammering the weathered wood, Lucy tried to summon proper feelings of gratitude but found only resentment and bleak expectations. She rested those on the man dressed in black, his tall form a dark silhouette set against the approaching night. She hated accepting his help almost as much as she hated returning to Boston.

Don't do either.

The thought startled her. She paused at the edge of the platform, walking around the idea in her mind, examining it, searching out possible flaws. She recognized the obvious hurdles—no money, no job, no friends or family. Yet, the notion remained solid, clear, and gleaming, far brighter than her prospects in Boston, where the same problems awaited her, except for the lack of family. She refused to be an added burden to her aunt and uncle. She couldn't go back, only forward.

"Watch your step, Miss Drummond."

Lucy frowned at the marshal's deep-voiced intrusion, then realized he couldn't know her thoughts. Still, his dark presence couldn't be ignored or dismissed. Her book of romantic notions lay heavy in the crook of her arm. She couldn't make another mistake in judgement.

Marshal McQuaid stood on the road directly in front of her, his eyes level with hers, his hand raised to assist her down the steps. Lucy hesitated, the decision she must make her only concern.

"A moment, Marshal." She looked past his impatient grimace to the busy thoroughfare behind him. Her eyes narrowed, bringing the nearest buildings lining the wide, rutted road into focus, while the more distant shops and businesses gradually dimmed into tiny splashes of light and evening shadows. Starlight, New Mexico.

An excitement built in Lucy, an excitement fueled by all the stories she had ever read about the West, all the possibilities waiting to be discovered. Perhaps her journey here hadn't been a mistake after all.

"Not much to look at, is it?"

Lucy's gaze swept upward to the worn mountain peaks looming above the town; she breathed in the fresh scent of pines and new lumber. No more tall, dingy buildings that blocked the sunlight, no more dirty, narrow streets, no more cooked cabbage with its smell of poverty.

"That depends," Lucy replied.

"Depends?"

Lucy met his blue eyes so worn and hardened. "On what you've been used to looking at."

"While *one* is looking," Sam tugged at her hand and gave her no choice but to descend the steps, "one had better look carefully. In this country, second chances are as few as the men who live to tell about them." He released her hand once she stepped to the road.

Lucy turned away from Sam's steady regard and faced Starlight. Marshal McQuaid failed to understand one thing—second chances came to those who looked for them, expected them, and when necessary, reached out and grabbed them.

Without further comment or knowing exactly where she was to go, Lucy set off down the road, confident she would find her way.

CHAPTER 2

Six shots ripped through the morning in one continuous blast of gunpowder and exploding glass. Birds burst into the morning sky. A cloud of thick blue smoke rode the silence that followed, giving lazy chase to the birds. Surveying the now empty fence rail forty feet away, Sam tapped the spent cartridges free from the Colt's chambers, his focus directed inward where timing, distance, and wind crystallized into a steady hand and an expert eye.

Shards of broken glass glimmered beneath the fence among the new shoots of grass and the first tiny purple blooms of spring. Shivering in the fresh morning breeze, the delicate flowers held his gaze and his hands stilled, his thoughts straying to a cluster of faded violets trembling upon a straw hat, the soft hazel eyes beneath the brim. His brows drew downward in a frown.

A light jingling sound lifted his mood and drew his attention to the path leading up from town. Cleve Hardesty stepped from a stand of cottonwoods, spurs ringing, a brown hat pushed back on wavy auburn hair. His deputy wouldn't have lived long chasing Apaches, Sam thought, and proceeded to reload his Peacemaker.

"Dave's little problem is on her way," the young man announced from the edge of the clearing.

Sam nodded an acknowledgment, then, in one smooth motion, slid the big ivory-handled revolver into its holster. He stared straight ahead, the scattering of purple flowers edging the periphery of his vision, his hands held loosely at his sides. In a blur of motion, he drew the Colt, spinning to a low crouch, and fired.

Five tin cans, one flying after the other, shot into the air from atop a wide dispersion of boulders and tree stumps. Echoes of the rapid gunblasts flowed into the distant sound of a train's whistle, which slowly drifted away with the blue smoke floating toward the treetops.

Sam rose to his full height, his attention claimed by the one remaining can winking at him from its rocky roost, an irritating reminder to make more time for practice. He turned his back to the can, gave a glancing regard to Cleve who busily rolled a smoke, and emptied the Colt's cylinder.

"Too many distractions lately," he muttered under his breath.

The train wailed its imminent arrival once more, calling to his mind a picture of Lucy Drummond standing alone at the station, waiting. His frown deeper than ever, Sam looked up at Cleve.

"You're sure about Miss Drummond?" he asked, remembering David's discarded bride had shown a stubborn streak yesterday.

"That'll be the eastbound coming in," Cleve replied, then touched a match to his cigarette. He shook out the flame, then blew two smoke rings into the air. "The Boston woman will be on it, I reckon."

The frown continued to hover between Sam's dark brows.

He loaded five cartridges into the Colt's cylinder, resting the hammer on the sixth empty chamber, and dropped the pistol home. Lifting his head, he listened to the sound of the train drifting up from the valley below. Cleve hadn't sounded as sure as Sam wanted him to be.

"You saw her leave for the station?" he asked, his eyes tracing the perimeters of the small clearing, taking in every shaded grove of trees, exploring every shadowed hillside.

"Clear as day," Cleve replied, and handed Sam his black coat. "Blond, baggy black dress, beat-up ol' carpetbag and a straw hat with little purple flowers bunched on it. She left the hotel about eight-thirty."

Sam didn't answer; he was neither pleased nor satisfied, simply relieved the awkward situation was over. He gave the coat a brisk brush-down with his hand, then pulled it on. Straightening the collar, he caught a smile lurking somewhere beneath Cleve's thick auburn moustache.

He gave his deputy a long look. "You think something's funny, Cleve?"

All signs of mirth dropped from the younger man's face. "No, sir." He threw down the cigarette and crushed it beneath a boot heel. "No, sir, I don't."

"Good," Sam replied, jerking at the cuffs of his coat. "Because I'd hate to think you found something funny in someone's misery. That girl came out here on David's promise to marry her. There's nothing funny about running out on a commitment, or shirking your duty. David should have met that train and faced the consequences of his actions."

"Yes, sir." Cleve gave his boots a thorough inspection, then looked up at Sam. "Hell, I didn't mean—"

"I know you didn't," Sam said, having made his point. "The whole mess is finished now and we can forget it."

Sam gave Cleve a good-natured slap on the shoulder and

started down the rocky path to town. Cleve fell in behind him, silent except for the jingling spurs he favored wearing.

Refusing to dwell on his brother's disappointing actions, Sam concentrated on the narrow trail that wound through fragrant piñon pines and junipers, every sense tuned to his surroundings. He had experienced too many years of fighting hostile Indians and wearing the star to drop his guard.

The dappled sunlight and cool morning breeze roamed through the trees and thick brush, and his thoughts soon wandered to the anxious young woman who had stood alone in a strange place, expecting to share her life with a man she didn't know. Daring or desperate—he wondered which description fit Lucy Drummond. Perhaps both.

She was no great beauty but certainly attractive with her unusual eyes. Too reckless with her decisions, he supposed, but she had plenty of pride. She had made that fact more than obvious. Probably trying to hide the hurt. Hell, she was better off without David, anyway.

He looked ahead and saw several small clapboard houses scattered among the thinning pines. By the time they reached Main Street, the train would be pulling out of the station. He wished all of his problems could be solved with a train ticket out of town.

"Has the mayor been to the office this morning?" Sam asked, recalling two newlywed problems he'd like to ship to Australia.

"Not yet," Cleve replied. "When do you expect the mayor to calm down? It's been nearly a week since Dave and Caroline ran off."

"Mayor Jones was quite attached to his girl, Cleve." Sam stepped over a thick, exposed tree root. "And was against that match from the beginning." Not that he blamed him, Sam thought.

After a flurry of jingles and a soft curse, Cleve said, "I thought for sure Caroline and that lawyer fella down in Silver City were headed toward the hitchin' post."

"So did her daddy," Sam replied. "Now the mayor is on my tail, badgering me to find them. Hell, the damage has been done by now. The mayor will have to accept it."

Keeping the rest of his thoughts to himself, Sam led the way up one of the side roads that would eventually take them to Main Street. He couldn't imagine his well-meaning but irresponsible brother married to the willful Jones girl. Sam gazed down the road ahead, finding it as rocky and meandering as David's future. Maybe pleasing his new bride would make a man out of his little brother, or, at least, make him keep a job.

Weary of chasing down David's troubles, Sam considered another brewing tempest he hoped would stay in a teacup. "Heard any more about those temperance women?"

Cleve stepped up beside him. "Ma says they're organizin' over at the newspaper office."

"Maggie Thompson and those 'demon rum' editorials of hers are a damn nuisance," Sam replied. "That's all I need. A bunch of psalm-singing do-gooders mixing it up with the saloon owners, including Sarge O'Reilly and myself."

Cleve studied the rutted roadway. "You think you've got trouble." He drew his shoulders back as if to prove he was fully grown. "Ma's after me night and day to sign the pledge."

A low chuckle rumbled from Sam's chest. "You oughta mind your ma, Cleve." His deputy's frowning glance only encouraged him. "Keep you out of trouble."

"Hell," Cleve muttered, aiming his frown toward the town, "I oughta sign the damn thing so you and Sarge wouldn't get the better half of my wages."

"We'd miss you over at the Outpost," Sam replied, his

face drawn in a serious pose. "But, when a man's ma is after him, well, anybody would understand."

"You'll understand plenty when she comes after you." Cleve said.

Sam chuckled at the image of kindly Mrs. Hardesty, who always smelled of apple pies, coming after him with a pledge in one hand and a rolling pin in the other.

Stepping up to the boardwalk in front of the hotel, his smile dimmed as he turned to Cleve. "I doubt if anything comes of all this temperance talk." He pulled his watch from a small vest pocket and consulted the time. "The ladies will probably get together, have their meetings and tea, then something else will come along to occupy them." He snapped the watch closed and glanced down the road, confirming the departure of the eastbound train, then dropped the watch back into its pocket. "I've seen it before."

Cleve looked beyond Sam as he swept a finger along each extravagant sweep of auburn hair beneath his large, straight nose. Lines crinkled in deep fans around his brandy-colored eyes and a dimple appeared in one lean cheek.

"Is that right, Marshal?" Cleve gave a nod, indicating Sam should look behind him.

Passing a curious look to Cleve, Sam faced the other way and his frown deepened. He'd like to buy about fifteen more train tickets. Maybe one ticket would do, he thought, and singled out the tall, thin woman leading a string of tight-lipped ladies from the small office of the *Starlight Observer*. Maggie held a placard, but he couldn't read it from this angle. Several of the other women carried signs, too. It looked like "demon rum" had poured out of the editorial page onto the streets of Starlight.

"Is that Leila Miller with her husband's base drum?" Cleve asked. He stepped up onto the boardwalk beside Sam.

Sam examined the big woman taking up the rear guard of the marchers. At just under six feet tall, Leila couldn't be missed. "None other," Sam replied. "How could Dolf let her use his drum?"

Cleve gave him a long look, one brow drawn into a questioning bow. "You don't know much about women, do you, Marshal?"

Sam passed a sidelong glance to Cleve. "I don't get any complaints."

"Maybe I shoulda said you don't know anything about wives . . . mothers . . . you know . . . ladies," Cleve replied.

Sam shrugged, thinking of the mother who had died too young and the long, hard-riding years wearing a uniform. "I've managed to stay clear of that sort," he muttered.

"Yeah, well, those days are over, Sam." Cleve gave a nod toward the assembling females. "When their sort goes on the rampage, they take no prisoners."

Sam propped an arm above his head on a nearby post and turned to Cleve, a smile teasing one corner of his mouth. "Sounds like you're ready to show the white feather to this bunch of hens, Cleve." He gestured toward the younger man. "You want to turn in your star?"

"No, sir," Cleve said in a strong, clear voice. "The only feathers that'll be flyin' around here are a certain rooster's tail feathers. I figure I'll be needed to help pick 'em up."

Sam's deep, rich laughter turned a few heads his way, but he disregarded the curious stares and gave his attention to the marchers busily forming ranks, an altercation or two seeming to have slowed the starting time.

"Don't gather the wood for the stew pot, yet," he said. "I doubt any feathers will fly."

Cleve raised his brows and gave a long sigh. "I hope you're right, Sam."

With a wide swing of her arm, the blacksmith's wife sent a thunderous boom through the town. The ladies scurried into place. Soon, the morning air filled with steady, vigorous drumbeats and the fervent voices of women with a cause rose in song. Marching down the center of the wide, dusty road, stopping traffic and generally raising havoc with the wagon teams and horses tied along the hitching rails, the ladies proceeded through town with their message of pure living and salvation.

Cleve stepped to the edge of the boardwalk and shook his head. "Ma never could carry a tune," he said.

Sam raised a brow, agreeing with Cleve, but kept that opinion to himself. He noted the boardwalks filling with onlookers, many from the saloons and dance halls across the road.

"Keep a watch on things, but I doubt anyone will make trouble today," Sam said. "I'll be at the office. Nell Taylor and that Englishman who owns the Mine Shaft will be down there complaining soon enough—maybe some of the other saloon owners, too."

Cleve signaled he had heard with a wave of his hand and stepped down to the road. He hooked his thumbs into the front of his double-rigged gunbelt and watched the little parade advance toward them.

Sam started down the boardwalk, his long strides keeping time with the beat of Leila's drum. He tipped his hat to two ladies who had stopped to view the noisy procession down Main Street and nodded to the customers gathered around the entrance of Pollett's Mercantile. He drew to a halt as three ladies pushed through the spectators and hurried to join the temperance marchers.

"Hey, Marshal," Oscar Pollett called out from behind his glass counter. "What're you gonna do?"

"Yeah, Marshal," a lounging miner added above the din

of the approaching drum and singing chorus. "You gonna throw the lot of 'em in jail for disturbin' the peace?"

Sam gauged the mood of the small crowd around him. Some faces bore serious expressions, others appeared amused, but they all looked to him for an answer. Everyone knew he owned the finest saloon and gambling hall in town. Naturally, they wondered how he was going to react to Maggie's marchers.

No use giving either side something to spread around, he thought. "I think I'll ask Leila to take over Dolf's position in the band," he replied, a slow smile joining the laughter starting around him.

Sam continued down the boardwalk and waved at the passing ladies with their white ribbons fluttering on every bosom. Several waved back, though their leader aimed her nose straight ahead. He knew all those women. They were mothers, daughters, and wives of his friends, with the exception of Maggie Thompson, who owned the *Starlight Observer*. She was a widow, he had heard. Again, Sam considered if he should take some action, but the fact was he hoped he wouldn't have to do anything except ride out the storm until it blew itself out.

Sam headed toward an adobe brick building standing alone just ahead. The jailhouse and marshal's office was only two years old, and already the white framing around the windows and door needed a coat of paint. When the mayor came in to harass him again about finding the newlyweds, he'd hit him with a demand to repaint the place. Requests that cost the town coffers usually sent Benjamin Franklin Jones on his way in a hurry. For now, he'd ignore the temperance ladies. More than likely, they would stumble upon their own detour.

Sam crossed an intersecting road, the righteous chorus now out of range, leaving the drum's resounding baritone booming over the town in solemn testimony. Eager to escape into the quiet of his office, he rushed up two steps to the peeling white-painted door and, giving the doorknob a quick turn, strode inside. He stopped abruptly.

"Damn," he muttered.

Lucy twisted around on the wooden chair, her arm resting on the back rail, and pushed at her spectacles. She'd forgotten how tall the marshal was, how intimidating with his black clothing and grim expression. Marshal McQuaid didn't look pleased to see her, but then she hadn't expected a pleasant welcome.

She sat very still, barely breathing as he stood in the doorway, staring at her. He was holding the doorknob as if frozen to it, and his long shadow filled the shaft of morning sunlight coming through the open door. Drawing strength from the small notice she had read in the *Starlight Observer* last night, Lucy's hazel eyes met his hard blue ones.

The crease between his brows deepened. "You're wearing spectacles."

Lucy self-consciously touched her steel wire frames. She had imagined all kinds of reactions to her unexpected appearance but never a quiet remark about her eyeglasses.

"Yes," she replied, not knowing what else to say. "I usually wear spectacles." Her hand gripped the wooden slat, her one attempt at vanity discovered. "I . . . I simply didn't yesterday."

Sam frowned at the peculiar conversation he had started, but he had been caught off guard by the Boston woman's sudden appearance, by the round, glass lenses that fairly drowned the early autumn color from her eyes with reflected light. He quickly recovered, however, determined to learn the reason he was once more presented with his brother's dilemma.

"Miss Drummond," he said, his voice sharper, more direct, "you missed your train."

Lucy sat straighter and pushed at her eyeglasses. "Is it a crime in Starlight to miss a train, or is it a crime only for me to miss mine?"

Sam gripped the doorknob as if he wanted to strangle it. "Of course not. I . . ." He nudged his hat back, mumbled a soft curse, and regained his usual control. "What happened?"

Lucy cleared her throat and prepared to deliver her much-revised speech, but her attention strayed to the approaching sound of jingling steps.

"Sam," a masculine voice called from outside.

Without taking his eyes off her, Sam slammed the door. Lucy's heart skipped a beat, then pounded as hard and loud as the drumming outside, but she managed to stay seated. Unsure what to expect, she followed the marshal's slow progress as he crossed the room and sat behind a large, paper-strewn desk.

He rested his clasped hands on a stack of wanted posters. Five muffled drumbeats passed. "Your train, Miss Drummond." His manner bore all the gentleness of a field commander dressing down his lowliest, most incompetent private.

Irritated with the marshal's stone-faced interrogation and resenting his high-handed tactics, Lucy fished a roll of greenbacks from her reticule and tossed the money on his desk.

"Thank you for your generosity, Marshal, but I cashed in your ticket. I'll be staying in Starlight for the time being," she said, quite satisfied with the firmness she had given her statement.

Sam gave the ticket money a dismissive glance, then

studied her for a moment, striving for the patience that had taken the nine o'clock train east.

"That's not a good idea, Miss Drummond." His tone rougher, his meaning clear, he added, "Starlight is not a town for a single woman with no man to protect her."

His implication brought a hot blush to her cheeks, but Lucy refused to waver in her purpose. "You have no authority to make me return to Boston, Marshal."

Sam stood, having heard enough. "I am obligated to send you safely home."

Lucy rose to her feet. "I am a grown woman, Marshal. I am perfectly capable of seeing to my own needs. Consider your obligation ended."

Her mouth set in firm disapproval, she retrieved her bag and turned to leave.

"Wait, Miss Drummond."

Something different in his tone, a weariness perhaps, prompted Lucy to obey the soft-spoken command, though she refused to face him. Deep, constant reverberations filled the silence, adding to the pounding blood in her ears. She stared at the two racks of rifles on the opposite wall, waiting. Sam walked into her view and stopped directly in front of her, the money in his hand.

"Pride can be an admirable quality or it can be a millstone around a stiff neck." He held the bills out to her. "Take the money, Miss Drummond. Take the money and buy a ticket to anywhere you want to go."

Lucy stared at the small stack of bills and the strong, sun-browned hand that held it. "A ticket to anywhere," she said. No strings attached this time, no promises to keep, no future husband waiting for her.

"That's right."

Slowly, she raised her eyes, pausing to look at the small crossed-sabers insignia attached to his gold watch chain and the tin star pinned to his chest, then her gaze locked with the smoky swirls of gray and blue in his eyes. At this distance, she was close enough to smell the starch in his white shirt, the clean scent of his shaving soap, and a hint of something else, something sharp and burning—gunpowder. Sam Mc-Quaid was dangerous.

Every instinct, every thread of thought told her to grab the money and run. Run as far as his money would take her. Another sense, beyond thought, deeper than instinct, whispered to her to stay—stay and show this unyielding man she didn't run, she didn't take the easy way out, she made her own way. That's what her father would want her to do. Hadn't he refused to be run out of Boston?

Lucy remembered the notice she had read in last night's newspaper, still unable to believe her luck. The town's teacher had married and the school board was looking for another woman to replace her. She intended to be that woman.

Lucy pushed aside his offer with the back of her free hand. "I won't accept charity, Marshal," she said, and swept past him before she changed her mind.

"Don't let that millstone choke you, Miss Drummond." Sam almost smiled at the furious look she turned on him, noting her fingers gliding along the unadorned collar of her jacket. "When you change your mind," he slapped the greenbacks in his palm, "the money will be waiting for you."

Lucy whirled around and opened the door. She glared at the young auburn-haired man who fumbled his hat off while struggling to stand from his slouched position against the wall, then directed her steps to the Grandview Hotel. Mrs. Schindler, the hotel manager's wife, had been mentioned in the news report as a member of the school board. She would speak to her right away. Marshal McQuaid's greenbacks would turn to dust waiting for her.

Sam glanced up at Cleve's noisy entrance as he returned to his desk and sat down. He took an envelope from a drawer and stuffed the bills inside.

"I thought she took—"

"She didn't." Dipping a pen in black ink, Sam wrote "Miss Lucilla Drummond" on the envelope.

"Why?"

"Says she's staying in Starlight." He tossed the envelope in a bottom drawer and slammed it shut.

Cleve gave him a quizzical frown, glanced out the door for another look at the paradoxical Miss Drummond, then faced him. "Why?"

Instead of answering the deputy right away, Sam leaned back in his chair and watched the temperance ladies trail past his window on their way back to the newspaper office, their voices raised in reproving ardor and Leila doing her best to spook every horse and jackass in town. A braying burro went kicking down the road; a hapless white-bearded prospector chased after it.

Two drunks pushed through the swinging doors of Jack's Billiard Parlor across the road. Hanging onto one another, the duet staggered to the end of the ladies' parade. They joined voices in a bawdy, off-key, barroom song that gave stentorian competition to the frightened burro, soprano sanctimony, and Leila's drumming.

The portly mayor stood on the boardwalk in front of his law office, doffed his hat to the ladies, then charged across the road, his double whiskers bristling along his jowls. At that moment, Nell Taylor, shoulders swinging, red ringlets bouncing, strutted past the window, the tall, perfectly-attired Leslie Laughton following behind.

Sam leaned forward, resting his forearms on the scattered

papers covering his desk, wondering which irritation would reach his office first. He gave himself a moment to imagine a grand collision of scarlet petticoats, British bluster, and outraged whiskers outside his door. A faint smile crossed his features before he directed his thoughts to Cleve's question.

"Why has Miss Drummond chosen to stay in our little patch of paradise?" He looked at Cleve. "I'd have to guess for the hell of it."

CHAPTER 3

"Mr. Schindler said you wanted to see me."

Slamming her book closed, Lucy looked up with a guilty start and found the hotel manager's wife standing in the doorway of the small office tucked into a back corner of the hotel's lobby. My goodness, she thought while poking *Marshal Earp Tames Tombstone* into the endleaves of *Ivanhoe*, Mrs. Schindler moved quietly for a large woman. Lucy hadn't heard her approach at all.

Lucy pushed at her spectacles. "Yes, I did," she said, and decided to broach the subject of the teacher's position at once. "I wanted to speak to you about Starlight's need for a schoolmarm."

Mrs. Schindler set the placard she carried on an oblong table in front of Lucy, and with a brisk yank, she scraped back a chair and sat. Leaning forward, Mrs. Schindler clasped her hands together in a grip any lumberjack would envy and leveled small, intelligent blue eyes at Lucy.

"Miss Drummond, is it?" she asked, a slight German accent flavoring her straightforward tone. At Lucy's nod, she continued. "I have great sympathy for your unfortunate situation, but the schoolmarm's post is one of considerable responsibility and should not be taken lightly."

Lucy forced a calmness to her voice, though she flushed at the mention of her abandoned circumstances. "I'm not interested in sympathy, Mrs. Schindler," she replied. "All I ask is a chance at the teacher's position."

Mrs. Schindler tapped her thumbs on the table, her eyes moving rapidly from Lucy's hat to the book lying in her lap. "Do you have references?" she said, the r's rolling off her tongue like a snare drum's tattoo.

Lucy took heart from the request and, after tucking her book away, pulled a large brown envelope from the carpet-bag at her feet. Bent at the corners and worn about the edges, the envelope bore evidence of repeated handling. Lucy set it on the table and unwound the string closure at the back. She slid a sheaf of papers out and placed them beside the envelope.

Selecting the first page, Lucy studied the sheet of thick vellum, her official notification testifying to her completion of instruction at the Loring Academy for Young Ladies. Her mother's name should have been inscribed among the seals and stilted language after six long years of scrimping and saving for Lucy's education. Her father's death had not been allowed to interrupt her parents' plans for her schooling. She didn't come from a family of quitters. Marshal McQuaid had seen evidence of that and now so would Mrs. Schindler.

More determined than ever to secure the teacher's position with its twenty dollar a month salary and house included, she handed her certificate to Mrs. Schindler. "The Loring Academy for Young Ladies is very respected in Boston."

Mrs. Schindler examined the document and gave a short nod. "Very good, but what of personal references, Miss Drummond?" She laid the certificate on the table.

Her heart taking up the beat of her rising hopes, Lucy presented two letters to Mrs. Schindler. "Miss Theadora Loring is headmistress of the school her parents founded, and Mr. Clancy owned the bookstore where I worked summers and holidays."

She watched the woman's earnest reading of her letters, her stomach twisting at the scowl that formed between Mrs. Schindler's brows. Neither Miss Loring's nor Mr. Clancy's recommendations should spark such a disapproving look. Lucy's hands closed tightly together. The teacher's position she thought so close drifted slowly out of reach.

Mrs. Schindler gathered Lucy's certificate and recommendations together and arranged them in a neat stack between them. She joined her hands together once more and peered up at Lucy from her head's slightly bowed position.

"Everything appears to be in order, Miss Drummond, but I confess, I'm curious. You come to Starlight to marry David McQuaid and yet you carry character recommendations as if you had intended to apply for a teacher's position. I think an explanation is needed."

Lucy glanced down at her white-knuckled hands, then raised her gaze to meet the older woman's. She didn't like discussing personal matters with strangers, but the school board had the right to know the circumstances that had brought her here. She took a breath and began.

"I had been visiting agencies in Boston for the purpose of finding a teaching position in a western community. My mother is ill and I had heard the climate would be beneficial for her." Her father's legacy of trouble with the precinct boss could go unmentioned. "One of the agencies, which handled a variety of positions to fill, convinced me to read David's request for an educated bride. As nothing developed for teaching positions"—*nothing that paid my travel ex-*

penses, anyway—"I decided to correspond with Mr. Mc-Quaid, and here I am."

The scowl lessened considerably but didn't disappear completely. "What of David and his bride? Will you be uncomfortable living in Starlight when they return?"

"The truth is . . ." Lucy hesitated, deciding which truth to reveal. She chose the least painful. "The truth is, Mrs. Schindler, I haven't the funds to search for other positions. Finding a need for a schoolmarm in Starlight seemed . . . well, it seemed the answer to a prayer."

Mrs. Schindler tilted her chin up, the thick iron-gray braid arranged in a coronet atop her head almost disappearing from Lucy's view. "A prayer . . . yes, I can see how it would."

Lucy sensed a change in the woman's attitude, a receptiveness that had been absent before. "When I saw the notice in last night's paper, I knew I should stay."

"I heard the marshal had bought your passage back to Boston."

News certainly traveled swiftly through this town, Lucy thought, but she continued as if she hadn't marked her popularity with the gossips, another group to which Mrs. Schindler no doubt belonged. She would have to word her reply carefully.

Lucy pushed at her spectacles. "That's correct. Marshal McQuaid bought my return ticket, but after reading about the opening for a teacher, I cashed it in and returned his money this morning."

Mrs. Schindler leaned forward, her eyes taking on an excited gleam. "Did you see our march?"

"I certainly did," Lucy replied, somewhat surprised at the change of subject but welcoming it.

"What did you think of our efforts?" the older woman asked, then sat back and placed a hand to her braided coronet as if it had slipped. "I mean, compared to a big city such as Boston?"

Lucy had never witnessed a temperance demonstration along the old cobblestoned streets. Everyone she knew was too busy working, forming labor unions, trying to survive, but she didn't want to disappoint the obviously concerned woman, not when the schoolmarm's position waited just beyond her fingertips.

"Your demonstration was the best I have ever seen." Not a lie exactly, Lucy assured herself. The expectant look on the older woman's face called for further explanation. "I think it was the drum and the . . ." She searched for just the right sentiment to add. Noticing the bit of ribbon tied in a knot pinned to Mrs. Schindler's dark blue dress she added, ". . . the ribbons. They added a unity of spirit, I think."

"Yes," Mrs. Schindler agreed, her cheeks taking on a rosy glow. "The white ribbons represent purity, you know."

"Of course," Lucy replied, though she hadn't known at all. She caught sight of a spool of white ribbon peeking at her from beneath a neatly folded sheet on the table and inspiration struck. "And the way the ribbons were tied—I don't know, something about them truly caught the eye."

Mrs. Schindler touched the knotted bow pinned to her bosom. "The ribbons were my responsibility."

Lucy dropped her gaze to her hands. Her chest felt tight, her skin prickly, and a slight queasiness assailed her. Lying was wrong, but in the great, dark world of black lies, hers surely were tiny white dots on the map. No one was hurt and she badly needed this position.

"You did a beautiful job," Lucy said, her voice so soft she wondered if she had actually voiced the words.

"They *did* turn out nicely. Now, as to your filling our teacher's post, I must first speak to the other board members, but I foresee no problems."

Lucy slowly raised her head, not quite believing she had heard correctly. She had waited so long, searched so hard, and to find her fondest wish hiding under the ugly rock of this marriage disaster made the discovery difficult to accept.

"I can be Starlight's new schoolmarm?"

Tilting her head slightly to the right, Mrs. Schindler gave a queenly bow of her head.

A smile eased Lucy's mouth from its firm control as a dim, incomplete picture grew stronger in her mind—a picture of herself teaching young students, of sitting in her own little parlor sewing with her mother.

"Thank you, Mrs. Schindler," she said, her tone almost reverent. "This position means a great deal to me."

Two index fingers extended from Mrs. Schindler's tight grasp. "Now mind, the board will have to vote and school doesn't begin until September."

"I understand," Lucy replied. She gathered her papers, tapping them against the table to straighten their bottom edges while ideas for lessons whirled through her mind so quickly she didn't stop to examine them. First, she must write to her mother and tell her the good news.

"What will be your plans for the summer, Miss Drummond?" the other woman asked. "I take it you won't be returning to Boston."

The papers stilled in Lucy's hands, the future's rosy picture fading before the present's pressing needs. "No, I'll be staying in Starlight," she replied, and slipped her certificate and letters back into the worn envelope.

"I can recommend several respectable boardinghouses in town."

Winding the string around the clasps, Lucy thought of her ten dollars and the four long months until September. "I'll have to find employment," she said, more to herself than to Mrs. Schindler.

"Do you sew?"

Lucy looked up. "I have a great deal of sewing experience," she said with all the confidence of too many nights bending over piecework she and her mother had contracted from a coat factory.

Mrs. Schindler slid a sheet of paper in front of her, and selecting a pencil from several collected in a cup, she began writing. "Take this note to Mrs. King. She owns the dressmaker's shop two blocks down on Main Street. You'll see her sign in the window. Though Ella hasn't joined our movement yet, she's a Christian woman and might need help."

Mrs. Schindler folded the note and handed it to Lucy. "If she can't hire you, there are several dry goods stores in town and, of course, Pollett's Mercantile."

Lucy put the note away with her envelope into the carpetbag at her side. Feeling a twinge of guilt at her manipulations, she pulled the bag to her lap and fussed with the strap rather than face her benefactress. "Thank you again, Mrs. Schindler," she said. The simple words didn't convey the depth of her gratitude. "I can't tell you how—"

"Just be a good teacher, Miss Drummond, and *please* don't get married over the summer."

A rush of hot color warmed Lucy's cheeks. She raised wide-opened eyes to Mrs. Schindler. "I have no intention—"

"Every young woman has intentions, and you've come to the right place with yours. Men are desperate for marriageable females in the territories."

Lucy gave her spectacles a poke. "Desperate or not, a man searching for a wife will not find one in me. My arrangement with Mr. David McQuaid was made purely out of necessity."

Mrs. Schindler leaned back in her chair, a smile cracking

the stern line of her mouth, her hands lying flat on the table. "What is your first name, *Liebchen*?"

The woman's changed demeanor gave Lucy a warm and hopeful feeling of impending friendship. "Lucy."

"You must call me Tildie. My friends do." She slapped the table. "Now, we two are friends and I will be frank. Our schoolmarm must be single and above reproach. Strict rules of propriety must be met. When the right young man comes courting—"

"I don't want—"

Tildie held up her hand and the rest of Lucy's protest died on a long breath.

"When the right young man comes courting, necessities will fly out the window, but you must be certain proprieties don't. A whisper of scandal will be the end of your employment."

Not wishing to argue, and more than a little embarrassed, Lucy conceded with a quiet nod.

Tildie pushed back her chair and rose to her feet. She offered her hand and Lucy quickly stood and shook it. Tildie's grasp was warm and firm, and it was easy to reciprocate her enthusiasm.

"Congratulations, Lucy. I will speak to the other members tomorrow evening. I'm sure they will be just as impressed with your qualifications as I am."

"Thank you . . . Tildie." Using first names with an older woman felt odd, but Lucy smiled. She was no longer a schoolgirl but a schoolmarm, now. Lucy bent to retrieve her bag.

"I must warn you, too. Starlight can be a dangerous place."

Immediately, Lucy thought of Marshal McQuaid in his black clothes and gun, the smell of gunpowder mingling with the clean scents of soap and starch. "I'll be careful," she replied.

"Don't forget, *McQuaid*, we expect the law to protect our interests."

Sam hated the way the Englishman said his name. Laughton gave it a snide twist, a kind of private sneering quality. He had listened to the dandified saloon owner's nasal posturings all he was going to today.

Sam tossed down the mail he had been scanning while Laughton, Nell Taylor, and the mayor had discussed, demanded, and dictated for the last half-hour. "Nell, get Laughton out of here," he said.

Nell rose from her chair in a quiet rustling of satin petticoats and green silk skirts. "Come on, Leslie. We've done all the damage we can do."

Remaining in his chair, Laughton crossed his arms and lifted his long nose. "He's given us nothing, no guarantees, no assurances that these . . . these—"

A boot scraped on the floor with a jingling reminder that one of the marchers had close ties to the marshal's office. Laughton arched a brow and crimped his thin mouth with irritation.

"That these ladies," he continued, "will indeed retire their placards before damage has been done to our business."

Sam leaned forward, his hands clasped loosely on his desk. "Laughton, you're irritating me."

Nell slapped Laughton's padded plum-colored shoulder, the diamond rings she wore winking on her hand. "Come on, Leslie," she said. "Sam's right. We'll only set those Bible-thumpers flappin' around the barnyard if we go rufflin' their feathers. Let 'em lay their eggs and they'll go to roost."

"How colorfully put, Nell." Laughton stood and gave his

jacket a jerk, peering down his long nose at Sam. "We pay you an extra ten percent to keep the peace in our establishments, McQuaid. Earn it."

Sam rose to his feet, topping the Englishman by several inches. He fixed his gaze to the other man's shifting dark brown eyes. "I'm paid to keep the law, Laughton. Those ladies haven't broken the law. Now get out."

"They aren't paying you—"

The mayor broke in quickly. "You haven't been here long enough to know about our arrangement with Sam. We couldn't afford our own marshal without revenue from the saloons."

Nell grabbed a handful of plum sleeve and tugged. "You're irritatin' me now, Leslie. Come on, I've got a new girl come to work for me. She's been dyin' to meet a real Englishman."

Laughton looked as if he would like to say more, but Nell pulled on his sleeve again. Catching hold of her hand, he tucked it inside the crook of his elbow and turned to leave. Giving Sam one last deprecatory glance, Laughton accompanied Nell to the door and opened it for her.

Gus Schindler sidled inside, with a quick look over his shoulder. Laughton ushered Nell out with a nasal complaint against rude little men.

Sam sat down and propped his feet on his desk, taking a moment to calm down. Gus was about to bust with whatever he had to say, but that could wait. He gave a look to the mayor that told him he could wait, too.

Outside, the ore wagons rumbled and rattled down Main Street, hammers announced the newest building going up—an opera house, he had heard—and folks passed his window in a hurry to stake out their claim to the town's prosperity. Everything was back to normal, as if that newspaper woman had never led her marchers down the middle of the road. A few more weeks, and everyone would forget the marches and songs, even if that drum would take a while to fade from memories.

Gus fidgeted by the door. Earlier, Sam had asked the hotel manager to keep his ears open and report back to him with any information about the Boston woman. He couldn't understand why she wanted to stay in Starlight, but he was sure the excitement would wear off when she saw what living here was like. She wouldn't stay long. Feeling calmer, he gave Gus a nod.

Gus stepped forward and wiped a white hanky over his balding head. He glanced over his shoulder as if he expected his wife to burst through the door at any moment, then turned back to the marshal.

"Tildie told the girl she can have the schoolmarm's job next September," he blurted.

"Damn!" Sam crumbled an old wanted poster into a ball and threw it at a trash can across the room, where it bounced off the rim and fell to the floor. With a disgusted grunt, he pulled his feet from atop his desk and turned to Gus.

"Why did she do a thing like that?" he demanded.

"Miss Drummond has a good education. They talked about temperance marches, too," Gus replied. "The girl said she wanted a schoolmarm's position so she could bring her sick mother out from Boston and marrying Davy was a necessity."

"A likely story, Marshal," Mayor Jones was quick to say. "I'm on that school board as well, and Tildie Schindler will have to convince me that a young woman who would sell herself into marriage would be a suitable schoolmarm."

Sam gave the mayor a deep frown. "She didn't sell herself into marriage, B.F."

The man's bald pate grew as red as his cherry lips, which always appeared squeezed into a pout by his thick muttonchops. "Why are you defending her, Marshal, when we both agree Miss Drummond must leave Starlight? Trouble, she is. I know trouble."

"Now that I won't argue with," Sam replied. "You raised trouble for seventeen years."

The mayor pushed his chair back and stood abruptly. "See here, you can't talk about Caroline that way." He pointed a finger at the ceiling, waving it about as he deemed necessary. "Spirit—my Caroline has spirit, and your idiot brother took advantage of her."

Sam grew very still, leveling his gaze on the pompous man. "Don't ever let me hear you say that again." His voice was quiet, his tone low, controlled, deadly serious.

For a reply, the mayor cleared his throat and jerked at his collar. His lips formed a tight pout that resembled a kiss and he began to pace the office. Sam exchanged a look with Cleve, who sat slumped in a chair by the entrance to the two jail cells in the back. His arms were crossed over the brown loose-fitting vest he wore over a burgundy shirt, his long legs extended before him.

Sam turned his attention to Gus once more. "What's Miss Drummond doing now?"

"Cleaning up, she said, before she went inquiring about a job at Ella King's or one of the dry goods stores."

A corner of Sam's mouth hooked downward, the only sign of his displeasure. Finding the crossed-saber insignia hanging from his watch chain, he rubbed it between his thumb and finger while he thought through this new development. He didn't like it, not at all. Every instinct told him Miss Lucy Drummond didn't have any business in Starlight, and his instincts had gotten him through twelve years of chasing renegade Comanches and Apaches from the Red River to the Rio Grande. Lucy talking to Tildie about the temperance nonsense confirmed those instincts.

No, Lucilla Drummond belonged back in Boston, taking care of her sick mother. He knew what was good for the stubborn woman, even if she didn't.

"Cleve," he said at last. The young man's eyes met his. "I have a job for you." Sam took a deep breath and let it out. "The mayor doesn't want Miss Drummond hired. He's president of the bank. You won't have to say more."

Cleve was on his feet and crossing the floor in pounded jingles before Sam could change his mind. Sam looked past the mayor's pleased expression and returned to sorting through the week's wanted posters. He didn't feel particularly good, but duty rarely permitted that pleasure.

CHAPTER 4

"Sorry, miss. I'm not hiring."

Mr. Pollett gave Lucy a cursory glance, then returned a can of peaches he held to the stacks of canned goods behind him.

Lucy curled her gloved hands into fists. Presented with the back of Mr. Pollett's blue-and-white striped shirt, she didn't bother offering some polite comment to his shiny pink bald spot. At least the other shop owners she had approached that afternoon had been courteous in their refusals.

With little regard for the pressed smoothness of her best dress, Lucy grabbed up handfuls of cream-colored skirt and turned to leave. She strode swiftly past a display table of tangled yard goods, her high-heeled footsteps echoing through the now quiet store.

She paused at the door, her hand resting on the brass knob, and looked back at Mr. Pollett, who was hastily straightening his merchandise after a busy day. The stiff line of her mouth faltered, fought to regain its firmness, then collapsed to a sad frown. With a sigh as soft as the gathering of her petticoats, Lucy left the store.

"Afternoon, Miss Drummond."

The deep voice sent Lucy's heart to her toes. Not him, she thought, not now. Forcing the disappointments of the day from her features, she stopped and faced Sam McQuaid with a studied composure. His big frame lounged against a post, his arms casually crossed over his brocade vest. The faint shadow of a beard darkened his lean cheeks, deepening the cleft in his chin, delineating his solemn mouth.

Smoky blue eyes met hers, then wandered from her upswept hair to her cousin's hand-me-down shoes in a lazy appraisal that warmed her cheeks and sent an odd little tickle to the pit of her stomach, but his expression remained as remote as the dark peaks surrounding the town.

With a marked effort, she straightened her shoulders. "Good afternoon, Marshal."

The proper courtesies observed, Lucy quickly changed directions and proceeded down the boardwalk, in no mood to deal with the marshal's demeaning inspections and badgering demands. She wasn't sure where she was going, but knowing she was moving away from Marshal McQuaid was enough to set her pace at a brisk walk. At least she appeared to have a specific destination in mind. She could head back to the hotel later and ask Tildie for some advice.

Sam stepped up beside her and adjusted his long strides to the full retreat that had set Miss Drummond's skirts in an eye-catching sway. She slanted a disgruntled glance at him but kept walking as if she was headed for a sale on new feathered bonnets.

Considering this particular female, war bonnets were more likely, Sam thought. He took another look at the lifted chin, the frown hovering over her brows, the defiant pout that held his interest a step or two before he recalled his purpose in seeking out Miss Drummond. Sam quickly shifted his attention to the nearly deserted boardwalk ahead and considered the best approach.

"Any luck?" he asked, though he knew the answer. He wanted to test the waters a bit, see how ready she was to admit she had made a mistake and accept his ticket money.

"Luck?" Lucy replied, trying but failing for a noncommittal tone of voice. She cleared her throat. "Whatever do you mean?"

"I hear about most everything that happens in Starlight," Sam said. "Did you find a job?"

Lucy debated telling the marshal anything. She supposed he would hear the truth anyway. The news might as well be told in the way she wanted him to hear it.

"Not yet," she said.

Not ever, Sam thought.

He walked on, wondering where the Boston girl was headed. "The places where you'd want to work are closing up now. Anybody tell you Starlight's not safe for ladies after dusk?"

Lucy didn't miss his intended reminder of their morning talk. No man to protect her, indeed. She refused to be intimidated by his threatening innuendos.

"I'm aware precautions are necessary, Marshal. I grew up in a big city."

"Just my point, Miss Drummond. Look around you. This isn't Boston."

Despite her pique, Lucy followed the marshal's suggestion and ventured a hurried inspection of Main Street. Few women walked the boardwalk now and the shopkeepers were indeed closing their stores. Traffic along the wide roadway had dwindled to a few riders and a slow-moving market wagon headed out of town.

Across the road, a large man wearing an army cap was

lighting the brass lanterns on each side of an establishment called the Outpost. She caught the strains of a lonely guitar melody that drifted to her on a cooling breeze. Horses tied to hitching rails switched their tails in a desultory manner and a man wearing a long white duster sat with his feet propped up, his hat tipped over his face, napping in the late afternoon quiet.

The only disturbing quality of the day was that it had almost ended and she hadn't discovered even the possibility of a job. She certainly wasn't going to discuss that setback with the marshal. Instead, she launched into a reply that stated clearly she was not to be fooled so easily.

"You're right, Marshal McQuaid. This isn't Boston. Starlight is much more peaceful." She glanced up at him and found aggravation added a definite edge to his good looks but welcomed the change from his usual cool disinterest. "In fact," she said, aiming a satisfied half-smile at the end of the block, "you can go about your business now."

"I'd like to, Miss Drummond, but," he caught her elbow and turned her around so she could see he meant what he said, "while you're in Starlight, you *are* my business."

Any notion of a smile forgotten now, Lucy jerked her arm free and stepped back. "Forget this ridiculous mission you have set for yourself. I don't want or need your assistance." Lucy didn't wait for his response, but started down the boardwalk once more, wishing he would leave her be.

Sam caught up with her and walked along beside her, admiring the color rising in her cheeks, the sparkle in her eyes the spectacles couldn't dim. He'd bet a pair of deuces to an ace showing that the Boston girl had no idea how a little fire affected her pale looks and warmed a man. That is, men who found the marrying sort appealing, he was quick to add.

Hell, he had things to do. She didn't show any signs of

picking up any sense. Time to put a stop to this foolishness. "The hotel's in the other direction. You can stop running from me and head that way now."

Surprised, Lucy darted a glance at him, then searched frantically for some excuse to be in this part of town, one that would make it clear she hadn't taken off to avoid him. She spied the dressmaker's shop wedged between the bakery and the drugstore and grabbed on to the only idea she could come up with.

"Running from you?" She added an indignant look for good measure. "As a matter of fact, I need to speak with Mrs. King," she said, and hoped the marshal would go on to his office in the next block. "I'll return to the hotel when I'm ready."

Lucy didn't know what to make of his silence, but he continued to keep pace with her, slowing as she approached the shop. She wasn't certain about her reception here. Mrs. King had been the first person she had spoken to that day, and the interview hadn't gone well.

Finding a nervous smile, Lucy lifted her white-gloved hand to Mrs. King, who was closing the door to her dressmaking shop. Peering at them through the glass window in her door, the kindly white-haired woman gave her a faltering smile with a sliding glance at the marshal, then quickly lowered the windowshade. The tick-tick of the pull ring swinging against the door testified to the woman's hasty retreat.

Lucy dropped her own smile with her hand, embarrassed and hurt but determined not to show it. She turned to the marshal, her fingers worrying the cords on her reticule, thinking of what to say as she spoke.

"I can't say I'm surprised by Mrs. King's odd behavior," she began. "I . . . I stopped here earlier to speak with her about a job and she had been complimentary about my sewing skills. I made this dress before I came out here, you see."

Sam noted the lace insets at bodice and sleeves, the coral ribbons trimming the creamy material. It was the kind of dress a young woman would like to wear on her wedding day.

"It's a pretty dress, Miss Drummond," Sam said, affected more than he wanted to admit by the hurt and confusion the young woman tried to hide. He'd add some extra money to that envelope when he got back to the office.

Once begun, Lucy saw no other course but to finish telling what had happened. "Then I introduced myself and Mrs. King became so nervous she could barely talk. Mrs. Schindler's letter of recommendation didn't help at all. In the end, I found myself comforting the poor woman, telling her not to feel badly, that I understood."

She looked down at her entangled fingers, realizing her story didn't blend well with the excuse she had given for walking down here. "But, I didn't understand. I . . . I thought I might try again."

For the first time in his life, Sam couldn't face the person with whom he spoke. He turned away, gazing down the almost empty roadway. "Mrs. King's a decent woman," he said. "She must have had her reasons." Like a loan at Caroline's daddy's bank, he thought. Too bad Miss Drummond's stubbornness had forced him to make these tough decisions.

"Maybe so, but she needed the help," Lucy replied, more curious than careful now. "She had backed-up orders everywhere and two ladies came in complaining while I was there." She looked up at the marshal, a sudden fear taking shape in her mind, growing stronger than her reluctance to tell him more. "In fact, mostly everyone I talked to today could have used some help, but no one was interested in me."

Before she approached him with her suspicion, Lucy studied the marshal's reaction to her story. She expected some caustic remark, a knowing look, another demand she give up. Instead, he looked everywhere but at her. The long grooves on each side of his mouth deepened in silent discomfort. Sam McQuaid knew something, something that made him mighty uneasy. She had to ask him. She had to know and the marshal had no reason not to tell her straight out.

She gave a quick glance to the left and right and saw the boardwalk was empty. Clearing her throat, she pushed at her spectacles. "I was wondering if perhaps my . . . marriage arrangement with David . . . had . . . you know . . . had made people think badly of me." She looked up at him, seeking clues in those eyes that now appeared more worn and weary than ever.

Lucy's candidness put Sam in a quandary. He could say yes, and she would most likely give up this schoolmarm notion of hers, but David's impulsive tom-foolery had hurt her enough. A good reputation was valuable to her kind. David was at fault, not Lucy. He refused to use or add to that hurt. She would go home soon enough when she couldn't find a job.

"No one thinks badly of you, Miss Drummond." He looked into her autumn eyes. "I guarantee it."

Lucy believed him. Sam McQuaid wasn't a man who lied. He wore his honesty as openly as his badge, in his direct, unsettling gaze, in the no-nonsense manner he spoke. "Thank you, Marshal," she said quietly, and started back to the hotel.

She took a few steps, pondering Mrs. King's strange behavior and the other shopkeepers' refusals to hire her. "I still don't understand. . . ." She remembered that odd look Mrs. King had given Sam.

Lucy stopped so abruptly, the marshal had to turn back to face her. "You don't want me to stay in Starlight," she said. "If I can't find employment for the summer, I can't stay." Lucy saw more than truth when she looked at Sam. Determination, authority and, yes, arrogance had carved his features into a forbidding presence. "*You're* behind all of this."

Sam had no trouble meeting her accusing glare. "You don't belong in my town, Miss Drummond. I've told you why, but you won't see reason."

"Reason? So that's what you call it." She gave him one of his own top-to-bottom inspections. "I wouldn't be frightened out of town this morning, so you resorted to backroom manipulations."

Regretting nothing, Sam replied, "I did what I had to do."

Lucy curled her hands into tight fists. "I know your type. I was raised with your kind of corrupt power, lost my father to it." She thought of her mother, ill and destitute, living on her uncle and aunt's charity. "I won't let you destroy my dreams."

Sam had reached his limit. "Time to wake up, Miss Drummond. Girls with no money, no menfolk, no one who gives a damn about them, end up working at Sweet Nell's place, doing all their dreaming on their backs."

Lucy flushed to her toes. No one spoke of such matters to a lady. Angry tears stung her eyelids. "Sam McQuaid, stay out of my life." Not trusting herself to say more, she pushed past him.

Sam grabbed her arm, pulling her around to face him, holding her when she tried to jerk free. "You have no idea what can happen out here," he said, his voice low, gritty, filled with the ugliness he had seen. "I do."

Lucy looked up into eyes where hope no longer dwelled, where hard, bitter experience left him blind to others' dreams. He would never understand people like her, only those like himself.

"I'm staying in Starlight," she said. "I'm staying whether you like it or not."

She looked at his hand on her arm, then slowly raised her gaze to his face. For a moment, when her eyes met his, when her heart pounded so hard she thought he must hear it, she feared he might not release her. What then? She couldn't guess, and the unknown opened before her in all its dark, scintillating possibilities.

Sam wanted to shake her. She wouldn't listen to him; she wouldn't believe him. Maybe he'd show her what she could expect. From more impulse than thought, the desire to kiss the defiance from her mouth caught him off guard, a wild punch to the gut that forced him to release her. Without a word, he stepped out of her way. With one flash of bewildered vexation, she swept past him.

He couldn't explain that instant of desire and his tone of voice expressed his irritation. "Save yourself time and more embarrassment, Miss Drummond. No one's going to hire you."

Lucy kept walking, lengthening the distance between herself and the marshal as quickly as possible without running. Her anguish had no tears, her anger no words. Hard cold fury settled in her heart with a heaviness that ached. She stared straight ahead, seeing nothing, only the endless journey back to Boston, back to her aunt and uncle's crowded little house, back to the legacy of the day her father's life had been snatched from her by ruthless, corrupt men; men like Marshal Sam McQuaid.

Sam retrieved a long, thin cigar and a match from his coat pocket. Keeping his eyes trained on the Boston girl, he struck the match on his bootheel and lit his cigar. The welcome bite of tobacco cleared his head. As he watched her walk away, he took special note of the ramrod stiffness of her back, the proud tilt of her head. Hell, he'd dealt with army mules more cooperative than this girl. She'd have given David a good kick in the ass, given the boy some sand, maybe. The idea of his brother married to Lucy Drummond ruined the taste of his cigar.

Upon reaching the corner, city-bred caution halted Lucy's steps, and without conscious thought, she checked for cross traffic. To the right, an empty country lane led up a hill into the pines. A loud, sharp popping sound jerked her attention to the left. The man who had been napping so peacefully moments before lunged to his feet and whipped a rifle out from beneath the long duster he wore. In a heartbeat, the weapon was cocked and aimed at a spot behind her: the marshal.

"Look out," she cried.

"Get down."

She heard the shout as she twisted around and saw Marshal McQuaid, his revolver drawn, dive onto the road. The glass storefront behind him exploded in a hail of lead. She held her breath as more shots kicked up tiny fountains of dust that followed his rolling body to a water trough. She didn't breathe again until she saw him throw his hat to the side and flatten his shoulders to the rough wood, waiting for the rapid shots to slow.

Forgetting the marshal's order, caught up in the sudden violence, Lucy held on to the post beside her, her attention rivetted to the scene in the street. The man with the rifle gave a sharp whistle, then leaped over the hitching rail, ducking among the skittish horses. Seconds later, another man dressed in an identical long white coat burst backwards through a saloon's swinging doors, his revolvers blazing, the sounds of shattering glass coming from inside. Her view was blocked by a runaway team racing down the road, pulling a loaded haywagon.

Sam rolled to his feet and ran to the center of the road, every sense connected to the gun in his hand. He waited for the wagon to roll past him, cursing stubborn women who took his time and haywagons that blocked his shots. He needed a clear target. A miss might kill a bystander.

Lucy's position farther down the block afforded her a better view through the dust and gunsmoke hanging over the road. The big man in the army cap charged down the boardwalk, a double-barreled shotgun clutched in his hands. He fired from the hip, sending the second man into a bloody sprawl over the hitching rail. A rifle shot clipped the big man in the shoulder, spinning him around.

Lucy caught sight of a white duster fly open as the remaining gunman sprang into his saddle and dug his spurs into his mount's flanks. The horse screamed and plunged in her direction. Drawing his revolver, the man fired behind him, sending the men rushing from the saloons for cover. Her eyes wide and staring, Lucy watched the man head straight for her.

Sam stood in the center of the road, his arm outstretched, his aim following the rider, waiting for his chance. Too many people had run out to see the excitement. "Get down," he shouted. "Get down."

The son-of-a-bitch didn't give him much to hit the way he clung to the side of his mount like a damned Apache. He waited, waited, closing out the uproar surrounding him. When the man popped up into the saddle, as Sam hoped he would, a cream-colored dress appeared in his line of fire. Sam jerked his weapon up, firing the round his instincts had squeezed off into the air, a filthy curse falling from his lips. He broke into a full run for the corner.

Lucy looked up into black eyes as cold as death. The gunman was going to kill her. Before her thought was completed, she saw the hand holding his pistol rise as the outlaw galloped past. She slammed herself against the wall. Three gunshots deafened her. Splinters of wood sprayed from the post where she had stood. She closed her eyes, breathing in deep gulps of air, listening to the retreating thunder of the gunman's horse.

"Don't move."

The marshal's harsh order opened her eyes as he ran to the center of the intersecting road. He took his position, his legs braced, and fired at the fleeing gunman, filling the air with gun blasts and the smell of gun powder. Lucy cupped her hands over her ears but couldn't take her eyes off Sam. Return fire spit dust around his feet, but he didn't stir, taking aim and firing again.

During a lull in the shooting, Lucy caught an odd but familiar jingling sound approach from her left. A quick peek around a window casing identified the marshal's deputy running down the road, half of his shirttail shoved into his pants, his vest hanging off one shoulder. He carried his gunbelt in one hand, his pistol in the other.

She was relieved to see help arriving. Dear God, the marshal had been right. Starlight wasn't Boston. Lucy shivered as if a cold breeze had blown through the little town.

Out of pure frustration Sam fired one more shot as the gray horse disappeared around a bend in the road. Damn! The bastard had gotten away. He spun around, emptying his revolver's chambers, then tugged cartridges from his gunbelt. He looked up at hearing Cleve.

"Where were you?" He took a look at Lucy, assuring himself she hadn't been hurt, but lingering long enough for her to read the justification he felt. She could have been killed, and by the look of her she knew it. She dropped her gaze, crossing her arms tightly around herself.

Cleve trotted up, out of breath and worried. "At supper."

Sam raked a look over the deputy's disheveled appearance while he punched bullets into his Colt. "Buying dessert at Sweet Nell's?"

Cleve shoved his revolver into his holster and shook his head, then looked up at Sam. "Sam, I—"

"Get some men together," the marshal said, his tone curt and uninterested in excuses. "I'm going after the bastard. You stay here and see what information you can piece together."

Cleve sighed, gave him a nod, and trotted off, shouting for riders and horses.

Dropping his Colt into his holster, he accepted his hat from a half-grown boy, who brushed the dust from it with his shirt sleeve. "Thanks, Gil. How's Sarge?"

The towheaded boy looked up at Sam, one eye squinting against the sun. "He's cussin' a blue streak over yonder, yellin' at the sawbones to let 'im be so's he can ride with the cap'n."

"Old warhorse," Sam muttered, but a tightness in his gut eased. He brushed at the dust on his coat, looking across the road to see his old regimental sergeant giving the doctor hell. "Tell Doc if Sarge O'Reilly gives him any trouble to hit him upside the head with a whiskey bottle. That's been known to get his attention."

"I'll tell 'im, Marshal," the boy replied, and started across the road, pushing through the small crowd of men making their way toward him.

"The dead one tried to rob my place, Marshal."

Sam recognized Red Grady, owner of the Painted Pony Dancehall, leading the group. The round-paunched little man hooked his thumbs in his red suspenders. "Killed a new fella around here named Otis Tyler."

"Anybody else hurt?"

"Naw. We all hit the floor pretty quick."

"Good." Sam scanned the crowd, picking out Leslie Laughton's long, haughty face in the back. Most of the men gathered were other saloon owners and a few miners from Red's place.

"Anybody see the other gunman?" Sam asked, searching the crowd for possible witnesses. "I never got a good look at his face." He'd have put a bullet in it if he had. Sam muttered a soft curse under his breath, remembering his lost chance.

Low mumbles and shaking heads gave him his answer. Sam nodded, a hard frown closing over his features. The outlaws were professionals, probably wanted, he thought. The federal marshals might know something about them.

Sam spied Cleve leading a saddled and feisty Colonel MacKenzie toward them. Mac was ready for the chase. It looked like his posse was going to be Dolf Miller and a couple of boys from the Triple Creek spread.

Several more miners and a few drifters joined the little group of saloon owners. "Any of you see that bastard who got away?"

"I saw him."

Everyone looked behind Sam. He turned around slowly, wishing he hadn't heard that low, soft voice. Lucy Drummond couldn't be his only witness. She stood at the edge of the boardwalk, her hands clasped at her waist, her brows gathered above her spectacles, a picture of nervous indecision.

"I saw the gunman's face," she said, somewhat louder, but her face remained white-sheet pale.

Sam lifted his gaze to the heavens. "Damn."

CHAPTER 5

Lucy sat at a small table beside her bed. Lamplight spilled across a neat stack of writing paper. A pen and a bottle of ink waited beside the blank sheets. Five crumpled wads of paper had been pushed to the side and *Duel at Deadwood* lay open before her.

The story unfolded with new insight. A dark-suited figure recited the lawman's dialogue in a deep familiar voice. Blue eyes were filled with "righteous vigor" and were "as piercing as an eagle's." A once forbidding expression was now "firm and unyielding" and a "prominent chin" featured an intriguing cleft. Masked robbers rode the Black Hills and the "remarkably pretty young miss" was in danger. The young miss didn't wear spectacles, however.

A soft knock at her door sent *Duel at Deadwood* under the thin stack of papers. Lucy resettled her spectacles and rose from the table. Tildie must have sent someone up for her supper tray, a kindness she appreciated after her experience on the street that had culminated with two hours of examining wanted posters.

Lucy crossed the room, wondering if she would sleep at

all tonight. So many faces, but to the deputy's disappointment, not one resembling the man with the cold black eyes.
She had done her best at describing him, but other than a
dark complexion, dark hair and eyes, she hadn't been too
helpful. Cleve Hardesty hadn't thought so anyway. She
hadn't appreciated him taking his ill humor out on her
simply because he had been . . . well . . . occupied
when the marshal had needed him.

Lucy picked up the tray of dirty dishes sitting on a small
bureau, then opened the door. "Tildie," she said, surprised to
see the manager's wife, who had been bustling about the
closed restaurant earlier, arranging a place for the temperance ladies to meet. "Is your meeting over so soon?"

"No, no, dear," Tildie replied. "I've come to get you. The
ladies want to hear all about the marches you saw in
Boston."

The dishes on the tray slid forward. Lucy jerked it
straight. "I . . . I . . ." She couldn't speak about something she had never seen. "I'm so sorry, Tildie. I . . ." She
glanced over her shoulder, hoping for inspiration but thankful for the momentary stall, and she thought about the failed
attempts at writing to her mother. She faced Tildie with the
proper look of regret. "I really must finish a letter to my
mother. She'll be worried."

"Nonsense, girl," Tildie replied, tilting her head back, her
coronet of braids tilting out of sight. "You need to get out of
this room, enjoy a little female companionship after your
terrible ordeal today." She took the tray from Lucy's tight
grip. "Come. Finish your letter later."

Lucy ran a hand down the navy-blue skirt she wore. "I'm
really not dressed to meet anyone, Tildie."

"Ach! You look fine. The ladies are so anxious to hear
from you. Don't disappoint them."

Seeing no gracious way to extricate herself, Lucy accepted the inevitable. "I'll get my things."

Tildie waited for her in the hall while she retrieved her reticule from the table. She hadn't had a chance yet to talk to Tildie about leaving. She didn't really know what to say. Words hadn't come easily to tell her mother she was coming home, either. More immediate was what to tell to these women about temperance marches, something she knew nothing about.

As if wading through rapids, Lucy followed Tildie down the darkened hallway; weak knees hardly suited for walking down the stairs. The small lobby was empty save for Mr. Schindler, who stood behind the registration desk, reading a newspaper. Tildie set the tray of dirty dishes next to her husband.

"Take care of this, Mr. Schindler."

The flustered man fumbled the pages closed. "Be happy to, *Liebchen*. The meeting almost over?"

"Miss Drummond is about to speak to us about the marches she attended in Boston," Tildie replied, giving her a deep nod and smile.

The hotel manager's lips stretched into a thin smile. "How nice, *Liebchen*," he replied, and rattled the paper open once more.

"We are very fortunate to have Miss Drummond among us," Tildie relied. "Come along, dear."

Tildie urged her along before Lucy could correct the impatient woman. She had never claimed she had *attended* any meetings, only had seen them. Lucy turned to address the misunderstanding, but found Mr. Schindler peeking at her around the edge of his paper with sharp speculation. He quickly ducked back behind the paper. A frown flicked across Lucy's features and she faced ahead, no longer concerned with misunderstandings but with Mr. Schindler's odd behavior.

Something about the little man disturbed her. He appeared harmless, with his tufts of white hair sticking up from the top of his head and over his ears, but she sensed he hid something behind his obsequious manner. She supposed marriage to Tildie wasn't easy and would make a man the nervous type.

Gaining a deeper understanding of Mr. Schindler's burden to bear with each step, Lucy followed Tildie's regal advance into the closed restaurant. A large chandelier made of wood and beaten copper lit a small group in the center of the room. Tables had been pushed into the surrounding shadows, and at least fifteen ladies filled the chairs aligned in several short rows facing a tall, strong-featured woman. Lucy recognized her as the woman who had led the march down Main Street that morning.

"There you are, Tildie, and you've convinced Miss Drummond to join us," the woman said with a smile.

The ladies sitting in the chairs twisted around almost in unison. Every eye trained on Lucy. She almost wished she was back in the marshal's office with his surly deputy looking at bankrobbers and murderers rather than these smiling, expectant faces. A few heads tipped together, nodding at whispered statements, and Lucy was ready to leave.

Tildie took hold of her arm and provided strong assistance to the front of the room. "Lucy, meet Maggie Thompson, publisher and editor of the *Starlight Observer* and the leader of our endeavors to break rum's hold on our town."

Lucy accepted the firm handshake offered her, meeting the woman's sharp, gray eyes. "Good to meet you, Miss . . . Mrs. . . . ."

"Mrs. Thompson, Lucy," Maggie said. "Widowed by the evils of strong drink."

A low murmuring met this declaration. Lucy said a soft, "I'm so sorry."

Maggie turned to the ladies. "I'm sorry, too, Lucy. I'm sorry that demon rum robs us of our husbands, snatches our sons into sin and"—she directed her gaze to a plump, pink-cheeked woman wearing a chip bonnet festooned with ribbon, lace and a white plume—"impure pasttimes." Pink cheeks deepened to rose and Maggie continued, including all of the ladies with a sweeping look. "And attacks our sacred homes."

The murmuring grew to assertive "yes's" and the pink-checked woman's white plume bobbed vigorously. "We must save our homes," she repeated.

"Ladies, ladies," Tildie said, her hands clasped together, her index fingers extended toward the audience. "It's time to meet our guest, who has kindly agreed to share her experiences from the East and possibly give us new directions to take."

Lucy linked her fingers in front of her, thinking of only one direction she would like to take: out the door. She hadn't a notion of what to say to these women. Tildie gave her a little push forward.

"You have all heard about Miss Drummond, and her unfortunate trip to Starlight with the promise of matrimony only to be abandoned by the marshal's brother," Tildie announced. "But, our Lucy would not be undone. She came to me and bravely sought another course. She wants to stay in Starlight and replace Miss Little in teaching our children."

Applause broke out among the ladies. The nods to one another were now enthusiastic and the faces lifted to her showed smiling approval. Lucy thought of the naive girl who had walked into Tildie's office that morning, full of hope and dreams, and how much she had wanted this favorable reception.

Tonight, after blood, gunsmoke, and chilling terror, after looking death in the eye and having him smile at her . . .

Lucy blinked and looked inward, seeing once more the gunman's smirk she had forgotten, the nasty grin that had revealed a gap between strong white teeth, feral teeth, like an animal's. She could almost smell the gunpowder again, hear the ear-numbing blasts, see the splinters of wood. She hated this fear that consumed her resolve, sapped her strength. Hated it, but couldn't rid herself of the pestilence.

She wished she had talked to Tildie earlier, explained she couldn't find a job, ended this journey to Starlight. She was a fake in more ways than one.

Tildie raised her hands and the clapping died away. "During our interview, Lucy praised our march, which must have seemed amateurish to a well-educated woman from Boston. That's why I have asked her to speak to us tonight. Please welcome Miss Lucy Drummond, Starlight's next schoolmarm, if I have anything to do with it, and I think you ladies will agree that matter is as good as settled."

Titters and quiet applause followed. Tildie and Maggie took seats in chairs up front and arranged to the side. Lucy nodded to the two ladies, Tildie looking pleased and Maggie holding her opinion behind a noncommittal closed-mouthed little smile.

Lucy cleared her throat and faced the gathering. The women looked up at her, settling down with a polite cough or two and the rustling of petticoats. They waited for her to begin, and Lucy knew she must. Tildie had been willing to give her a chance. She wasn't going to embarrass the proud woman by appearing less than what was promised. Lucy decided that sticking to the truth as much as possible should keep her out of deep water.

"As I told Tildie today," she began, her voice steadied by the pact she had made with herself, "I have seen few, if any, temperance organizations give such a rousing demonstration as I witnessed on Main Street this morning."

She smiled at the applause that statement elicited. This wasn't going to be that difficult. She spied the tall, robust woman sitting in the back, the woman who had beat that infernal drum. "The drum playing gave special emphasis and drew attention, while the white ribbons added"—what had she said to Tildie?—"unity and a purity of spirit." More applause rewarded her efforts and she began to relax.

"What have you seen that proved truly effective in closing gin parlors?" Maggie asked.

The women quieted, waiting for her answer. Lucy sent a frozen smile to the newspaper woman, adjusted her spectacles, and tried to catch one thought from the many that scampered through her mind like a rabbit chased by a coyote. She straightened her skirt, discarding the aching smile along with the few ideas she captured. What had she seen, indeed? Vaguely, Lucy recalled reading about the temperance crusade of the early seventies and decided she *had* seen the methods used then, if only in books.

She cleared her throat and assumed a suitably serious expression. "Some groups used entire bands, but I considered those a bit showy, taking away from the . . . the simplicity of the message."

Feathers and flowers and big, bright bows bobbed approval over the gathering, especially from the large woman in the back. Her two ostrich feathers threatened to take flight.

"What did they do to close saloons?" Maggie's voice rose once more above the soft chattering.

"Thank you, Maggie," Lucy said, her tone surprising her with its pleasance. "I was just getting to that." She turned to the ladies. "The methods that proved most effective were setting up tables, where names were taken of those who visited these places. Prayer vigils also proved helpful."

Arms crossed with purpose and quiet nods followed. Lucy stepped back, hoping Maggie didn't have any more questions she would have to dig up answers for.

"Thank you, ladies," Maggie said. She turned to Lucy, curiosity and a touch of humor adding a subtle softness to her eyes. "And thank you, Lucy, for a most informative talk." She didn't wait for a response but urged the ladies to take their seats once more, indicating with a gesture Lucy should take the one she had vacated, and began taking suggestions for the next march.

Tildie gave her shoulder a pat, then joined the discussion. Lucy found herself becoming more interested in the woman who printed the newspaper and led the temperance marches. No feathers, lace, or ribbons for Maggie Thompson. Her faded brown hair was twisted up in a careless knot atop her head, and she wore a beige skirt and jacket of the plainest cut, trimmed only with thin braiding.

Lucy imagined something similar for teaching purposes. Only now she wouldn't be teaching, at least, not here. No point in dwelling on any of that. Sam McQuaid had been right about Starlight. A woman alone . . . she sighed. What did it matter? She couldn't get a job for the summer. That was that.

Lucy listened to the excuses coming from the floor at Maggie's urging for another march to be held soon. Ice cream socials, washing day, baking to be done, and a child's birthday narrowed the choices; too many demands on busy lives. Maggie finally chose Friday, three days from today.

"Those who can make it should meet at the newspaper

office by nine o'clock," Maggie **said**. **Shakes** or nods met this announcement. "That's all **for this** evening, ladies. Tildie has set up coffee and cake for us. We are adjourned."

Conversation settled into a pleasant hum and the meeting broke into a social gathering. Tired, and wishing to avoid further half-truths and misrepresentations, Lucy turned to give her excuses to Tildie but was interrupted by a woman who wanted to meet her, then another. More filed by, each with a gracious welcome to Starlight, awkward references to David's perfidy, and more questions about temperance leagues she had seen in action.

Lucy accepted the first with a smile, even for the wives of two of the men who wouldn't hire her, had no response for the second, and fielded the third with quick assertions that she had been too young to be more than an interested observer to temperance league activities. All the ladies went away with pleasant smiles and promises of support for her as Starlight's new teacher. At last, she shook the last hand and hoped to make a quiet escape.

Several ladies stood among the chairs chatting with Maggie, while others had gathered in pairs and threesomes around a table set up by the kitchen table. Tildie was speaking to the small, pink-cheeked woman with the plumed chip bonnet. Lucy slowly made her way around the pair.

"I've tried to get him to sign the pledge," the woman said, her feather dipping and shivering, "but he won't listen." She continued relating her trials.

Lucy turned to side-step them, but Tildie caught her arm. She didn't look at her but nodded to the older woman, an understanding frown knitting her brow. Lucy waited, wishing the woman would end her tale of the prodigal son. If he was anything like Aunt Ada's oldest boy, the story had no end.

"Dolly," Tildie finally interrupted, "it is young men just like your Cleve we hope to save from the clutches of demon rum."

"Yes, yes, I know," Dolly replied with a long-suffering sigh. "That's why I'll make time for Friday."

"Good." Tildie turned to her. "Lucy, I'd like for you to meet Dolly Hardesty. She's our deputy's mother."

Lucy had suspected as much when she had heard the son's name. She now understood that piercing look the woman had received from Maggie earlier.

"I'm happy to meet you, Mrs. Hardesty," she said.

"Please call me Dolly," the woman replied, smiling up at her. "People in Starlight don't stand on ceremony. Cleve told me about your ordeal today." Dolly gave her a sympathetic pat on the arm. "I'm so sorry. Nothing like that has happened since Sam McQuaid took the marshal's job two years ago."

"Yes, it was unpleasant," Lucy replied, striving for a note of understatement. "I'm relieved no one in town was hurt badly."

The tall drum-playing woman arrived, a cup of fragrant coffee in one hand and a plate of cookies in the other. "The posse hasn't returned yet."

Tildie made the introductions, then said, "Leila's husband, Dolf, always rides with the marshal."

"He was a blacksmith and in the regimental band posted with Captain McQuaid," Leila Miller announced, her head held high. "Retired from the regiment with him and Sarge O'Reilly."

"That old drunken Irishman," Tildie murmured.

Lucy watched the ladies, listening closely to what they had to say about Sam McQuaid. An army officer, too. Not much imagination was required to picture him in a blue uniform, so straight and tall. And those blue eyes . . .

"Sarge O'Reilly is a good man," Leila replied. "He helped the marshal out today."

"He's a bad influence on young men like Cleve," Tildie stated.

"Is that the man who was shot?" Lucy inquired, remembering the big man with the shotgun and beat-up army cap.

"Yes, but Doc says he's doing fine," Leila replied.

Tildie crossed her arms. "He's a saloon keeper."

Leila stood straighter, topping Tildie's coronet by two inches. "He manages the captain's gambling house just like your husband manages the captain's hotel and . . . billiard room."

Tildie's eyebrows shot up. "We only serve beer in there. Good, healthy German beer."

Dolly made a quick retreat, and Lucy thought she had a grand idea. "Think I'll turn in now," she said, not wanting to leave without saying something.

Tildie broke off the staring match with Leila and replaced her scowl with a look of concern. "I know you must be tired, but come meet the rest of the ladies. This is a good opportunity for you. Two members have husbands on the school board."

Lucy dashed a glance to Leila, who quietly sipped her coffee. She wasn't going to leave, but Lucy decided her presence didn't matter. "Thank you so much for your help, Tildie, but . . ." She looked down at her hands. "I couldn't find a job today. No one was hiring."

She didn't mention Leila's captain's behind-the-scenes maneuvering. Marshal McQuaid's interference still rankled, but considering the circumstances, not nearly as much as before the shootout. She met Tildie's scowl. "It looks as though I'll have to return to Boston."

"I can't believe this." Tildie clamped a hand on her arm

once more and pulled her toward the ladies gathered around
the refreshment table.

Lucy had no idea what the woman had in mind, but she
didn't have a say in the matter—that was clear. She certainly
would like to take control of her life again. First the marshal
interfered, and now Tildie dragged her from one thing to
another. At least, Tildie meant well.

"Ladies, Lucy tells me she was unable to find employment today." She aimed her scowl at a brunette woman in
the back. "Etta Hamilton, I suggested your husband's dry
goods store because you were just saying you wouldn't be
able to help him much longer, being in the family way and
all."

Etta, a young woman wearing a plaid, full-cut Mother
Hubbard, looked down, her face growing red. Lucy wished
Tildie hadn't embarrassed the poor woman. It just made the
situation more awkward.

Another woman stepped forward. "Etta won't tell you,
Tildie, but I will. Cleve told everyone who might hire Miss
Drummond that the mayor didn't want her staying in town.
The marshal went along with it. Mayor Jones owns the
bank, and the bank owns the town. There you have it, plain
and simple."

"Oh, that man!" Tildie said.

"Which one?" someone piped up.

"All of them," Tildie replied. "Think of it. Lucy has a sick
mother to care for and all that mayor can think of is that
silly, spoiled daughter of his."

"And the marshal—his brother," a thin, sharp-featured
woman added.

Lucy hadn't known about the mayor, but he was only a
tool, she was certain. Sam McQuaid was his own man. She
wanted to be fair. "Marshal McQuaid was concerned about
my safety, I believe."

"Look how just this woman is," Tildie claimed. "Taking up for the man." She turned to Lucy. "I assure you, Lucy, Sam McQuaid looks out for his own interests. I suspect he and the mayor heard of your temperance experience and did not want us to profit by it."

A general consenting mood swept through the ladies. Lucy was surprised to hear one or two mention they had heard something to that effect. She remembered Gus Schindler's sly look. No doubt he had overheard her morning conversation with Tildie and reported back to the marshal. After all, he owned a gambling establishment and the temperance ladies would certainly be troublesome. The most frustrating part of the whole scheme was that Marshal McQuaid's warnings of danger had proven too real to ignore.

"It really doesn't matter, Tildie," she said. "I don't want to make trouble for anyone. Starlight will find another schoolmarm."

Tildie tilted her chin up. "Not with your credentials or courage, Lucy. This young lady has a finishing school education and the heart of a lioness, I tell you. She did not falter this afternoon when others might have swooned at the first shot."

"Cleve said Lucy's description could lead to the arrest of a professional outlaw," Dolly added. "Those kind do not like being identified, I can tell you."

Lucy's eyes widened, then blinked back her surprise at the disquieting news. "I appreciate your support, ladies," she said. "Really I do. I would love to teach your children." Lucy swallowed back the sick feeling crawling up her throat. "But, I guess I wasn't meant to be Starlight's schoolmarm."

"Remember what you told me?" Tildie inquired.

Lucy shook her head, thinking she had told Tildie too much.

"You told me when you saw that notice in the paper stating Starlight needed a schoolmarm, you thought you had found an answer to a prayer."

"Yes," she replied, "that's true, but . . ." She made a valiant effort to find that spark, that determination, that will to make her dreams come true once more. But all she found was a sore, empty place in her heart and an excuse. "I won't be the cause of problems for anyone. It's best I return to Boston. I can try again through the agencies." That bone thrown to her pride gave her a little peace.

"If I could give you a job for the summer I would," Tildie said. "And the marshal could go to blazes, but I have nothing."

A silence fell over the little group, the soft sounds of cutlery on china and cups returning to saucers an indication of the ladies' sudden interest in finding something to do other than volunteer a job or meet Tildie's challenging survey. Lucy took pity on the dismayed assemblage and decided to end their misery. She understood the pressures they faced.

"I've enjoyed meeting all of you ladies," she said, looking at each tense face. "I . . . I admire you all for your pioneering spirit," she added, and the warmth in her voice gave no doubts she meant what she said.

A lighter mood settled over the group. Ladies she hadn't met yet ventured forward, shaking her hand, thanking her for her information. Lucy slowly made her way to the door, relieved it was almost over.

"Miss Drummond," Maggie called out to her.

Lucy tipped her head to the side and peered around Deputy Hardesty's mother and Etta. She hadn't seen the newspaper woman standing among the shadows. The ladies parted, giving Maggie a clear path.

Maggie stepped up to her. "Miss Drummond . . . Lucy, with all the extra time I must give to the cause, I could use extra help at the newspaper. I can't pay much, but I can provide room and board and an inside look at the newspaper business." She pulled her head back, looking at Lucy through a skeptic's eyes. "Are you interested?"

Tildie rushed over to them. "Of course she is. This is wonderful, Lucy."

"Yes, wonderful," Lucy replied, her attention still held by those measuring gray eyes that saw a great deal more than they should.

They provided a mirror Lucy didn't care to look into. No excuses, now. She had to face herself. What did she see? A coward running home to her mother and the same dead ends she had tried to escape. What did she want to see? A woman who grabbed her chances when they came her way. A woman who didn't let those opportunities go when they became too difficult.

Maggie didn't prompt her with word or look but simply met her eyes with a steady directness. Lucy swallowed her nervousness and replaced it with a determined smile. "Thank you, Maggie. I accept." She folded her arms over her jumpy stomach and locked her gaze on Maggie's. "When do I start?"

A smile broke out on the newspaperwoman's face. She grabbed Lucy's hand and shook it. "Start tomorrow morning at eight, Lucy. The sooner the better."

Etta led the ladies in rushing forward to congratulate her. "You should see the charming little house the town provides," Etta said. "It will be just perfect for you and your mother."

"It has four rooms and an inside pump," Leila added. "We value our schoolmarms in Starlight."

Lucy smiled, feeling better than she had for hours. "Yes, I'll want to take a look at it so I can describe it to Mother."

Other ladies crowded around, offering tidbits about their children, telling her she had their full support. Lucy smiled more, offering appropriate remarks and thanks.

Far back in her mind, she recalled the marshal's curse at finding she was his only witness, and she wished she *had* swooned at the first shot that afternoon. She pushed the image of cold black eyes from her mind and filled it with imaginings of her little house—a home for her and her mother. She bit her lip, hoping she had made the right decision. A soft touch to her elbow interrupted Lucy's thoughts.

"Do you have a moment?" Maggie said, her expression giving no clue she had noticed Lucy's nervousness.

"Of course." Lucy welcomed the distraction and the opportunity to finally talk with Maggie alone.

Maggie drew her to the side. "I saw you talking to Marshal McQuaid today."

Lucy colored, remembering the heated discussion. "Yes, I'm not sure how he will take the news I've found a job. Are you certain you want to do this?"

Maggie waved aside any difficulties with a simple lift of her hand. "Newspaper editors thrive on conflict," Maggie replied. "I've taken on a good helper. But the marshal isn't an easy man to stand up to." She slowly nodded her head. "Don't you worry, Lucy. You've got what it takes."

Maggie had seen right through her but still liked what she saw. "Thank you, Maggie."

The woman gave one of her brief, closed-lipped smiles and walked out of the restaurant. Lucy watched her, even as she pictured the marshal's face when he learned she had found a job despite his maneuverings. A small smile played at the corners of her mouth. She eagerly awaited her next meeting with Marshal Sam McQuaid.

CHAPTER 6

Lucy vowed never to be the last in line again. Each strike to the big bass drum echoed through her head, crawled under her skin, vibrated her very bones. She tried not to blink at each reverberating boom, but the task proved impossible. The result was a rather dizzying view of a jeering, laughing crowd of onlookers gathered along both sides of the road or, if she stared ahead, Dolly's bobbing white plume.

As a counter-balance to Leila's pounded rolls of percussive exuberance, Lucy sang as loud as she could, hoping an equalization could be found somewhere between eardrum and tonsil. The songs weren't familiar to her, and she frequently referred to the lyrics she and Maggie had printed up the evening before.

Maggie had held high hopes for a strong turnout with each voice raised in simultaneous song. To the newspaper woman's disappointment, only nine of the faithful had shown up this morning. Lucy feared the drum overwhelmed their meager lung power and the sad message from "Father Dear Father Come Home With Me Now" was lost to its intended audience.

Sliding a glance at the saloons and dance halls they passed, Lucy wondered if this whole effort was useless. Those smiling, laughing faces hardly appeared chastened by the plight of a young girl sent to a drinking establishment to beg her father for money to buy medicine for her dying baby brother.

Lucy felt more than a little ridiculous and wished Maggie hadn't insisted she join today's march. Refusing had seemed mean-spirited, but she must come up with a plausible excuse next time. Finding Dolly's plume easier to view than the mocking assaults on either side, Lucy faced ahead, blinking, marching, and singing. September looked mighty far away.

Through the thicket of brandished placard signs, Lucy saw Maggie's arm stretch upward, their signal to halt. The drumming stopped at last and Lucy breathed a sigh of relief. She stood still, relieved to hear only the quiet of barking dogs, braying donkeys, and a bucking horse, its owner raining curses either on the dumb animal or on them: his colorful choice of invectives didn't make his target clear.

Leila turned and side-stepped closer. "Is there a problem? We didn't stop by the depot last time."

Lucy took hold of the drum. "Let me help you get this off and we'll see."

"Thanks."

Leila lifted the broad strap over her head, then helped Lucy set the heavy drum on the ground. The other ladies had collected around Maggie. Clearly, another debate was taking place, a regular occurrence that had grown tiresome, but Lucy welcomed the lull from Leila's contribution to the cause.

Lucy followed the tall woman, keeping to the fringes. She hopped out of harm's way. She didn't like deceiving these ladies. Since her talk to the league, she had avoided the temperance subject whenever possible and Maggie hadn't pursued it, concentrating instead on newspaper business. They had settled into a comfortable working friendship, but the temperance cause was another matter. Maggie left her uneasy with her zeal. Reluctantly, Lucy moved in closer and caught Maggie in mid-argument.

"No one is asking any of you to enter a saloon, but we must do something to make our message heard." Maggie crossed her arms and encompassed them all with a stern look that discouraged rebuttal. "Our ranks might be thin today, but we can still make those rumsuckers take notice with a prayer vigil outside one of the saloons."

"How many rumsuckers do you suppose are in the saloons at nine-thirty in the morning?" Leila asked.

Maggie shot her chin a notch higher. "I wanted to march later in the day, but suppers had to be prepared, remember?"

A flurry of protests, excuses, and emphatic denials muddled the issue into an argument over exactly what they had hoped to accomplish. Lucy longed for the living quarters located over the newspaper office, a refuge she had sought during other debates. The middle of Main Street provided no alternative but to appear interested if disinclined to comment.

Tildie held her hands up in a quieting gesture and the dissenting voices faded one by one. She gave a slight bow of her head, then clasped her hands together at her waist.

"Our mission is to encourage the citizens of Starlight to sign the pledge," she said, "not to disrupt our families and abandon our responsibilities. Mornings offer the best compromise for the most people."

"How many have signed?" Maggie shot back.

Tildie ground her hands together as if she were crumbling Maggie's question like a handful of crackers. "Two, as of today. Mr. Schindler and that traveling preacher, Reverend Brown. But our marches have only just begun."

Maggie looked from one lady to the next until those gray eyes landed on Lucy like a lodestone settling north. Lucy swallowed hard and managed to return the steady gaze.

"Correct Tildie, we *have* only begun," Maggie said. "Lucy has told us we must carry our banner to the very doors that lead our youth into ruin. Morning or evening, our message will be heard by those who profit from sin." Once more, she caught the eye of each of her followers. "We must ask ourselves if we are truly up to the battle. Demon rum is a mighty enemy."

Silence met this ultimatum. Lucy wondered how she had managed to get herself into this mess. She had never thought to find herself praying at saloon doorsteps, and she suspected the same thought had occurred to more than one woman attending this morning's march. They weren't on their knees yet, and if she could plant such ideas, she could certainly do her best to nip them before they budded.

Lucy edged closer to the center of the self-searching group. She gave her spectacles a poke and cleared her throat. "I suggest we take our argument back to the office, where—"

"Onward Christian so-o-oldiers," Dolly sang out in off-key fervor, "marching as to war." She held forth her placard quoting Proverbs 23:31 and turned about, the words of the old song pouring forth as she started up the street.

Leila scrambled for her drum while Maggie and Tildie fell in behind Dolly, their voices adding rich embellishment to Dolly's high soprano. The other ladies quickly followed suit with Leila taking up the rear, leaving Lucy to stare after them. September seemed years away now.

Feeling partially responsible, Lucy saw no recourse but to follow. She quickly caught up, pacing off the drum's tempo behind Leila. Maybe a few strategically placed prayers would do some good. Starlight had need of several from what she had observed.

Lucy gave the boardwalks a quick study and saw the angry frowns mixed among the laughter and thought of the marshal's three-day absence, chasing after a professional gunman. Maybe they all could use a prayer or two.

Dolf turned in his saddle. "Suppose they're finished now?"

"Let's hope so," Sam called back.

He rubbed at his eyes in an unsuccessful attempt to rid them of gritty fatigue and waited for the drumbeats to begin again like they had earlier. They had caught the first session booming through the valley like thunder. A storm was promised, all right, but the only rain to come of it would be complaints on his head.

Dolf's hurry to return to Starlight had slowed considerably while his wife banged away on his drum, which had been fine with Sam. He wanted the marchers tucked inside Maggie's office before he rode into town. Maybe then he could get a bath and a bite to eat before the complainers found him.

With a turn of his wrist, Sam urged Colonel Mac down a shallow embankment to a lane leading into Starlight. The roadway was wide enough for two riders, so he pulled up beside Dolf.

"Sounds like Leila's put away her war drum," Sam said. "You think it's safe to ride in now?"

Dolf took off his hat and ran a hand through his dark blond hair. "About as safe as it ever is now that Maggie's got the womenfolk all stirred up."

Sam twisted a corner of his mouth into a wry smile. "Considering we just wore our tails out chasing after a fella that shot up the town, we can't blame Maggie for all the trouble.''

Dolf gave a disgruntled huff and shoved his hat back on his head. "If we had caught that yahoo, I'da thanked him for the vacation.''

"This temperance business will all blow over soon enough," Sam replied. "But, damnit man, get that drum away from Leila.''

Dolf shifted in his saddle and tugged on the wide brim of his gray hat. He stared at the road ahead. "I'd rather take a cub from a she-bear, Captain.''

Sam chuckled. "That's a sad thing for a man to admit, Dolf.''

Dolf gave him a brief glance and blew out a sigh. "You wait, Captain." He nodded his head with sure knowledge. "Someday it'll happen to you. You'll get corralled like the rest of us.''

Sam slid his curled left hand down his reins and sat up straighter. "Not me," he stated. "I smoke my cigars whenever I want, play cards and drink good whiskey in my own saloon, and—''

"And go to bed lonely every night.''

Sam tipped his hat back and gave the big blacksmith a sharp look. "The hell I do.''

"Paid company ain't the same.''

"It's all the same under the covers, Dolf.''

"I can't explain it, Captain, but believe me, it ain't.''

Sam met Dolf's sincere frown, then turned his attention to the road as quickly as the other man stared ahead. Sam had never considered Dolf the sentimental sort before. He was a hell of a fighter, didn't cheat at cards, and could drink nearly any man under the table, but he wouldn't take that drum away from Leila. Sam slipped a finger in around his collar. Damned if he'd ever get roped and tied with apron strings.

As they topped a hill, a short stretch of Main Street came into view between the hotel and the drugstore. Sam breathed a deep sigh. Trouble or not, Starlight was a welcome sight after three days in the saddle. A bath, a meal, and the defiant Miss Drummond waited just around the next corner. Home sweet home.

He'd bet David's mail-order bride was anxious to get home by now. That woman had needed a good dose of reality and had been lucky to receive it without getting hurt. There would be no more speeches about corrupt power. His kind, she had called him. Now that he didn't need a witness, Lucy Drummond had better be glad *his kind* was willing to bankroll her return trip to Boston.

"Did you see that?"

Sam gave a sharp look to the trail ahead and saw nothing unusual. "No, what was it?"

"Two men went running by the hotel," Dolf explained. "There goes another one. You suppose somethin's goin' on?"

Sam gave the Colonel a nudge with his knees, urging his mount into an easy canter. "We better find out."

Dolf took the lead, and Sam followed him down the last hundred yards of lane. Colonel Mac sensed his stable near and didn't need much encouragement to pick up speed. Sam scanned the rooftops, but no smoke drifted into the pines. Not a fire. Several more people rushed past the hotel. Shouts could be heard above the clatter of their horses. Sam drew his Colt.

Like Dolf, he pulled up to a slower pace as they rode between the buildings and entered Main Street. A quick sweep of the road revealed a crowd gathered in the road in front of the Painted Pony. From this distance, he couldn't make out what they were looking at, but several of Red's dance-for-hire girls sat on the upstairs windowsills, looking down on the scene below them. Sam cursed beneath his breath. Not another shooting.

"Here comes the marshal," someone shouted.

The small gathering parted just in time for him to see pails of water pouring down from the upstairs windows onto a semicircle of kneeling women, all of whom jumped to their feet like puppets jerked into action. Squeals of surprise and howls of laughter mingled into one big noisy commotion. He supposed Leila's thunderous drumming had brought on an unexpected shower after all.

Putting away his revolver, Sam had to force a smile of his own into a disapproving scowl. The view of wilted feathers and fuming females almost got the best of him, until he recognized a new member of Maggie's prayer party.

Lucy Drummond stood among the women, her upswept hair tilted in a tangled mass to one side. She held out her hands and shook the water from them, scolding with the best of them. Sam swung down from his saddle and, dropping the reins, strode toward the disturbance. He had a bad feeling about this.

Lucy pushed at her hair and peered through her water-speckled lenses at the other members of the temperance group. Unaccountably, she wanted to join the gales of laughter coming from all sides. Never in her life had she seen such a bedraggled array of femininity. Hair hung in dripping snarls around surprised or angry faces, and white ribbons clung limply to heaving, soaked bosoms. Poor Dolly blew at her defeated plume and blinked like an owl. Tildie's corset showed through her white blouse as she fluttered her arms and walked about, exclaiming, "Good heavens, good heavens." Maggie wiped the water from her face and, Lucy suspected, a smile behind one swipe. The other ladies shook their skirts and muttered imprecations. One had tears rolling down her face. Leila glowered at the women hanging out of the windows upstairs, their raucous laughter nearly as coarse as the men's. Lucy noted that one smoked a cigar.

Leila glared at Tildie. "Good heavens, woman. Shut up!"

That drew an instant scowl from Tildie and a spattering of applause from their audience. Tildie advanced on Leila and a hot argument ensued, the subject of which couldn't be discerned from the many other boisterous discussions taking place. Lucy considered routes for the most dignified retreat possible, but found the prayer group was ringed in by onlookers.

She was about to collect the still-addled Dolly when a man wearing red suspenders stepped through the swinging doors of the saloon. Lucy remembered him from the day of the shooting and gathered he was the owner of the Painted Pony Dancehall, the object of today's prayers. Through her water-distorted vision, Lucy recognized the saloon owner's disgust with their efforts. He gripped Dolly's unsuspecting shoulders and gave her a shove.

"You crazy women get on out of here, now," he said, and shoved Dolly again. "Your sorry appearance is scarin' off customers."

Lucy wasn't tempted to laugh along with the crowd any longer. The man had no right to handle Dolly in that cavalier manner. She pushed at her spectacles and covered the short distance between the pair in two long strides.

Pointing a finger in the man's face, she leaned forward. "Take your hands off that woman, you . . . you bully." To her surprise he did, and Dolly scurried away.

He cocked his head to the side and stepped up to her. "If you're looking for trouble, lady, you've found it."

Wrinkling her nose at the smell of stale beer on his breath, Lucy propped her hands on her hips and glared at him with watery disdain. She saw all the belligerent precinct bosses she had ever known in this man's pudgy face.

"What a big man you are," she said, and made the most of his short stature with an up-and-down inspection. "Picking on defenseless women." She reached over and popped one of his silly suspenders, then stared up at him, wondering at her own audacity.

The man appeared stunned, while the crowd laughed uproariously. His nose turned as red as his braces and his eyes narrowed into mean slits. "I know who you are. You're that damned eastern whore David sent off for. Get off my property." He stepped in close and raised his hands to shove her, too.

Hiding her hurt feelings behind a stiff frown, Lucy raised her arms to fend him off. Beefy hands grazed her shoulders, but a man dressed in black reached in front of her and pushed the saloon keeper back, then stepped between them. Shocked by the marshal's whirlwind appearance, Lucy had to be dragged out of the way by Maggie.

"What's going on here?" Sam demanded, looking from the owner to the ladies assembled on the boardwalk and steps.

Lucy took off her wet spectacles to see more clearly what was happening, but jingling boots stomped up the steps and Cleve rushed past her and Maggie, blocking their view.

"Red Grady put his hands on my ma, that's what," Cleve said. "I'm going to beat the hell out of him."

Lucy ducked to the side and saw the marshal's hard scowl that stopped Cleve in mid-stride. The deputy took a step back, clenching and unclenching his hands. A sheen of sweat broke out on the saloon owner's beet-red face, and he inched toward the swinging doors.

"Stay put, Red," Sam warned. "I'm not finished with you."

Maggie tugged at her shoulders, but Lucy wouldn't budge. She had to see what happened, had to know how fairly the marshal handled a disturbance with a fellow saloon owner.

"Take your ma home, Cleve." The marshal's calm, almost gentle tone surprised Lucy. "Take her on home now," Sam reiterated, a bit firmer this time. "I'll take care of this."

"That damned Leslie Laughton had me holed up in the office, Sam."

"That's all right, Cleve. This mess was more than one man could handle. Go on. Your ma needs you."

The tenseness eased out of Cleve's body, and Lucy drew a deep breath. Cleve turned to leave and, seeing her, gave her a nod. As he walked past them, he paused.

"I won't forget what you did for my ma, Miss Drummond."

He tugged at the brim of his hat, then left the boardwalk. Placing his arm around Dolly's narrow shoulders, he guided his mother through the crowd. Dolly was so proud of her son, and now Lucy understood why. Too bad he wouldn't sign the pledge. Then his mother would forget this nonsense.

Lucy returned her attention to Sam and found his gaze on her, an odd expression on his face—a weighing, measuring kind of look.

Sam turned back to Red. "You're lucky I didn't let him have you."

"Just protectin' my property, Marshal," the saloon keeper said. He licked his lips but wouldn't meet McQuaid's eyes.

"You better think about protecting your mouth, Red," the marshal said, his voice low and hard. "If you can't keep it shut, I'll shut it for you. You understand?"

Red cut his eyes to Lucy. "I think I do, Marshal."

Sam grabbed Red's shirt front and rammed the gaping

88   Pamela Litton

man against the wall. Lucy crossed her arms, uneasy with
the sudden violence unleashed to protect her name. She
might be inexperienced, but she understood the man's ugly
remark.

"I don't think you do understand, Red."

"I understand now, Marshal. I understand real good."

The marshal let him go, and the saloon keeper sagged
against the wall. "That's the kind of cooperation I like to
hear from the citizens of Starlight."

Just as she was about to change her opinion of the
marshal, a shiver slid down Lucy's spine, and not because
she was wet. She must be the least cooperative of Starlight's
citizens, as Marshal McQuaid would soon discover. She
couldn't say she looked forward to confronting him with her
success at thwarting his schemes.

Sam turned around and Lucy saw the deep furrows of
fatigue that marked his face, but his blue eyes remained
steady. His clothing was dusty but neatly arranged, right
down to the bow in his string tie. Marshal McQuaid was a
man in perfect control of himself and any situation he
encountered—except maybe where she was concerned.

Lucy feared she had made a formidable enemy, yet she
was satisfied with her decision. She waited with the rest of
the murmuring townspeople, wondering what the marshal
was going to say about this debacle. She was sure he would
have plenty more to say if he learned her part in the new
direction the temperance ladies had taken.

He gave a long look to the crowd. "I'm going to say this
once, so listen up. No women are roughed up in my
town—not even temperance women."

His last comment brought a few chuckles, but Lucy didn't
smile. This man confused her, scrambled her conceptions of
him until she didn't know what to expect anymore. She
didn't totally trust him, yet couldn't dislike him. He was an

enigma, this marshal: a man who wore black and seldom smiled. How far would he go to make her leave Starlight? Lucy couldn't guess, and that made her wary. She must keep her guard up at all times.

Sam stepped down the stairs with a loose-limbed grace and the crowd began to disperse.

A tall, broad-shouldered blond man stepped out of the crowd. Lucy remembered that he was the man who had ridden with the marshal after the gunman. He must be Leila's husband, Dolf. Looking past him, she didn't see a prisoner and wondered what had happened. Had they killed the dark outlaw or simply not found him?

"Collect the drum, Leila, and come along," Dolf said in a raspy, quiet voice. Leila nodded and took hold of the drum. She followed her husband through the thinning crowd.

"These wet clothes feel ghastly," Maggie said, shaking her dripping skirts. "Let's get back to the office and change. We have those handbills for Pollett's to do up today."

Lucy didn't reply but gathered her skirts and started out after Maggie. She had no wish to confront Sam McQuaid in her present soaked and confused state. She needed time to prepare. Besides, a long list of tasks waited for her at the newspaper office, and she wanted to finish in time to run an errand of her own. She had finally discovered where the schoolmarm's house was located and thought she might make a quick sketch to send her mother.

"Miss Drummond."

The deep voice stopped her in her tracks. She had seen the marshal standing in the road but had hoped he might allow her to leave without discussing what must be on his mind—her presence with the temperance ladies. There was a great deal more to tell Marshal McQuaid, but the middle of Main Street was not the place. She slowly turned about and faced him anyway.

"Yes?" she replied.

"I'll talk to you later," he said, then walked to a black horse standing patiently in the road. He picked up the reins and, giving a peculiar tug at his collar, slowly led his mount down the road.

Relieved but anxious, too, Lucy watched the pair for a moment, the horse hanging its head, its long tail giving an occasional swish. She should have at least thanked Marshal McQuaid for helping her, but perhaps it was just as well. She sighed and turned to follow Maggie. This was hardly the victorious meeting with Marshal Sam McQuaid she had imagined.

CHAPTER 7

Sam found Lucy sitting peaceably under a pine tree, completely engrossed in sketching the ramshackle house. Serene, completely at ease, she appeared unaware of the snarl of barbed wire she had left in town for him to untangle.

The mayor had made a long, eye-popping, name-calling speech contending Lucy Drummond was out to make trouble for his Caroline for stealing away Miss Drummond's desperate chance at matrimony. B.F. hadn't explained how he had come to this conclusion, but then, making sense had never been the mayor's strong point.

Word of her little speech at the temperance meeting had made the rounds through all the saloons and dancehalls like promises of free whiskey. After the Painted Pony prayer party, the saloon owners had crowded into Sam's office, demanding to know where he stood. "By the law" hadn't seemed to cool any of the hotheads. Some, like Red Grady, were a rough crowd and would do most anything to protect their profits.

In all the ruckus, Lucy had earned the loyalty of one knight in shining spurs. Cleve had been quick to point out his mother's claim that Miss Drummond hadn't volunteered to speak or even attend the meeting until Tildie had dragged her downstairs.

Volunteered or dragged into it, the results were the same: she had found herself a job and poured more fuel on a fire that was about to sputter out. Only nine women had shown up for today's march. By the looks of the pow-wow Sam had walked into at Maggie's awhile ago, the sob-sisters of sobriety were flocking to their new standard-bearer, Lucy Drummond, abandoned mail-order bride, aspiring school-marm, expert temperance lecturer. A real pain in the ass.

Sam pulled out David's telegram, which had been waiting on his desk, and read the request for money once more. It looked like the newlyweds had taken off to Las Vegas, the railroad terminus north of here, and had run out of funds while staying in one of the best hotels in New Mexico Territory. Slowly, carefully, Sam wadded the thin yellow paper into a tight ball and dropped it into his coat pocket.

Sam watched Lucy a moment longer, satisfied with his plan to clear her out of town. However, she'd be expecting more use of *corrupt power*, which would only garner her more sympathy and cause more trouble. He had decided on different tactics—a flanking maneuver she wouldn't expect, a surprise attack. For her own safety and his sanity, Miss Drummond would board that train to Boston and be happy about it or . . .

Sam cut off the "or elses." They didn't belong in the new plan. He stepped away from the tree he had been leaning against, ready to cross the country lane into battle.

"How do you like it?" Lucy asked.

Sam froze, then noticed she was holding her sketch pad up toward the house, not looking back at him at all. He could have sworn she was alone. A frown pulled at his brows as he looked around for her companion. If that Cleve—

"I know it needs some work, but the light's fading." She placed the pad across her knees and leaned back against the tree. "It's nice and quiet out here. I suppose that's why you like it, too."

Who in the hell? . . . Sam searched every corner of the small clearing. His gaze slid over the house and caught a slight movement under the porch. On closer inspection, he made out a mostly black cat sprawled behind some broken lattice work. A black bushy tail gave a lazy flip and the cat licked a white paw, then gazed about in sardonic disinterest, displaying its white ruff to best advantage.

Amused, but not really surprised, Sam studied the contradictory woman who bet against the odds and spoke to stray cats. From where he stood, the dark greenery of the weed-choked yard outlined her slightly turned up nose, stubborn chin, and the white curve of her throat. His inspection dropped lower to the fullness of her white blouse, and he remembered another she had worn, wet and clinging to soft feminine curves wrapped in a lacy package, a little bow in the shadowed center waiting to be untied.

Sam blinked and jerked his thoughts back from the edge. He started to announce his presence, but his tongue was dry and his throat constricted. He pulled at his collar. Damn, but it had been choking him lately. She spoke again, and despite his principles, he listened.

"The evening star has come out already," she said. "I really should go, though I've enjoyed our little chat this afternoon. I hope you're here tomorrow but a little more friendly. I could use a friend."

The cat rolled to its back and batted its paw at her. She laughed, and Sam was taken with the joy in the sound and couldn't interrupt it.

"All right, all right, I'm leaving. First, I'm going to make a wish, but I won't tell you what it is because then it won't come true."

Sam watched the tantalizing movement of her lips, whispering her wish. He wondered what it was. Probably something that would bring on more trouble. He started once more across the road and didn't stop until he stood in the open.

"Be careful," he said. "You might get what you wish for."

Lucy popped her eyes open and twisted around to find Sam McQuaid standing in the lane. She scrambled to her feet and faced him. She covered her embarrassment with a quick grab at indignation.

"Eavesdropping is quite rude," she said.

She placed a hand over her frantically beating heart and struggled to attain the cool aloofness she had practiced in her imagined confrontation with Sam McQuaid. Once more he had her at a disadvantage, but she had prepared for the worst, knowing he would hear about her job and the temperance speech, too. Lucy readied her best retorts.

Sam pulled off his hat and held it to his chest. "Please accept my humble apologies."

His gaze wandered from her spectacle-shielded eyes to the small white hand resting on her breast. Images of lace and pink-ribboned bows came to him unbidden.

Lucy shifted the drawing pad up to her chest, suspicious and disturbed by the marshal's flip courtesies coupled with his ill-mannered inspection. Not one of her imagined conversations had included such behavior. He was ruining everything, even the quiet peace she had found in this hidden meadow.

"How did you find me?" She didn't bother masking her irritation.

"Maggie," he replied and put his hat back on. Watching

her carefully, he crossed the short distance separating them. "I need to talk to you about the shooting on the street the other day."

Lucy had expected talk about temperance and jobs, anticipated a small amount of polite gloating, but she was not prepared to discuss her run-in with death. She fought the sinking sensation draining the warmth from her body and turned her back on the hard blue eyes that had seen her fear that day.

"I gave Mr. Hardesty my statement," she replied, and noticed that the cat had disappeared. She wished the marshal would follow the cat's example.

Sam moved in closer, propping his forearm against the tree, allowing his hand to hang loosely, inches above her hair. "I thought you might remember something else. The description you gave Cleve covers three-quarters of the population of New Mexico Territory."

Lucy wandered a few steps to the left and pretended interest in a wild rose blooming among the tangled vines and bushes; anything to distance herself from the deep voice that had drawn too near.

"You didn't . . . find him, then." She regretted the disappointment that had crept into her voice.

"No, we didn't. He's . . ." Sam decided not to tell her that the gunman had made a beeline to the border. "He's still loose. Thought I'd send his description out on the wires. Maybe somebody will run across him. You sure you don't remember anything that might help pick him out of a crowd?"

"No," she replied instinctively, then she recalled that bone-chilling smile, a memory she had tried to forget with limited success. "Wait! Yes, I did remember something else. The man had a gap between his front teeth."

Sam caught a slight breathless quality in her voice and

knew his plan was working. He didn't like this, but it was necessary. She was moving closer to the train station every minute.

"That information narrows things some," he said. "Of course, since you're staying in Starlight . . ." He paused, giving her time to connect the gunman's escape with her own presence in the area. Then he pushed harder. "You can identify him face-to-face and testify at his trial, that is, when he's caught."

Lucy closed her eyes to the beauty of the rose, the quiet tranquility of the place she had already come to think of as her own. Those cold, black eyes had found her and brought the sickening fear that always followed. Little deduction was needed to know she posed a threat to this outlaw. She could be his next target.

Lucy turned from the battered old house and faced Sam. He stood there so easy, so sure of himself and her response. Bullets had sprayed dust on his boots and he hadn't faltered, yet he thought she would run.

To spite him and to prove something to herself, Lucy pushed at her spectacles and stepped forward. "I want to testify," she said. "Men who take shots at innocent, unarmed women should get what they deserve."

Sam pushed back his hat, bested but not bowed. This woman had more grit than he had expected and a sharp tongue to match. Too bad she didn't have the sense God gave a jackass.

"You're right, *that kind* should get what they deserve," he replied, "but they rarely do."

Her lips pursed with annoyance, causing Sam to think about all the promising aspects of her mouth. To clear his thoughts, Sam focused on something less distracting—the sketch book she clutched to her chest as if it were the last *Godey's Ladies Book* west of the Mississippi.

Sam leaned his head to the side so that he could get a better look at her drawing. "Not bad, but it doesn't look like the old Lockhart place."

Lucy gripped the sides of her tablet. "Maybe not now, but by September, when my classes begin and my mother arrives, the house will look very much like my picture."

Her spectacles caught the light from the sunset. Sam thought of an old saying that fit Lucy Drummond too well.

"You can't always look at the world through rose-colored spectacles, Lucy."

"Marshal—"

"Please, call me Sam," he said, hoping she would consent to a friendlier, perhaps more agreeable, relationship. "We've been shot at by the same man. Out here, that means we can drop the formalities."

The sky burned behind him and set his features in sharp relief, like those faraway peaks brooding along the horizon. Still, Lucy caught the slight crook at the corner of his mouth: teasing or laughing at her, she couldn't be sure. Lucy strove for a response that would suffice for either intention.

"I see very clearly . . . Sam, and I don't need advice from you." It felt a bit awkward dropping formalities, but keeping things friendly between them could only help her situation.

"So you've said before," he replied, "but after those bullets whizzed by your head the other day, I thought you might be more willing to listen."

Angry now, Lucy turned her shoulder to him once more and rested her gaze on the house that would become her next home. She had never met a more stubborn man! If bravado hadn't convinced him she was staying, maybe the truth would. Goodness knows she had started enough problems by stretching things a bit.

"I won't deny I was afraid," she began. "I'll even admit

you were right about the dangers here." She turned to look at him directly. "You've done your duty. I've been warned, but I'm willing to take my chances."

"You want to teach a bunch of bratty kids that badly?"

"I want to provide a home for my mother and me." She might as well tell him the rest. "That's why I agreed to marry your brother."

"Lucy, you're only making a bad decision worse. David was a poor candidate for a husband. He couldn't have taken care of you and your mother."

Lucy believed him. Several of the ladies had taken great pleasure in relating David's many faults. Sam must think her a fool and that rankled. She looked off toward the mountains.

"He wrote such nice letters," she said. She didn't mention she had been drawn to the name of the town as well. Starlight. It sounded like a place where dreams came true.

"David has a way with words, all right, and he always has great intentions, but . . ." Talking about David brought up too many bad memories, too many regrets.

Lucy worked up the courage to ask him what she couldn't ask those ladies. "Why did he do it?" She shifted her attention back to the tall, solemn-faced man. "Why did he send off for a bride, Sam?"

Lucy could see that her question disturbed him by the way his mouth tightened, as it always did when he was uncomfortable or irritated. He looked over her head and rubbed his thumb over the pads of his fingers, thinking over an answer. Sam McQuaid was easy to read but it took close and careful watching.

He looked down at her, and she felt the weight of those smoky blue eyes press against her heart. "You don't have to answer," she said. "It was forward of me to ask."

"You have every right to know, Lucy." His hand lifted in

a careless gesture. "David's reasons weren't clear to me, but I'll make a guess. He had been seeing Caroline Jones, but her father was against the match. Any father would be. Anyway, she was about to marry some lawyer fella, and my guess is David wanted to marry, too. None of the local girls would have him. Knew too much about him and Caroline and . . ."

He left the story unfinished; there didn't seem to be anything left to say. The run-down house caught his attention.

"This isn't the house the town provided for Miss Little or the two schoolmarms before her," he said.

Lucy stepped to his side, sharing his eagerness to move on to another subject. She didn't care to dwell on life with a husband who loved another woman. This old house promised much more.

"Yes, I know," she replied, "but the bank supposedly sold the other house, and this is the one Tildie was told about. It needs some work, but it's roomy. Mother and I will like it."

"It's too far out of town."

"I like the quiet."

"It's not safe out here."

Lucy thought of her father, murdered on a busy city street. "Sam, there are no safe places."

Dropping his hands to his sides, Sam looked down at her. "You're too young to know that."

Lucy met his gaze, almost told him about her father, then remembered who he was—a town marshal who wanted her out of the way. She decided to change the subject as he had done and walked down the worn dirt path toward the small clapboard house.

"Next time, I'll bring a broom and cleaning supplies," she said. Lucy looked over the gray, weather-beaten walls, the boards missing from the porch, the broken window and sagging front door. "Some paint, later," she added. "White, I think."

"You're so sure the school board will approve your appointment?"

She didn't look at him, only the house. "Tildie says—"

"Tildie can't speak for the mayor or the other five members."

Hearing the sureness in his voice, Lucy turned and faced Sam. At last she could use one of her practiced speeches. "I know you used the mayor's bank to make sure no one would give me a job, but I'm hoping to overcome any other obstacles you two cook up, just like I did the first one." She lifted her chin proudly. "I won't give up, Sam," she added.

"You really shouldn't do that with your mouth, Lucy."

Parting her lips in surprise, Lucy touched them with her fingertips then quickly dropped her hand to her side. He was trying to trick her, distract her in some way.

"I have no idea what you're talking about."

Sam shook his head. "Some people have to be shown everything."

He walked toward her, his pace sure and determined, like everything he did. Lucy stood her ground, not knowing what to expect but determined to prove she couldn't be intimidated—not even by a man dressed in black whose eyes looked through a woman, straight to her fears, maybe even her wishes.

He finally stopped, but he was so close. Still, she didn't back away but instead wrapped her arms around the drawing pad. "I meant what I said, Sam."

"So did I."

The low, rough texture of his voice was a warning she heeded too late. He took hold of her arms and pulled her closer. Protests died as half-formed thoughts, victims of a

restless, unnameable need that shook through her, holding
her prisoner more surely than Sam's warm hands.

"You try a man's patience, Lucy Drummond."

He bent his head toward her, blocking out the burning
sky, the dark mountains, the sighing pines. Lucy closed her
eyes, drifting with a sense of imminent discovery. Her
breath caught at the first touch of his lips. Warm and firm,
his mouth closed over hers.

Another world opened for Lucy, another existence where
desire and passion ruled and surrender was the best choice.
Holding tightly to her drawing pad, she breathed in his
scent.

Sam pulled away slowly, the delicate, little sigh that had
brushed his lips a memory he wanted to forget but knew he
wouldn't. He looked down into unfocused, dreamy eyes and
damned himself for forgetting that Lucy was an inexperienced lady, too young to know where kisses and honey-
sweet sighs led. He was more dangerous to her right now
than any randy cowpuncher.

Disgusted with himself and angry with her for being so
trusting, so damned gullible and stubborn, too, Sam gave
her a slight shake. "Do you understand now, Lucy? Do you
understand what can happen when you challenge the wrong
man with that pretty pout?"

She blinked as if awakening, and bewilderment shadowed the green and gold depths of her eyes. "The wrong
man?"

"Hell, yes, the wrong man," Sam stated, he thought
perhaps too emphatically, until he saw awareness cross her
face.

With something like a wince, she stepped away from him,
tugging her arms free with a sharp twist of her shoulders.
Snatching her skirts up, Lucy set out for the road and
chanced no more denials. He had shown her something

wonderful and frightening and all together unacceptable. Sam McQuaid was indeed the wrong man.

"Lucy!"

She wanted to ignore the sharp command he gave her name but didn't. Stepping onto the lane, Lucy turned and forced herself to meet his gaze.

"What now?" she said.

Snapping his pocket watch closed, he slipped it into his vest pocket, his expression preoccupied, as if he had already concerned himself with other matters. Apparently, this afternoon's events held little importance or interest to him, while they had left her confused and—yes, she would admit it—somewhat thrilled.

He walked over to the tree and leaned against the trunk, then crossed his arms. "There won't be any more"—a corner of his mouth curled—"backroom manipulations."

A hundred questions crowded her mind, but Lucy didn't ask one. Better to stay on guard, see what transpired between now and September. If he had abandoned one method to make her stay in Starlight difficult, he had another in mind. She nodded once, then rushed into the cool shadows covering the lane into town.

Sam shuffled through the messages he wanted sent out in the morning and tossed all but one beside the chattering telegrapher's bug. Bob Jenkins didn't look up but continued translating the dots and dashes in a frenzy of pencil scratchings. Sam looked out the doorway at the view of Main Street lit up for the night. He tapped the single scrap of paper against his thigh and pondered an old problem—his brother.

Bob's scratching stilled at last and a jangling piano's rendition of "Camptown Races" drifted into the little office stuck in the corner of the train depot.

"This all you got, Marshal?" Bob asked.

Sam reread the note he held, then decided the problem would have to solve itself. "I need one of those back," he said.

Bob scooted back, peering up at him over the wire frames of his spectacles. "Help yourself."

Sam quickly sorted through the description of the gunman, a list of the various local lawmen, and a notice to the federal marshal's office until he found the instructions to his bank in Santa Fe. He quickly crumpled it with one hand and tossed the other message in its place.

Bob picked it up and, holding his chin high, read the new message. " 'A husband takes care of his wife.' " He dashed a glance at Sam over the top of his spectacles. "To Davy, I suppose."

Sam drew his brows together, the guilt eating at him again, but his resolve remained firm.

"Send it to the Plaza Hotel in Las Vegas."

Bob looked at it again, then scooted back to the desk. "It'll go out first thing in the morning," he said, and added it to the other messages. He spread them out with a finger. "Terrible what happened today."

Sam didn't remark on the puzzling case. "I want to hear right away if anything comes in."

Bob nodded and gathered the pieces of paper into a neat stack. "Who was it got hisself killed?"

"Another drifter thinking he could strike it rich," Sam replied. He caught a glimpse of the long message Bob had taken and thought he made out "Pinkerton" in the illegible scrawl. "Train robbed?"

Bob straightened in his chair and gave a quick, "Hmmm?" over his shoulder.

"That long message coming over the wire when I came in," Sam explained. "Trouble with one of the trains?"

"Naw." Bob shook his head. "Just some of the mayor's business."

"Glad to hear that," Sam replied, but he wasn't, and he knew Bob wouldn't tell him anything further. The station-master took his telegrapher's trust seriously, which the town appreciated. "I'll be at the Outpost if anything comes in. Want me to send anything over?"

"Thanks, Marshal," Bob replied. "A cold lemonade and a sandwich would be good."

"I'll have Gill bring it over." Sam pushed through the low swinging gate and walked through the deserted depot, then paused at the door. He took out a cigar and lit it, thinking over another of David's dilemmas.

B.F. must have called in the Pinkertons to find his daughter. Those two newlyweds would never be happy if Caroline's daddy found them too soon. Sam pulled on his cigar, then let the smoke curl out of his mouth. He was still tempted to send David some money.

Sam sighed and shook his head. Too much help had always been David's trouble. He had hurt too many people with his irresponsibility. One, especially. David was twenty-one years old now, and it was time he figured things out on his own. Maybe he would learn something.

Sam took another puff of his cigar and considered the possibility of learning something himself. Lucy Drummond. Talking to cats, wishing on stars, popping red suspenders. He had wanted to laugh with everyone else that morning. She was a scrapper, all right, and proud, too. That's why he had spoken to Lettie King. Maybe if the girl didn't have to ask him for the money she would leave.

Again, Sam wondered what she had whispered to the evening star. What hopes had she chased across a continent? A home for herself and her mother, she had said. What home had she left behind? *There is no safe place,* she had said.

He remembered something about *his kind* killing her father. His thoughts wandered back to her dreamy eyes and that defiant, tempting mouth; dangerous territory, indeed. Maybe something in her background would help him find some answers.

Sam tossed his cigar to the road and returned to the telegraph office. "Bob, give me a pencil and some paper. I have one more message for you to send."

Bob didn't question him, simply handed over the requested items and waited. Sam wrote out his inquiry, then handed the paper and pencil back to Bob. "Send this to the Boston Police Department."

Bob read Sam's notations with his usual curled down mouth. He dipped his chin and looked at Sam over his spectacles. "Mighty popular girl."

Sam cut the stationmaster a sharp glance. "Depends on which side of Main Street you walk on."

"And you, Marshal?"

Sam took a long, hard look at the noisy town, where silver flowed in like water every night and trouble waited behind swinging doors and rose-colored spectacles.

"I'm walking on both sides, Bob."

CHAPTER 8

Lucy focused on the eye of her needle, blurring out the rest of the press room, and guided the tip of thread through the tiny opening. Successful with the first attempt, she quickly prepared her needle and thread for sewing. After printing hundreds of handbills extolling the evils of demon rum, she looked forward to the quiet concentration required to execute fine handwork.

Lucy arranged a yellow bodice over her lap and began stitching white eyelet lace to the neckline. Gradually, as she had hoped, the women's preparations for the next printing project receded to a soothing background of friendly voices and her thoughts turned inward.

What a surprise this morning when Lettie King had appeared with a basket filled with sewing work. If she could spend more evenings sewing and less volunteered time printing broadsides, she would have her mother's fare to Starlight saved in no time. She could begin a nest egg now and count on extra income for later. The teacher's salary wouldn't be that much, and the sewing fit exactly into her plans.

The conversation spoken around the regular clink, whirr, clank of the printing press interrupted her thoughts. Tildie was holding forth on something or other, as usual, and though her subjects revolved around prayer vigils, marches, and impossible schedules, this time they included the marshal, and immediately Lucy thought about the kiss that had revealed too much to the wrong man. She still didn't understand what had happened, how she could have—

"Maggie Thompson," Tildie said in a sharp voice that cut through the printing noise and harping recriminations. "I don't know what you were thinking, sending the marshal out to the old Lockhart place when Lucy was out there alone."

Lucy's nimble fingers grew clumsy, her heart raced, and blood rushed to her head. That kiss! The whole town knew—no, someone would have said something before now. The roar in her ears crested, then receded, as she looked at the two ladies attending the *Starlight Observer*'s big Washington Hand Press. She hoped Tildie wasn't picking an argument. She didn't want to be caught in the middle.

With a roller in each hand, Tildie applied ink to type locked in the brass form. "It simply wasn't proper," she said.

Lucy drew comfort from Maggie's unconcerned expression as she folded the hinged wooden tympan over the type. Tildie appeared truly aggravated with Maggie as they slid the bed bearing the form to a position beneath the cloth-covered platen.

"Only gossips would make anything out of the marshal questioning Lucy out there about the shooting," Maggie replied, and pulled the wooden bar, which caused the platen to press the tympan against the type. "By the way, Lucy, that was a fine piece you wrote this morning, describing what happened on the street that day." She pushed the lever and the platen lifted.

Lucy met Maggie's gray eyes. "Thank you, Maggie," she said, more grateful for her attempt to change the subject than the newspaper woman's praise.

Tildie helped Maggie reverse the printing process, then placed her hands on her hips. "Are you suggesting that I'm a gossip?"

"Certainly not, Tildie." Maggie released the copy from the platen and passed Lucy a commiserating look as she crossed the adobe-walled room. She set the page with others spread on a table to dry, where Leila sat cutting individual temperance pledges from the sheets.

"Your concern for Lucy is commendable," Maggie continued. Picking up a blank sheet of paper, she returned to the press. "I'm only saying those who would be suspicious of Lucy's conduct—or the marshal's, I might add—would be very small minded." She fit the paper into the tympan's frame with an expert's ease.

"How about pea-brained?" Leila added. She finished cutting one sheet in half and looked at the other ladies. Lowering her voice to a conspiratorial murmur, she said, "Everyone knows Captain McQuaid sees that beautiful Creole woman over at Nell's place."

"Does more than *see* her," Maggie said.

Tildie gasped and jerked the rollers from the locked type. "We should remember Lucy is unmarried and inexperienced."

"My point exactly," Leila said. "My heavens, the captain would never be interested in a girl like Lucy."

The white eyelet suddenly gained new importance and Lucy poked her needle at it, stabbing a finger in the process. She pushed at her spectacles and smoothed a hand over the light-weight mull, giving herself a moment before attempting the delicate stitches again. Leila had only spoken the truth. She hadn't meant anything mean or hurtful. So why did it bother her so much?

Lucy took a deep breath and began the tiny stitches again. She had needed to put yesterday's incident—yes, incident was a good description—in perspective, and Leila had done that for her. She should thank the woman instead of wanting to take those scissors from her and snip, snip, snip at that awful drum. The press clanked, paper rustled, and Maggie's quick steps crossed the wooden floor again.

"Just the same," Tildie said, "the board votes in a few days and not a whisper, not a hint of scandal must touch Lucy. Our schoolmarm must represent everything decent and upright to Starlight's children. She must be the epitome of virtuous womanhood."

Lucy's needle slowed and the fumes from the coal oil lamp on the table next to her clogged her throat. She pushed it a few inches further from her, though she needed the light. The press clanked on.

"Leading the fight against demon rum and standing up as a witness against lawlessness should give the school board something more to discuss than whispers and hints," Maggie said.

Lucy gave the lamp another shove, which set the oil sloshing in the glass reservoir.

"Everyone is certainly talking about how Lucy popped Red Grady's suspenders," Leila commented. "That was worth the soaking we got."

"Lucy's spirited defense of Dolly won us many new friends," Maggie replied with a rustling of paper. "Even among the men."

"According to Dolf, she certainly gained one young man's favor."

"Now, don't go spreading talk about Lucy and Cleve

Hardesty," Tildie said. "I'm telling you, the board will consider such things."

"Did Dolf mention the marshal's reaction?" Maggie asked.

"Can't say that he did," Leila replied. "Lucy, did the captain speak to you about our baptism under fire, so to speak?"

Lucy drew her thread through the material but didn't look up. "No." She cleared her throat and found a stronger voice. "We mostly talked about the shooting. Had I remembered anything more. Things like that."

"How did he behave?" Tildie asked.

Lucy stabbed her thumb, bringing a bead of blood welling to the surface. She stuffed the injured appendage in her mouth, an unintentional, if convenient, cork.

"Oh, give it up, Tildie," Leila said. "A plain little schoolmarm wearing spectacles is not—"

"I think Tildie is concerned with how the marshal will tolerate our crusade," Maggie rushed to say. "We should remember the man is a saloon owner, too."

"Yes, Leila," Tildie said, giving the tall, brunette woman a regal bow of her head, "that's what I meant." Arching her brow at Leila's huff, she turned her attention back to Lucy. "Now, Lucy, when you spoke to the marshal, did you sense anything unusual or hostile?"

Her thumb planted in her mouth, Lucy shook her head. Kisses weren't unusual—not to him, anyway. Hostile? Thinking of a fitting reply, one that might relieve the ladies, Lucy withdrew her thumb. "He said there would be no more backroom manipulations."

"That's an odd phrase," Leila said, and snipped another pledge from the sheet. "What does that have to do with his feelings about our temperance work?"

"It shows a tolerant attitude," Tildie said. "And Lettie

King brought work to Lucy this morning. The poor woman is terribly behind with her orders but had to refuse to hire Lucy the other day. Maybe the marshal is easing up."

"Maggie's already hired Lucy," Leila pointed out, so it probably didn't matter. Why would he continue to deny an old lady help if he didn't have anything to gain?"

"Leila, you seem to know so much about Marshal McQuaid," Maggie said. She laid down the last sheet of printed pledges on the table. "Do you think he will uphold the law or make trouble for us?"

Tildie wiped her hands on a towel. "Or more trouble for Lucy?"

"Sam McQuaid is a fair man," Leila said, pointing with her scissors, then put them back to work. "But, when he's made up his mind about something, that's it. While serving in the Army, he always did whatever was necessary to accomplish his mission. He could be ruthless in his determination, and some of his scouting trips were downright incredible. He was promoted from the ranks, you know." She put down her scissors and addressed Maggie and Tildie. "I wouldn't want him against us." She looked at Lucy but went back to cutting and said nothing more.

"If he's fair, we'll have nothing to worry about," Maggie replied, gathering up metal type, then sorting it into a big wooden tray. "We won't break any laws."

Tildie picked up an extra pair of scissors and pointed them at Lucy. "Lucy, don't give Marshal McQuaid or the mayor anything to use against you. If you want to be Starlight's schoolmarm, don't even smile at that good-looking rascal, Cleve Hardesty."

Lucy managed a nod and, taking up her sewing once more, concentrated on every perfect stitch. A discussion began on whether they should plan another prayer vigil or set up a pledge table outside the Mine Shaft. Leila wanted another march. Scissors snapped, metal type clicked, and the conversation turned testy. But now all Lucy could think about was her position as schoolmarm.

Not even a smile for Mr. Hardesty, she thought. How about kisses? She could just imagine how the school board would react to kisses under a pine tree. Maybe Sam McQuaid already knew. Maybe Sam and the mayor were sitting over at the Outpost right now, laughing at her, laughing at how easily she had allowed a man she hardly knew to kiss her, how easily she could be discredited to the board. They were probably drinking to another mission accomplished by the indomitable Captain Sam, hero to all, defender of everyone, whether they wanted to be defended or not.

Pulling her thread through another stitch, she looked up at the ladies stacking the pledges into neat piles. Maggie insisted they must consider afternoon activities, while Tildie and Leila declared that few had the time to give late in the day.

"What of the new members?" Maggie asked. "Thanks to Lucy, we have a growing number of interested ladies."

Leila and Tildie nodded their agreement, and the three of them began planning another organizational meeting. Lucy heard her name mentioned several times as speaker. Frowning her dismay, she lost interest in her sewing.

She attached the needle to the material and put away the unfinished bodice. Instead of a quiet seamstress, she had become a temperance crusader. A saloon-owning marshal who didn't like trouble had more reason than ever to be rid of her, even though it was his fault she had landed here.

She looked about the heart of the *Starlight Observer*, its cracked adobe walls filled with wildly gesturing shadow figures, its rafters ringing with the temperance call to arms, and she wished she had a glass of Aunt Ada's peach brandy.

Her long sigh ended with the crashing shatter of broken glass.

Tildie screamed, Leila shouted an epithet she had picked up around her husband's stables, and Maggie retrieved the large rock that had rolled to her feet. Lucy stared in stunned silence at the jagged hole in the big front window until the viciousness of the act penetrated her shock. Outraged, she hopped from her stool and ran to the door.

Lucy rushed out onto the boardwalk and looked each way, but their rock-thrower had melted into the dark night, his escape cloaked by the raucous music from across the road. Not far down the way, light fanned onto the roadway in front of the marshal's office, and Lucy spotted Cleve Hardesty's auburn moustache the instant he strode out the door.

"Mr. Hardesty," she called, "come quickly. Someone threw a rock through the window." She dashed back inside.

Calmer now, Tildie and Leila each peered over Maggie's shoulders, while Maggie cut the twine which held brown wrapping paper to the rock. Lucy stepped gingerly over the broken glass to Maggie's desk. The sound of Cleve's spurs jangling down the boardwalk assured her that the law was on its way and she was *not* listening for another man's forceful tread on the boards.

"For heaven's sake, let's see it," Tildie demanded.

Lucy rested her palms on a jumble of journals and old newspapers and leaned across the desk while Maggie smoothed out the coarse paper. A nearby lamp illuminated broad black markings on the paper, but Lucy couldn't make out any words. She looked up at Maggie.

A frown deepened the crease between the newspaper woman's gray eyes as her mouth flattened. Tildie and Leila appeared equally disturbed.

Lucy stood straight away from the desk and addressed the ladies. "What does it say?"

"Garbage," Tildie said. "Plain and simple garbage."

Leila walked away with a disgusted "humph" and found a broom in a corner. Maggie's gray eyes searched Lucy's over the top of the wrinkled wrapping paper, but her expression was impossible to read.

Maggie tossed the note on the desk. "Someone just gave me the leading headline for our next edition," she said, and made a quick trip to the type racks.

Lucy snatched up the thick, scratchy paper and read: "*Leaguers Beware.*" She looked at Tildie, who shook her head and, muttering in German, left to help Leila sweep up the glass.

Lucy read the crudely written letters once more and frowned, not so much at the message or method of delivery, but at her own responsibility, intentional or not, in creating more tension in the town. The temperance ladies had now reached a crossroads. The others wouldn't say it, and neither would she, but if they continued, they would likely face more than laughter and pails of water.

Cleve Hardesty's jingling steps slowed outside the door and Lucy lifted her gaze to the entrance. The tall, wiry deputy stood in the doorway, one hand catching at the doorjamb. He faced the street.

"Hank, go look at the Outpost for the marshal," he shouted. In a lower voice, he added, "Charlie, you check Nell's place." Cleve advanced into the newspaper office, his eyes searching hers. "Anybody hurt?"

Lucy dropped her gaze to the black scratchings once more, too conscious of what Leila had revealed earlier. Young men seldom took notice of her, and she felt awkward somehow, as if on display. She didn't know what to do with herself.

"No," Tildie declared as she scooped up broken glass with a wide dustpan. "Thanks only to God for that. Glass sprayed over the whole front of the office. Luckily, we were working in the back."

"I'll say you were lucky," Cleve replied, looking about the room at the scattered shards of glass. "What do you think we've got here, ladies?"

Giving quick strokes of her broom to tinkling glass, Leila supplied the answers. "A polecat, a rock, and a broken window. Lucy's got the note that was tied to the rock."

Lucy looked up and found the deputy's fine brandy eyes fixed on her once more, but she didn't look away. Intelligent, warm, and interested, Cleve's eyes lacked the brittle patina of hard experience, yet they held an edge, a sharpness that advanced his years.

She looked past him, but the boardwalk was clear of Sam McQuaid, though others had gathered around outside the office. She wondered if one of those curious faces was their culprit.

Cleve kicked at a piece of glass with his boot, then looked up and walked toward her, surveying the room as he came closer. "Kind of late for you all to be working," he commented.

"Our work has just begun," Tildie declared, and waved her dustpan as if it were a placard.

"Tildie, you've just been quoted," Maggie said. She took a notepad from her pocket and a pencil from her bun, then wrote furiously.

Tildie looked at Leila, and a small smile curled the corners of her mouth at the taller woman's tight frown.

Maggie continued to write. "I'm using your polecat statement, too, Leila. It adds just the right tang."

Leila lifted her brows and patted a hand to her carefully poofed and pinned-up hair. Lucy decided to make no comments that might find their way into the next *Starlight Observer*. She feared she had already said enough.

Cleve drew beside her to read the note.

"Leaguers beware," Cleve repeated. "I guess that's pretty clear."

"You'd think so, Cleve, but some people don't see like everybody else."

The deep familiar voice sent Lucy's heart pounding and her hand pushing self-consciously at her spectacles—her rose-colored spectacles, she thought. With a steadying breath she met Sam McQuaid's accusing glare without flinching until a shattering rattle of broken glass startled her and she jumped. Her eyes grew round at Cleve's reassuring squeeze to her shoulder.

Cleve studied her face. "Are you all right, Miss Drummond?"

"Yes, yes of course," she replied. "Only a little jittery, I guess." She darted a glance to Sam and saw a fleeting glimpse of that slight, telltale tightening of his mouth.

Tildie tapped the side of the barrel with her dustpan and glared at Cleve. "For heaven's sake, Cleve, show the marshal the note."

Cleve lifted the paper from Lucy's fingers. "Not much to it." He joined Sam near the doorway and the two walked to a far corner, conversing in low tones.

Lucy looked about for something to do other than stand in the middle of the room, a target for the gawking crowd gathered outside, peering at her through the broken window. Only one broom and dustpan meant she couldn't assist in the cleanup. She searched about the untidy room until the stack of newly printed pledges caught her eye. A perfect solution to both of her problems presented itself.

Lucy gathered a handful of the sheets and marched out to

the boardwalk. She handed a pledge to an unsuspecting miner dressed in coveralls. "Won't you sign, sir?"

The man scratched his gray-sprinkled whiskers and held the paper up before his face, turning it this way and that. Others began to drift over and gather around him.

"Can't see too well, sister," the man said. "What does it say?"

After hours of arguments over the inclusion of beer and picking out type for the pledge four times, Lucy knew it by heart. "It reads," she said in a loud clear voice, "I hereby solemnly promise, God helping me, to abstain from all distilled, fermented, and malt liquors, including wine, beer, and cider, and to employ all proper means to discourage the use of and traffic in the same."

The man thrust the piece of paper back at her. "No thanks, sister." He turned and pushed back into the crowd.

Lucy stepped forward, pushing the fluttering papers at every person she encountered. "Won't you sign, sir?" she said to an older man. "Think how happy you would make your mother," she said to a peach-fuzzed cowboy. Spying a wedding ring on a drummer's hand, she said, "Think of your wife, your children."

Some threw their hands up and backed away. Others shook their heads and shoved their hands in their pockets. One or two accepted the slips of paper with a quiet, polite, "Thank you, miss." All of them made tracks back across the road.

Soon Lucy stood alone, the pledges fluttering in her hand, surrounded by the night and a cigar's rich aroma. She knew when she turned around whom she would face. The nutty, spicy scent was familiar, bringing back disturbing memories of pines sighing in the wind, and big warm hands holding her close.

She stiffened her shoulders and turned to face Sam

McQuaid. He stood by the door in a pool of lamplight, his arms crossed, the cigar she had smelled held between his fingers and thumb. Swirls of golden smoke guarded his expression, leaving her without a clue to his mood or why he watched her so intently. Vaguely, she wondered who had found him—Hank at the Outpost, or Charlie at Nell's.

He threw his cigar into the road. "I warned you, Lucy Drummond."

"What did he say?"

Lucy caught Tildie's failed attempt at whispering and answering "sshh." She snatched a glance inside the office. Maggie wrote furiously at her desk while Tildie, Leila, and Cleve pretended not to watch her and Sam. She looked back at Sam, her tongue darting quickly over dry lips. Surely he didn't mean—

"I warned you yesterday about challenging the wrong man."

He did. She swallowed hard. That kissing incident. He was taunting her with that business about pouting, as if she truly engaged in such a juvenile habit—or was he threatening her? She glanced once more at their interested audience in the newspaper office. Was he giving her a subtle reminder of what he could say?

Blackmail. That's what this baiting was all about. Leila had said he could be ruthless. Her father hadn't allowed blackmailers to silence his disclosures of the graft he had discovered in the precinct elections. She wouldn't allow blackmail to put her on a train to Boston.

She pushed at her spectacles and started for the door. He should be taking care of his duties instead of harassing her. Not giving him a glance, she brushed past him.

"Really, Marshal, some ruffian has destroyed property," she said softly. "That should be your concern."

"Of course it is," Sam replied right behind her. "What else would I be talking about?"

Sam watched the hot flush burst across her cheeks as she pretended to straighten pledges. He supposed he shouldn't tease her like that, but when he had seen her stepping over broken glass to hand out pledges, he had experienced the most perverse urge to rile her up. Maybe he had wanted to see if her eyes really sparkled as he had remembered, or if her pouting lips demanded kissing.

With a fleeting grimace at his wandering thoughts, Sam stepped over to the table and took the pledges from her hand, tossing them in an untidy pile on the table. "The ladies tell me you were the first out the door," he said. "See anything?"

Frowning her displeasure, Lucy looked up at him. "No," she said, hoping she wouldn't have to endure another two-hour session of questions.

"Too bad," he replied, his eyes searching hers. "You make such a good witness." He turned his attention from her and addressed the other ladies. "We've got something to discuss, and now's a good time."

Much to Lucy's relief, Dolf Miller chose that moment to barrel into the office at a full run. He grabbed up Leila in a bear hug around her waist and swung her around. "Oh Lord, honey. Are you hurt?"

"I wasn't until you came in, you big oaf." She gave him an affectionate box on the ear. "Put me down."

Dolf stood her beside him but kept his arm around her shoulders. "I'm taking you home right now."

Tildie gathered a shawl from a hook on the wall. "I better see that Mr. Schindler has completed the night duties," she said.

"Hold up," Sam called.

Having followed Leila and Tildie's lead, Lucy halted her

retreat to the stairs leading up to the living quarters. She turned to see Maggie toss her pencil to her desk and the other two ladies swing around to face Sam.

Sam paced the room, his boots crunching on an occasional piece of broken glass missed by the broom. "I want you ladies to think long and hard about this temperance thing you've started. It's going to bring trouble down on all our heads, and someone's going to get hurt."

"Especially your saloon business," Maggie stated.

Sam gave her a deep frown. "The business I'm concerned with right now is keeping law and order in Starlight. The Outpost won't lose business no matter how hard Leila beats that drum."

"Don't count on it, Marshal." Maggie stood, resting her fingertips on the desk. "Ladies, the next organizational meeting will be—"

"Not at my hotel," Sam said.

"Here, then, tomorrow evening," Maggie replied. "Can I count on you to pass the word, or are we going to allow ourselves to be defeated by a poltroon throwing rocks?" She wrote a quick note, then looked up.

"You can count on me," Leila said.

"And me," Tildie added.

They all turned to her, but Lucy looked directly at Sam. That kiss, she thought. That stupid, weak-willed kiss. Unknowingly she had given Sam the power to ruin her, and she didn't doubt he would use it. If she was going to lose everything anyway, she'd rather go down fighting.

Lucy cleared her throat. "I'll start passing out the broadsides in the morning."

CHAPTER 9

"I'm telling you, Marshal, something must be done about that Drummond girl." The mayor stopped his pacing and executed a perfect about-face. "Starlight doesn't need any outside, eastern agitators."

Agreements rumbled through the gathered saloon owners, an indication of the ugly mood spreading over the town and at whom it was directed. Waiting for the grumbling and growling to subside, Sam sat back in his favorite leather chair and checked his watch.

According to Gus's report on the meeting last night, Leila's drum should be kicking off the *clean sweep* at any minute. He snapped his watch closed and regarded with growing impatience the angry proprietors he had assembled from the east side of Main Street. They looked back at him with equal irritation.

They expected him to do something about this temperance nonsense, and he had. The saloon owners were up here in his living quarters over the Outpost and the marchers were down on the street, a temporary solution at best. He had to come up with something permanent, and fast. The latest telegram from his brother and Caroline had shortened the fuse on the whole mess, and it was about to blow up in his face.

Sam fixed his gaze on the portly mayor, who was doing his best to wear out his new Navajo rug. "What do you suggest, B.F.?" he said. "Should we tar and feather the girl, send her out of town on a rail because Caroline won't come home until Lucy Drummond has left town? That is what Caroline's telegram said."

"Yes it is," the mayor replied, his side whiskers fairly quivering with agitation. His pointing finger rose with the tone of his voice. "But that doesn't change the fact that the Drummond girl has caused nothing but trouble since she arrived. Just as I predicted," he finished with a flourish of his hand.

Sam couldn't argue with that, but he blamed David for this mess, not Lucy. Besides, he admired the Boston girl's grit, if not her aim. And no matter what he had tried, Lucy had stuck to her guns.

Sam glanced over at Nell Taylor, who stood by the big corner window, looking down on the activities taking place on the street. "Have they formed up ranks yet, Nell?"

Morning sunlight glinted through her copper hair and sparkled off her bracelet and rings as she held back the gold velvet curtain and leaned forward. The light revealed deep lines in her rice-powdered face, and Sam wondered how old she was. Women like Nell belonged to the night, he supposed, while others . . . well, the others made trouble for a man twenty-four hours a day.

Nell rested a hand on her hip and turned to Sam. "They're almost ready to climb on those brooms they've been waving around and fly down Main Street," she replied.

Her meaning was clear, and a few of his guests laughed, while more mumbled references to witches and another word that rhymed. Sam noted those men, remembering who to question next time the leaguers received a warning. Whoever had delivered the last one had only made matters worse. Most folks didn't hold with threatening women, and the leaguers had gained support.

"How many marchers this morning?" he asked.

Nell squinted her eyes. "I'd say around twenty."

"Damn, Marshal, twice as many as last time," the owner of the Sundowner said. "You told us this thing would die down."

After listening to Cleve's talk about plucked tail feathers all morning, Sam was in no mood for more reminders that he had underestimated the ladies. "I also hadn't counted on anyone being stupid enough to start throwing rocks and threatening women."

"Balderdash," the mayor exclaimed. "That girl is the problem. She's either making inflammatory speeches or passing out pledges and broadsides or—"

"Or working on that old house the bank is supposedly providing the new schoolmarm," Sam said. He hated admitting he'd made a mistake, but he couldn't avoid the obvious, and he wasn't going to let the mayor off the hook either. "If we hadn't interfered, she'd probably be sewing peacefully over at Lettie King's, waiting to be the schoolmarm."

"No, you don't, Marshal," the mayor replied. "This is all David's fault. David brought that girl out here to trick my Caroline, to lure her away from the good match I had arranged."

Though Sam had cursed David forward and backward for skipping out on his mail-order bride, David was family and Sam wasn't going to let the mayor place all the blame on his brother. "B.F., that doesn't make sense," he said. "Caroline is too willful to be tricked into anything, and the whole town knows it. She probably ran off with my unsuspecting dupe of a brother to escape your arrangements."

"Now see here, Marshal—"

"Gentlemen, gentlemen," Leslie Laughton said with his disagreeable nasal superiority. "The answer is really very simple."

Sam gave reluctant attention to the Englishman, who sat in a matching chair with one knee-high shiny boot crossed over his impeccably creased trousers. At this point, Sam would welcome a solution, simple or otherwise, from any source. Laughton tapped his walking stick against his boot and slid a glance from the mayor to him.

"If the school board doesn't hire her, then she'll leave and our agitator is no more."

Red stepped forward from the corner where he had been standing, his thumbs hooked into his suspenders. "What about that, mayor? You're on the board." He cast a quick glance in Sam's direction, then took on an obstinate expression. "Fix that girl good and send her on her way." He jerked a nod that shook his jowls.

Sam didn't like the threatening undertone. The look he passed to Red said so, and the man scuttled back to his corner. He waited for the mayor's response before deciding if he needed to remind everyone of his promise to close down anyone caught breaking the law.

He still didn't know who had instigated the rock-throwing incident, though he had his suspicions. He looked at Red once more and the man backed against the wall, knocking a Comanche war shield askew.

"Don't you think I've thought of using my influence on the board?" the mayor replied. "But, it's too late. Tildie Schindler has done a bang-up job talking up the girl, and several of the members' wives are involved in this temperance thing. I can't even dig up any gossip about her."

Laughton gave his boot a good whack with his walking stick. "I've already seen a slowdown in business. What are you going to do about this woman, *McQuaid*?"

Sam returned the languid glance sent his way with a cool study of the Englishman. "If you're having trouble down at the Mine Shaft, it's because you water down your whiskey and run crooked games. In fact, I've been meaning to—"

"You know, boys," Nell said, and sauntered over to a sideboard where she poured herself a cup of coffee, "like a girl who should have said no, the damage has already been done and can't be undone." She turned around and took a sip.

"She's right," Jack Shipley said. "Even if the Drummond girl left town, those Bible-thumpers are loaded up and ready to fire."

A resounding boom filled the room, and Sam was amazed at Leila's damnable timing. Low curses greeted the thunderous news that Starlight was headed for sweeping changes. Sam rose from his chair and walked to the window, leaving the others to their carping. Little was going to be settled because there was nothing they could do, nothing legal. What a mess.

Sam brushed back the heavy curtain and surveyed the street below. Formed up in double ranks, the marchers shouldered their brooms and set forth down Main Street. Dolly and the barber's wife led the way with a big banner held between them that stated: SWEEP STARLIGHT CLEAN.

Sam searched through the group of ladies, looking for a blond wearing spectacles. But Lucy wasn't marching, which surprised him. He thought she would be leading the parade.

Lucy Drummond defied all logic or good sense, which made her damned difficult to deal with, but she was hardly the crusading ringleader the mayor described. No, he didn't like what he had heard this morning at all. The whole situation was frustrating, and with the mayor's help, everyone was focusing those frustrations on Lucy.

He spied Cleve's wave from the boardwalk in front of Pollett's and nodded. Cleve shouldn't have any problems today, not with the saloon owners up here with him and Lucy absent from the march. He had to admit she did have a way of finding herself in one foolhardy predicament after another.

Sam considered putting together some kind of parley between the ladies and the owners, but didn't have any compromise to propose. He wasn't about to sign the pledge and close down the Outpost, and he was certain the other saloon owners felt the same way. The temperance ladies had to give it a rest. Sam listened to the grumblings behind him grow louder. And soon, he thought.

He saw Lucy, then. Prim white blouse, dark-colored skirt, and neatly arranged hair. Curiously enough, she didn't join the broom brigade but pulled a hand-wagon filled with a collection of boards, buckets, and a broom. Probably on her way to the Lockhart place.

Lucy stopped and spoke to his deputy. Sam noted how her hand fluttered up to push at her spectacles before she moved on. He watched her progress down the walk until she turned into the lane that led to the old house. Cleve looked up at him, but Sam couldn't make out his expression.

Cleve and Lucy. Sam frowned and let the curtain drop. He poured himself a cup of coffee and sipped it while the mayor ran on about his daughter and Laughton demanded action. Sam couldn't stop thinking about Lucy peering up at Cleve and that odd little way she had of pushing at her spectacles when she was nervous. Surely she wasn't looking in Cleve's direction. His deputy had potential, certainly, but he was too wild, too . . .

Sam took another sip of his coffee and tried to think of exactly what it was about Cleve that wasn't right for Lucy. Hell, Lucy Drummond couldn't marry Cleve, and he would think of all the reasons later. Right now, he had to figure out how to make sure she and the whole town didn't get caught in the cross fire between demon rum and the pledge.

"I say, *McQuaid*?"

Sam set down his coffee cup and turned to the Englishman. God, he hated the way Laughton said his name, like he was high lord of the land.

Laughton flipped his walking stick against his boot in time with Leila's deadly dull drumming. Sam waited to hear what had put that sly smile on Laughton's face.

"We have concluded our discussion, and it is generally agreed that you should arrest these women for disturbing the peace, or we will use whatever means necessary to protect our businesses."

Sam examined each face in the room as the drum boomed out the seconds, a constant reminder of his time running out. Some met his eyes, some wouldn't, but no one disagreed with Laughton. He should have known better than to turn his back on this crowd, he thought.

Sam concentrated his displeasure with the Englishman's ultimatum by singling him out for silent disfavor. The walking stick tapped double-time.

"I've got as much or more to lose as any of you." Sam spread his solemn censure to the other owners. "But, arresting those women would only make them dig in harder and probably give them more supporters."

Laughton's smile slipped to the side and several heads nodded in agreement. Sam crossed his arms and leaned against the sideboard. "If we keep our heads, those women can parade and pray all they want, but the miners and ranch hands will still flock into Starlight every night."

"What if they decide to start praying outside my billiard parlor like that Drummond girl suggested?" Jack Shipley asked. "Or the Mine Shaft or the Outpost? Customers aren't going to like that. They can take their wages to Kingston or Hillsboro for a good time."

"You see, Marshal," the mayor said, "Miss Drummond causes all our problems. We have to do something about her before she leads those women right through every swinging door in Starlight."

"For God's sake, B.F.," Sam replied, "Lucy isn't going to do that."

"How do you know, *McQuaid*?" Laughton cut in. "They've already blocked the entrance to Red's place with their praying. Do you expect us to do nothing?"

Sam didn't move but set his gaze on the Englishman. "I've had my say about roughing up any women in Starlight."

"Seems to me only one woman is causing us most of our problems," Nell said, "and I know how to get rid of her pronto." She waited until she was sure she had everyone's attention, then continued. "I can't believe any woman would want to stay cooped up with a roomful of little heathens for months at a time when she could make more money easier and faster."

The mayor cleared his throat and darted hopeless looks about the room. "Well, Nell . . . dear . . . ladies—"

"Shelve the explanation, Mayor. I know what I'm talking about." Nell rested her hand on her hip. "I'd pay the Drummond girl a hundred dollars to leave town. How about you, Jack?"

Jack's face brightened. "I see where you're going. I'd pay

her a hundred. I bet every saloon owner in town would pay her a hundred. That comes to—"

"Fourteen hundred dollars," Sam replied. He remembered all of Lucy's talk about corrupt power and, keeping to his earlier decision, wouldn't venture a guess as to how Lucy would respond to the saloon owners' offer. "Miss Drummond has some far-fetched notions about things and—"

"A woman on her own is practical," Nell said. "She's gotta be to survive."

Sam uncrossed his arms and stepped forward. "Practical is not in Miss Drummond's vocabulary."

"Sounds like a good idea to me," the mayor said, and made a quick check to see that everyone in the room appeared agreeable, too. "Once she leaves, I predict the other ladies will no longer find her ideas so intriguing." He drew himself up. "Marshal, as the mayor of Starlight, I commission you, our peace officer, to take this more than generous offer to Miss Drummond."

Sam started to object, then hesitated. He had to think of the town. Not only would the saloon owners lose money, but the merchants would suffer, too. Right now, he didn't have any better ideas and couldn't guarantee this one wouldn't work. He gave the owners the nod they were waiting for.

"I'll talk to her this afternoon," he replied.

"The sooner the better," the mayor said, and joined the others as they started to leave. He turned to Nell as they filed out of the room. "If only David had married that girl, if only someone would show an interest in her, or if I could find out something unsuitable about her," he mumbled. "She couldn't be the schoolmarm then, you know."

"Caroline will come home when she runs out of money," Nell said, giving him an assuring pat on the shoulder. "You took my advice and didn't send her any cash."

"No, no," B.F. replied. "Haven't sent her a dime. Told her I would send her a train ticket for one." He stabbed a glare at Sam as he left.

Sam gave him a bored sigh and lit a cigar. He had some thinking to do. Approaching the proud and unpredictable Lucy Drummond with the saloon owners' money wasn't going to be easy. Too bad he wasn't as good as the mayor at predictions.

Jack Shipley pulled the door closed behind him, and Sam was left with Leila's beating drum to keep him company. Finally that stopped, too.

He walked over to the window and looked down at the ladies milling around in front of the boarded-over window of the *Starlight Observer*. A heated discussion appeared to be taking place. Maggie pointed across the road, and Sam thought he might have to arrest the mothers, sisters, and daughters of his friends.

Ladies on the fringes began to wander away in pairs, and finally Leila left with the drum. The last of the ladies dispersed and Maggie went inside. Apparently, not all the sweepers shared their leader's cleaning zeal. Maybe Lucy didn't, either.

Sam returned to his big leather easy chair and sat back, smoking his cigar and examining the bits and pieces of his life that hung on the walls. Comanche war lances, an Apache peace pipe, his company pennant, and a framed letter from Colonel Ranald S. Mackenzie, his former commander. Duty, honor, country—the cornerstones of his life. Order and discipline—the bricks and mortar.

He had subdued renegade Indians, chased down bandits, and made men out of green troopers, but he hadn't been able to convince a certain blond young lady that she would have been better off in Boston. Now he had to convince her to take what amounted to a bribe to leave town. Suddenly, he longed for those easy days of riding with his regiment.

"What do you think of blackmailers, Blackie?"

Lucy tore the last shred of meat from the piece of fried chicken and placed it on a chipped saucer she had found in the house. The big cat sniffed, then ate the sliver of meat. He licked his chops and looked up at her with his great golden eyes.

"You've already eaten a thigh and a leg." She gathered up the remnants of her lunch. "I don't have anything more to give you."

Blackie blinked, then began licking his white paw and cleaning his face. Lucy stowed cup, towels, and a jar half-filled with water into a basket, then fastened the leather strap. She sighed and leaned back against the tree, crossing her legs at her ankles, her hands laced together over her full stomach. As she looked at her new home, Lucy resolved that she would not let Sam McQuaid pressure her to leave town over one silly kiss.

"Would you, Blackie?"

He walked away, his long, bushy tail held high, curled just so on the end, then plopped down a few feet away. Looking about his kingdom, Blackie blinked at her once before turning his head and meditating on the intricate patterns of lacy shade shifting over wildflowers.

"No, I can see you wouldn't," she said, and smiled. Blackie had come a little closer today, and she hoped after a few more feedings he would allow her to pet him, maybe even curl up in her lap and purr with contentment.

Lucy closed her eyes and rested her head against the rough bark, breathing in the scent of pine. Her back ached from scrubbing and her hands stung from the strong soap she had used, but they were good aches and pains, filling her with a satisfaction she had seldom experienced.

The outside of the house was going to need more than scrubbing, but the interior was coming along nicely. She had found some pretty tile work under the thick grease and grime in the kitchen, and Cleve had said the wood floors were in good shape. He hadn't seen any dry rot or water damage, and Dolly had promised to help her wallpaper. Hopefully, everything would be ready by the time her mother arrived.

Next, she would work on those steps, but not right now. She had stayed up late last night helping set up the next edition of the *Starlight Observer*. A few moments of rest would help her stay up tonight and sew.

Thank goodness Maggie had given her the day off, an unexpected surprise supplied by an unexpected source. Old Pete Cassidy hadn't realized his grumblings about "amateurs clutterin' up the place" was music to her ears. His surliness would mean a day away from the newspaper every Monday. Today, he had delivered her from Leila's drum, as well.

She had been unable to mask her obvious relief when Maggie had asked her to forego the parade and set up the type for the advertisements that had arrived that morning from Hillsboro. The marchers had entered the office about that time, and she didn't think Maggie had noticed her momentary lack of eagerness to spread the word.

Lucy drew her bottom lip between her teeth. Every day she grew more uncomfortable with the role she had begun so innocently in Tildie's office, a role that had lead her further into danger and a moment of intimacy with Sam McQuaid. Still, she couldn't leave this lonely high place. Something waited for her in Starlight, something she must discover or lose forever.

Suddenly beset with unknown longings and doubts, she opened her eyes and took in every weathered board of the old house sitting in the quiet glade, every rusty hinge, every broken window or slat of wood. A quiet peace settled over her as she imagined the house painted white, with green shutters and the lattice work under the porch repaired.

Next spring, she would plant rose bushes along the front and put in a vegetable garden in the back. She could almost see herself and her mother sitting in rocking chairs on the broad porch. Blackie, too. Sometimes, if one imagined things hard enough, they came true. Hadn't she left Boston? Wasn't she living in the West?

She blinked back her drowsiness. Mother would like it out here. The air was so fresh . . . the sun so warm . . . so quiet . . . so . . .

Her eyes closed again, and she listened to the wind whisper through the pine, the faraway drone of insects, a soft whistling from the house. Thoughts unraveled and wandered, seeking, finding, settling on a tall man dressed in black. *The captain would never be interested in a girl like Lucy.* She sighed and frowned and slipped past consciousness to dreams of running through a dark house, searching, searching, but never finding.

"Lucy."

The deep voice entered her dream, and Lucy ran down a hallway to find it; doors opened and voices called to her—Aunt Ada, Tildie, Maggie—but Leila's shouted "never be interested in you" crowded out the others. She saw her mother step out of the last room and beckon with her hand. Lucy ran faster.

"Lucy."

The voice drew her attention from her mother to a dark figure of a man standing at the end of the hall. Light shone behind him, shadowing his features, but she knew who he was. Her mother gestured to her, urging her to come to her. She looked pale and sad and tired, so tired. Lucy ran harder, but her mother and the dark figure never drew closer. Her feet grew heavier and heavier until she could hardly lift them; still, she struggled forward, pushing at the hands that reached for her.

"Lucy."

The sharp command opened her eyes, and she stared at smoky blue eyes that peered into hers as unguarded as she had ever seen them. So startling was the effect, she released Sam's arm to touch his face, making certain she wasn't experiencing one of those strange dreams of waking.

Kneeling beside her, his hands tightened on her arms. "Are you all right?" he asked. "I thought . . . never mind what I thought. Are you awake?"

Lucy slid her hand from his face, his whiskers prickling her palm. Every sensation was intensely real, the nutty, spicy scent of his cigars mingling with bay rum and soap, the warm cloth of his sleeves beneath her hands, the hard strength beneath the cloth. *Let go of him.* She gathered the black cloth into her fists. She couldn't.

Sam was at a complete loss. Lucy looked up at him with a kind of desperation, soft and uncertain, lost. He remembered an old Chinaman had once told him to never waken someone too suddenly: the sleeper's soul wandered and must have time to return. He dismissed the story, yet couldn't explain her odd behavior. He hadn't known she was asleep. The house had been reflected in her eyeglasses. He hadn't meant to frighten her.

"I'm sorry, Lucy."

Her hands eased their tight grip and she lowered her gaze. "I'm sorry, too, Sam," she said, and slipped her hands from his arms.

Sam never expected to hear those words from Lucy.

Maybe she regretted the troublemaking ideas she had given the leaguers. Hell, he had put her in that situation.

Sam lifted her chin with a gentle touch so that she looked into his eyes again. "You don't have to apologize about your speeches."

"What?" Her brows drew together with bewilderment, then sharpened with irritation. She slapped his hand away. "Apologize for . . . I should say not."

Sam sat back, resting a hand on his raised knee, more than a little confused. "What were you apologizing about, then?"

Lucy didn't know if she could put the sudden sadness she had felt into words, but even if she could, she wouldn't tell him now. "What about you?" she said. "You apologized first."

Sam suspected he would never hear an explanation for her strange apology. A shame, too, since whatever it was had riled her up so much. "I was sorry I woke you up."

Lucy pushed at her spectacles. "And well you should be, frightening me like that." She stood up and shook out her apron, giving him the most indignant look she could muster. A little crook rose at the corner of his mouth and she launched into another subject before he could pursue her unfortunate slip of the tongue.

She planted her hands on her hips. "I suppose you've come out here to . . . to cause talk . . . to further your blackmailing schemes," she said, flinging the last at him with a wide gesture of her hand.

He stared at her, looked off to the side, mouthing the words she had said, then unfolded his long legs and stood. He raised his hand toward her. "What the hell are you talking about?"

Lucy narrowed her eyes at him. "You know." She lifted the hem of her skirts and marched toward the house.

Sam watched her stride up the path, arms swinging, head held high, shoulders straight. All she needed was a carbine on her shoulder—or a broom. Where had he lost control of this situation? Hell, he hadn't had control since his brother's abandoned mail-order bride had turned her forlorn, near-sighted eyes up to his at the station. Taking a deep breath, Sam lowered his head a notch and started after Lucy.

Lucy grabbed a hammer that sat on the knee-high porch and selected a nail from a can. Ignore him, that's what she would do. Lucy positioned the nail on one of the new boards Dolf had cut to her measurements, one she had already situated to replace the first step. Sam McQuaid *did not* upset her. She gave the long, thick-shanked nail a whack with the hammer.

The board plopped up and tumbled off the brackets; the nail pinged out of sight. Rude laughter twisted her around to face Sam, hammer held in her fist.

He slipped it from her grasp. "Lady, you're dangerous."

"Give me back my hammer," she said, ignoring his lazy smile with difficulty. At last, he wore an expression that matched the intriguing cleft in his chin, but why did he have to be laughing at her?

"Not until you tell me what you were talking about. Blackmail is a serious charge," his smile broadened, "to fling at someone."

She crossed her arms and gave a huffed sound of disgust. "Please, *Marshal*, don't pretend."

"The only pretending going on here is you pretending to be a carpenter." Sam tossed the hammer onto the porch, his humor at her outrageous charges settling into waiting patiently for an explanation. No telling what other mischief she would stir up.

Lucy faced the steady calmness in his eyes, the quiet confidence he wore like steel armor, and the ground shifted beneath her feet; her ears buzzed with the warmth rushing to her face. Maybe she had made a mistake.

Sam McQuaid was a lawman who faced outlaws with a gun and a star. Surely he wouldn't demean himself by carrying tales about a woman he had kissed. He was ruthless at times, but he wasn't a weasel. The notion seemed so absurd now. Her fears and doubts had played upon her imagination and now she must apologize once more.

"I'm waiting, Lucy."

Oh, this was going to be difficult. She turned slightly away from him and rubbed her hands along her arms. She didn't want to use the word "apologize" again for fear he would bring up her earlier reference. She decided a simple explanation would suffice.

"You may have noticed I get a little carried away at times," she said.

"On occasion," Sam replied, and marveled at his restraint.

Lucy plucked at her sleeves, looked along the road, admired the sleek black horse cropping grass nearby, and found that Blackie had abandoned her once more. She cleared her throat, hating her stalling, then hating prolonging this ordeal more. She plunged ahead.

"I had thought . . . it sounds so ridiculous . . . I had thought that . . . well . . . that you would threaten to tell the school board about your . . . visit out here the other day."

Sam began to understand, and with understanding came resentment. He turned her to face him. He wanted to see her eyes. "Tell them what, Lucy?"

Again, a warm flush rushed to her face. "That . . ." She took a deep breath. "That I allowed you to kiss me, that I was unfit for the schoolmarm position." She hurried to add, "I know I was wrong now, that you would never—"

"Is that right?" he said, feeling more than a little put out by her constant railings against his character. "You know, that's not a bad idea."

"Sam . . ." She shook her head.

"You've caused me and the town more trouble than drunken miners, payday cowpokes, or the day the stock fences broke."

"What about you?" she was quick to say. "All I wanted was to be the next schoolmarm so I could take care of my mother, but you and that . . . that mayor—"

"I know," Sam replied, not wishing to go into all of that now. Not when he was about to tell her the mayor's latest scheme. The burden of what had to be said pulled his mouth into a tight frown. "I came out here to make you an offer, one that will calm things down in town and go a long way toward taking care of your mother, too."

Lucy gave him a suspicious look, finding this sudden concern for her mother difficult to believe. "I'm listening."

Sam looked over her shoulder toward the wreck of a house she found so damned important. He rubbed the brass crossed sabers hanging from his watch chain between his finger and thumb. He hadn't come up with any favorable way of saying this, and after her accusations of blackmail, he understood the full extent of her distrust. Finally, he met her cautious appraisal.

"Some of the businesses in town have taken up a . . . a collection to help you resettle, Lucy. They've asked me to offer you fourteen hundred dollars to relocate. I'll still pay for your ticket home."

Sam waited for the explosion, that flash of temper and spirit to light up her eyes and form her sweet mouth into that inviting taste of defiance. Instead, her eyes darkened with the odd expression that had confused him earlier when he had awakened her. Like a lost child, she looked up at him, her eyes peering deeply into his. Quickly, she lowered her gaze, and the corners of her lips eased into a small frown. Her shoulders sagged under the weight of the world. She sighed.

Sam tipped back his hat and blew out a long sigh of his own. Without a doubt, Lucy Drummond had just been dealt another losing hand.

CHAPTER 10

Completely confounded, Sam struggled with the urge to comfort her, but he clamped down hard on that impulse. Hell, she had just been offered a sum that would take her years to earn as a schoolmarm, and she acted like he had told her to go to blazes.

Sam shifted his weight from one foot to the other, uncomfortable with the burden of her continued silence. Accusations or stubborn refusals he could handle. A nice "I'll think about it" would be ideal. But this subdued silence pulled him toward her, made him want to tell her that things would look up. Only he knew they seldom did and the saloon owners' offer was the best hand she was going to be dealt.

Sam crossed his arms to keep himself from touching her. "Lucy, I don't know what you—"

The distant rumble of an approaching horse claimed the rest of his attempt to draw Lucy out. Sam lifted his gaze from her troubled expression and watched the shadowed roadway. Lucy took the opportunity to distance herself by several steps.

Sam didn't know whether to be irritated or relieved by the interruption. Irritation won when Cleve appeared at the bend in the lane, his roan gelding striding out in a fast canter. Sam uncrossed his arms, hooking his thumbs in his gunbelt, and cast a disapproving eye toward Lucy's eager wave to his deputy. She stepped farther away from him, and he experienced an uncomfortable jab of ill temper.

Sam ran a finger around the inside of his collar and aimed a scowl at Cleve, the safest target for his aggravation. He didn't wait for the harried-looking young man to dismount before stepping forward and expressing his disgust with the whole sorry day.

"This better be important."

Cleve's startled reaction sent his horse into nervous dancing. He gave his mount a firm hand at the reins and looked from Sam to Lucy. "You all right, Miss Drummond?"

Lucy stood between the two men, looking from one to the other, and found the calm concern on the young deputy's face as disconcerting as the black scowl on the marshal's. Suspecting Cleve might harbor an affection she couldn't return, she faced her own foolhardy yearnings.

Sam stood in the shadow of the pine tree, framed by the neglected house behind him, his mouth a grim testament to iron-willed expectations, his eyes a dark, remote mystery of conflicting emotions. Lucy tried to imagine Cleve's warm and caring expression reflected in Sam's features. Surely she couldn't be in love with Sam McQuaid.

His smoky blue eyes met hers, and Lucy turned away from wishes that could never come true. "I'm fine, Mr. Hardesty," she replied with more conviction than truth. "The marshal was just finishing a distasteful errand for the mayor and the task put him in a foul mood."

"Yeah, I heard," Cleve answered and flicked a noncommittal look behind her. "A deputy federal marshal is waiting at the office. Wants to talk to you and Miss Drummond about the shooting last week."

Caught off guard, Lucy placed a hand to her mouth as if she could hold back the softly spoken, "Oh, dear."

Still chafing under the errand-boy label Lucy had pinned on him, Sam kept his comments to a deepening of his scowl and set out for his horse. The significance of what Cleve had said hit him as he picked up the Colonel's reins. He slapped the ends of the leather straps against his palm and directed his bewilderment to Cleve.

"I never mentioned Lucy in any of my wires," he said.

Cleve pulled out a folded newspaper from one of his saddlebags. "While the deputy was waiting for you, the newest edition of the *Starlight Observer* hit the streets." He dismounted and strode over to Sam in long, jingling strides. Handing the paper to Sam, he glanced over at Lucy. "You know about this?"

Lucy wasn't sure what *this* was, but thought she should investigate. She joined the two men in time to hear Sam's long and colorful description of the fourth estate before he thrust the paper into her hands.

"This wasn't a good idea," he announced.

With a sinking sensation, Lucy noted Cleve wore a stern expression that almost matched Sam's for disapproval. Knitting her brows at the two, she gave the paper a crackling snap, then searched for an explanation for their odd behavior. She didn't have far to look.

Beneath the bold masthead, illustrated with a curved half-moon and a sprinkling of stars, Lucy encountered a headline she had never seen. "WITNESS TO MAYHEM" she read. And below that: "In her own words, Miss Drummond relates the horrendous explosion of violence that ripped through our town. Read how this stalwart young educator describes the villainous pestilence wrought by rum's hold on Starlight." Hair prickled along her neck as Lucy continued down the page. In smaller print, but larger than the lettering in the long columns of articles, several lines raved over the bravery of the young eastern woman seeking Starlight's schoolmarm's post. The passage ended with a quote from Cleve claiming that few would have stepped forward and identified the dangerous outlaw who had escaped, or volunteered to testify at his trial should he be caught.

She looked up at the young deputy, her brows drawn up in surprise. "Cleve?" That's all she could manage.

"I was talking with my mother. I didn't know Maggie would use what I said in the paper." He smoothed his moustache with a stroke of his finger and cast a quick glance at Sam, then looked back at her. "Read the rest of the paper. You'll see what I mean."

Quickly scanning the article she had written, Lucy discovered two long paragraphs had been cut. Her stirring description of Sam's stand in the road exchanging fire with the fleeing gunman was summed up in one cursory sentence: "Sam McQuaid, town marshal, fired several rounds after the escaping outlaw."

Seething over Maggie's editorial butchering of the bravest act she had ever seen, Lucy declared, "She cut my story."

"The space was needed," Sam said in a low, clipped tone.

Lucy had already moved on to a story about the rock-throwing incident with Tildie's and Leila's quotes included as promised. To her dismay, Lucy found herself mentioned again. "Miss Drummond would not be daunted by a poltroon's tricks," she read, "and waded into the crowd of rum-soaked gawkers with pledges in one hand and righteousness in the other. The children of Starlight could have no better example of a brave and pure spirit."

Feeling neither brave nor pure but embarrassed by the heavy-handed compliments, Lucy couldn't look at the two men. "I knew nothing about any of this," she said, and realized Maggie had never meant for her to know. Obviously, she would have objected, and Maggie didn't want to deal with her objections.

The newspaper rustled in the heavy silence that followed. Lucy wondered if Sam and Cleve accepted her feeble denial. She glanced up to find both men regarding each other with grim solemnity until Cleve noticed her anxious expression.

"You sure that fella hightailed it across the border?" Cleve asked.

"Just as sure as I know he could hightail it back," Sam replied.

Lucy closed her eyes and cursed Maggie's zeal and her own cavalier attitude. Just like Maggie, she hadn't wanted to recognize possibilities that had conflicted with her desires. She truly hadn't believed the outlaw would return, but seeing her name and actions splashed across the front page of a newspaper forced her to see the very real threat.

Seeing her pale distress, Sam believed she had known nothing about this front page endorsement. Instead, he saw the fear in the quivering lower lip she caught between her teeth. Good. He wouldn't have to waste time explaining that she was now most likely the target of a cold-blooded killer. Any woman with sense, even Lucy Drummond, would take the saloon owners' money and go home to her mama. She'd be out of his hair at last, and out of that killer's reach.

Sam snatched the paper from her unresisting grasp. "Go on back to town, Cleve, and tell the deputy we're on our way."

"He was in a big hurry to see you, Sam," Cleve replied. "Maybe you better ride back. I'll walk along with Miss Drummond."

Giving his deputy a long look, Sam folded the paper into a precise, tight-cornered square. "I have business to discuss with Miss Drummond," he finally said. "Private business."

Sensing trouble brewing between the two, Lucy spoke up. "Why don't both of you walk with me?" she said. She did not wish to engage in any more private discussions with Sam until she had thought all of this through.

Sam looked from his deputy, who had never before questioned an order, to the small blonde at his side. Lucy pushed at her spectacles, peering at both of them through round, light-distorting lenses, and fiddled with a pearl button at her throat. His gaze lingered on her smooth coral lips, shiny now with nervous wettings from her tongue. Running his own tongue over his lips, he looked away and tried to decide what to do. He needed to talk to Lucy now. She was his responsibility and his alone, but he had problems enough without forcing a rift between himself and Cleve.

Giving a quick nod, Sam agreed to Lucy's suggestion. "Get your wagon and let's go," he said, and continued to watch her as she gathered her skirts and hurried over to the small hand-wagon parked under the pine tree.

"She's got guts," Cleve said.

Sam cast a glance at Cleve from beneath a raised brow, but his deputy had eyes only for Lucy. Sam forced himself to unclench his fist. "And no sense," he replied.

Keeping his thoughts to himself, Cleve took off at a different angle toward his mount. Sam returned his attention to Lucy and gave the Colonel a pat on the nose. That fourteen hundred dollars must look mighty tempting to Lucy now, he thought. He hoped it did—for Lucy's sake.

Lucy quickly stowed her bucket, basket, and cleaning supplies inside the wagon and took up the handle. She examined the old house once more and compared it to the sizable sum of money the marshal had promised—fourteen hundred dollars and a ticket to Boston.

She took a deep breath and thought of the long train ride away from guns and outlaws and a black-clothed man who never smiled—almost never. She would return with money enough to give herself and her mother a good start anywhere they wanted to go. The possibilities were limitless and much easier to think about than those that faced her in Starlight.

Blackie poked his nose around the corner of the stone foundation and fixed his golden eyes on Lucy. He appeared to be waiting for her, waiting for her to return with bits of food and, perhaps, a scrap of affection. Her throat tightened painfully at the sight of the lonely cat and abandoned house. Both needed her.

"Come along, Lucy."

Sam's call prompted her to give the wagon a tug and turn away from the house. The two men waited for her, each holding the reins to his horse, both measuring her with a close scrutiny she found uncomfortable. She looked over her shoulder and saw the big cat slide around the corner, the white tip of his bushy black tail twitching with what she interpreted as annoyance.

"Good-bye, Blackie," she called softly, and wondered if she would ever see him again. Would he sit on the porch day after day, looking for her, while dust and time settled over the house? And what of her? she thought. Would anyplace else ever feel so much like home?

The white duster gave Lucy a start until she saw the badge pinned to it. The deputy federal marshal sat in Sam's chair, his worn black boots propped up on a corner of Sam's desk, his lips clamped around one of Sam's cigars. A flinty gaze met hers, and unclasping his hands from behind his neck, the lawman unfolded his long lanky body to stand behind the desk.

He pulled the cigar from his mouth. "Deputy U.S. Marshal Whit Prescott, ma'am." He touched the brim of a sweat-stained gray hat, and eyes the same ashlike color took a head-to-toe inventory, not unlike Sam's habit of quick, assessing inspections, Lucy thought. The deep lines that creased his beard-stubbled cheeks curved upward briefly.

"You must be the famous Lucy Drummond," he said, his voice rough, as if he had swallowed a good portion of the trail dust that covered his long riding coat.

Lucy gave her spectacles a poke, cleared her throat, and raised her chin a notch. "Yes, I'm Lucy Drummond."

He nodded and the long creases bent once more in what Lucy now recognized passed as a smile, hardly friendly or inviting, but not derisive or mocking, either. He slid his inspection to the two men following her into the office, and his features resumed their remarkable likeness to those of the wooden Indian outside Pollett's Mercantile.

The door closed softly and Cleve stepped forward with quick jingling steps. "Sam, Marshal Prescott rode down from Socorro to see you. He's interested in that fella who shot up Main Street last week."

Sam moved up beside Lucy, taking a position slightly in front of her. "I understand you have some questions," he said.

"A few," the lawman replied. He held up the cigar, his gaze fixed on Sam. "Hope you don't mind," he said with a casualness that gave a bow to courtesy and nothing else.

"Take some extras," Sam replied. "I've got plenty more."

The deputy marshal glanced around the office, gave Sam

another measuring look, then said, "I guess you do, Mc-Quaid."

Curious about this polite small talk, which held not one note of sincerity, Lucy studied the federal lawman's lean, weathered face but was unable to read much from his closed expression. She glanced up at Sam and saw the same wary reserve aimed at the other lawman. The silent exchange disturbed Lucy, and she wasn't sure why until she realized that Sam viewed everyone from behind a barrier of remote authority, including herself.

Aware she was staring, but caught in a darkness of spirit she couldn't escape, Lucy sought release from the unyielding firmness of his mouth, the forbidding command of his eyes, the warning grumbles of memories. She recalled a pine tree's whispers and smoky blue eyes displaying a glimmer of humor, perhaps a moment's alarm, certainly a flash of desire. Possibly the hint of . . .

So wild, so dangerous was her train of thought, Lucy refused to continue it. She faced Marshal Prescott, wishing to return to the newspaper office as soon as possible. She had much to think through: sensible recourses, responsible decisions, consequences. She certainly had much to consider.

Lucy grabbed a chair and set it before her with a thump. She sat down and said, "About those questions, Marshal Prescott?"

The federal lawman clamped the cigar between his teeth and moved around to the front of the desk. Resting a hip on the corner, he reached inside his coat pocket and pulled out a folded square of paper. With quick efficiency, he unfolded the thick paper and handed her the creased result.

"Is this the man you saw?" he asked around the cigar.

Lucy stared down at the crude drawing of the man who had aimed his gun and fired at her. Though stained and faint in places, the artist had captured that same, gap-toothed smile, the thick, straight brows with their devilish slant. She returned the picture without reading any of the notations at the bottom of the page.

"Yes, that's him," she said, her gaze meeting the lawman's, then sliding away. Fourteen hundred dollars, just for leaving town, she thought. She drew her brows together into a small frown. Just for leaving town. . . .

Removing the cigar from his mouth, Marshal Prescott took the drawing from her and looked it over. "Thought so from McQuaid's description that came over the wire."

"I'd like to see that," Sam said on his way to the big chair behind his desk.

The other lawman gave Sam the poster but quickly returned his attention to Lucy, then frowned and rubbed his tired eyes.

"Got any coffee around here?" he asked through his hands.

"Usually some there on the stove," Sam replied while studying the picture. He glanced at Lucy, then held the poster out to Cleve, who stepped over from his stance by the window. "What do you know about this man, Prescott?" Sam asked.

The deputy marshal eased off the edge of the desk and sauntered over to the small pot-bellied stove in the corner. Sam's question hung in the air, and Lucy suspected indecision plagued the man; she was sure it had something to do with herself and that outlaw.

Marshal Prescott poured himself a cup of coffee and slowly turned from the stove. He frowned down into the cup and, pulling the duster back, rested a fist above a wide gunbelt fashioned with double rows of cartridges, its holster holding a large revolver at his hip. A bone-handled bowie knife was secured in its leather sheath inside the waistband of his striped gray pants, which were tucked into his boots. The handle of another knife peeked above the dull leather. Lucy spotted one bid at fashion in the brass buttons that lined the square-cut yoke of his blue shirt.

Hard-bitten and trail-weary, Deputy U.S. Marshal Whit Prescott carried an air of reckoning about him, a demand for retribution and the strength of purpose to see it done. Lucy knew what he saw in that cup of coffee: trouble.

He sat down on a nearby chair and took a sip of the apparently bitter brew, if his grimace was any indication, then looked hard at Lucy. His expression didn't ease from his encounter with the day-old coffee.

"Miss Drummond, you are in a peck of trouble, and damn me, but I have to ask you to stay that way."

Sam beat Lucy to a reply. "I know where you're leading, Prescott, and Lucy's not playing the Judas goat for you," he said, his voice low, tight, and controlled. "You don't even know he'll come back across the border."

The marshal shifted a speculative glance between Lucy and Sam but gave no indication of his conclusions other than an instant's thinning of his mouth. "Raul Mendoza has already been spotted crossing the border at Columbus."

Lucy couldn't stop a panicked glance toward Sam. The cold hands of fear squeezed at her heart, and she longed for some kind of assurance to ease its chilling grip, but he only gave her a hard, almost angry, look in return. Of course, Sam had told her to leave, had warned her this might happen. She must face the results of her own stubbornness.

Lucy took a moment to gather her wits and calm her jitters. Tension sizzled through the room and beat down on her battered nerves. She curled her hands into tight fists. "Why didn't someone apprehend him in Columbus?"

"Ma'am, I do my best, but I can't be everywhere,"

Marshal Prescott replied. "And the locals missed him, just like McQuaid here did last week."

"Can't you call in some help?" Lucy asked, knowing she sounded desperate but not caring at the moment.

"I've called in two more deputies, but it will take a few days for them to get here," the deputy marshal replied. "I've done my best down here, but Raul is a wily one. Not easy to track, and ducking across the border whenever he needs to."

He transferred his attention to Sam, while Lucy's gaze followed a long-legged spider's progress across the floor. Her thoughts turned to fourteen hundred dollars and all that she could buy for her mother.

"Right, McQuaid?" Marshal Prescott continued. "The article in the paper said you trailed him that far."

Sam gave a sharp look to the deputy marshal. "That's right, Prescott," Sam replied. His gaze wandered to Lucy, and he remembered that lost shot at Mendoza when his sights had fixed on a girl in a cream-colored dress instead of the outlaw riding behind her. "He crossed somewhere between Hachita and Columbus." Sam poked a thumb over his shoulder toward Cleve. "Why hasn't that poster been sent out? If *we locals* had more information, we might grab some of this border trash before they rob businesses and kill our citizens."

"He's not wanted." Marshal Prescott took another sip of the bitter coffee and his expression showed his disgust for either the coffee, the situation, or both. He set the cup on the floor. "Kid, why don't you make us a fresh pot of coffee," he said.

Sam nodded at Cleve's inquiring look and was distracted from his demand to know more about Mendoza by Lucy's silent study of the floor. Her knuckles were white with tension and she held her mouth in a tight little frown. Again, he was confronted with the urge to comfort her, pull her close and tell her he would keep her from harm, but he couldn't guarantee her anything but a ticket to Boston and the saloon owners' money.

Angry and frustrated, Sam returned his concentration to the problem with this deputy U.S. marshal's plan to use Lucy to lure Mendoza back to Starlight. He needed more information, but Prescott was holding back.

"Not wanted, huh?" Sam remarked. Prescott had changed the subject quick enough after that revelation. "You rode all this way on the outside hope of catching some two-bit holdup man who isn't even wanted?"

Marshal Prescott had sat back, his long legs stretched out in front of him as he blew smoke at the ceiling. Then he laughed—a dry, scratchy sound from deep in his throat.

"Raul Mendoza is no saloon robber, McQuaid. Death for hire is Mendoza's specialty, and he's very good. What do you know about the man he killed?"

"Not much," Sam replied. "Nobody knew him and no papers were found on him that mentioned a family or where he was from. A drifter, like a lot of men who come through these boom towns."

Marshal Prescott raised a brow at Sam. "I doubt he was your run-of-the-mill drifter." He leaned his head against the wall. "Over the years, Raul Mendoza and various partners have murdered the *alcalde* of a village that didn't want to give up its water rights, a stubborn old sheep herder who loved his little patch of mountainside more than a mining company's paltry offer, and a rich widow up on the Colorado line who wasn't cooperating with a syndicate from the East that wanted to run cattle."

He took a puff of the cigar, then continued. "That list is only a few of the killings we know about, and we suspect more. By the way, the blacksmith showed me his partner's horse and gear over at the stable. Got any idea who he was?"

"Not a one." Cleve set the pot of coffee on the stove. "Couldn't find much identification on him after Sarge O'Reilly's shotgun nearly cut him in half."

Swallowing back the bile rising in her throat, Lucy looked at the three unaffected men, unable to comment on the marshal's information after Cleve's graphic reminder of the scene she had tried to forget. She thought she might be sick and took in a deep breath.

So much killing, and these men discussed it as if violent death was a business-as-usual matter, but then she supposed it was their business. No wonder Sam smiled so little and dreamed not at all. He had faced that final sleep too often, delivered it too many times. She turned to look at Sam's solemn features, but he looked away.

"Raul will be back, McQuaid," Prescott said. "He'll be back to guarantee himself no complications when he decides to take on another job."

Knowing she was the complication the deputy marshal spoke of, Lucy pushed aside her musings. She found the indignation to voice her frustration and fears. "Why hasn't someone caught this Mendoza fellow before now?"

"We've caught him, Miss Drummond," Marshal Prescott replied, all of his tired, weary miles revealed in his voice. "Put him on trial, too, but he's smart, like I said. Got off twice because witnesses tend to disappear and we never have enough evidence to prove murder. The villagers believe he has the devil's own luck," he explained. "I was beginning to believe them, too, until I read about you in the paper this morning."

"You don't need Lucy," Sam said, not wanting to hear any more. "You've got two more deputies coming. Surely you can track him down."

"Personally," the federal lawman began, stressing the word, his implication clear. "Personally," he repeated, "I would like to spare Miss Drummond from this dirty business, but my duty is to bring in lawbreakers and let justice take its course, which in Mendoza's case will be straight to the gallows. He knows she can put his neck in that noose. Our best chance is to wait for him. He'll come, McQuaid, and when he does, we'll be ready for him. We need her to testify."

Sam turned to Lucy. "What he's asking is too dangerous."

"Is it, Miss Drummond?" Marshal Prescott asked. "Is it too dangerous to lay a trap for a killer, then get rid of him for good, or let him go on to his next victim?"

Sam jumped to his feet. "You can't guarantee anything, not even her safety. You don't need her."

The deputy U.S. marshal slowly stood. "She can give us a decoy and him a distraction. She can put him in a hangman's noose and show any who would take his place that the law is more powerful than any devil's luck. She can save lives and he might tell us who hired him."

"Hell, Prescott, that kind never talks, and you know it. I won't let her—"

"You know I'm right, McQuaid. Damnit man, Mendoza is poison, and as a lawman it's your duty to do what must be done."

Sam couldn't say anything. The burden of his sense of honor and responsibility caught him by the throat and choked the very words from his mouth. The deputy marshal was right, but for the first time in his adult life, Sam told every principle he lived by to go to hell.

"Lucy's taking the first train out of Starlight," he said, his voice a shadow of its usual full timbre.

Marshal Prescott turned to Lucy. He pointed his finger at

her. "What do *you* say, Miss Drummond? Are you up to it? Will you testify?"

Lucy looked past Deputy Marshal Prescott's sharp, cutting gaze to Cleve, who slowly, almost imperceptibly, shook his head, to Sam who glared at her with absolute authority to do as he wished. She knew that look so well and had always ignored it. Only this time, she was tempted, very tempted, to obey him.

If the squirrels scurrying in her stomach were any indication, she wasn't up to Deputy Marshal Prescott's task. Yet, the idea of leaving Starlight, boarding a train with her fourteen hundred dollars of bribe money, made her feel ill.

Lucy considered her options while the Regulator clock on the wall ticked off the seconds. She made her decision and felt an uplifting relief, as if a huge burden had been removed from her soul. She stood and faced the hard, flinty gaze of the deputy U.S. marshal, her hands clasped together.

"I'll stay in Starlight," she said with calm and ease. "I'll testify."

CHAPTER 11

Lucy froze at the sound of a firm knock on the outside door. A glass globe in one hand and a lighted taper in the other, she looked over at Maggie who, like herself, had been in the process of lighting one of the two lamps in the small parlor. Lucy raised an inquiring brow. Since coming to live with Maggie, no one had used the outside back stairs to come calling.

Maggie lifted a shoulder. "I'm not expecting anyone," she said, then finished lighting her lamp.

Lucy did the same but encountered difficulties fitting the chimney's glass rim back within its brackets. Her quickened pulse hadn't slowed, though she told herself murderers rarely knocked politely at their victim's door. The floorboards creaked as Maggie passed behind her, and Lucy settled the globe at last.

"Who's there?" the newspaper woman called in a sharp, demanding tone.

Lucy stared at the tiny flame burning at the taper's end and listened for the reply. Clearly, Maggie didn't expect a friendly face on the other side of the door. Her front-page news had generated a lot of excitement on both sides of Main Street.

"Sam McQuaid," came the muffled answer.

The flame shuddered beneath Lucy's long sigh. She shook it out and turned to face the door. Sam's visit, though unannounced, wasn't unexpected. His stony silence had to end sometime. He had escorted her back to the newspaper office without speaking one word. Every thought had remained locked behind rigid lines of annoyance until he had delivered her to the *Starlight Observer*.

The glare he had aimed at Maggie had caused Tildie and Leila to cease their chatter immediately. The two ladies must have drawn a collective breath, because as soon as Sam had turned on his heel and marched away, a tidal wave of questions had sent her reeling through hurried explanations.

The ladies had known about her generous offer from the saloon owners. That hadn't surprised her—a secret in Starlight was more rare than a signed pledge to sobriety. Leila had been the one to point out how desperate the opposition must be, an observation that had brought smiles of satisfaction to everyone except herself.

Then Dolly had sailed through the door with Cleve's account of what had transpired in the marshal's office, including Lucy's personal danger made more precarious by the article in the newspaper. The ladies' subdued reaction had called forth a curt comment from Maggie about risks, rewards, and the daring to pursue both. Chores and errands had been suddenly remembered. Tildie had rushed out the door, claiming that the schoolmarm's position was guaranteed to a brave woman like Lucy Drummond.

That was the last comment regarding her situation Lucy had heard. Maggie had gone about the business of running a newspaper, giving instructions when needed but saying little else. As for herself, she had chosen not to pile blame and demands for explanations on the woman who had given her a chance, who, after all, had only published the truth. Yet, Maggie's secrecy and editorial shenanigans couldn't be completely forgotten. Lucy felt used, but it served as a reminder that she too had used the temperance movement for her own purposes.

The resulting disgruntlement with herself and Maggie was uncomfortable, the unspoken questions and suspected answers wearing. In a way, Lucy welcomed Sam's arrival. Even a storm was preferable to a stultifying calm. She kept a firm grip on the smooth mahogany trim of the wing-backed chair at her side and braced for another demand that she leave Starlight.

Maggie shot back the brass bolt with a loud click and opened the door. Sam strode into the small room without an invitation and fixed the startling intensity of his blue eyes on Lucy. She drew herself up with a quick indrawn breath. The faint scent of the smoking taper stung her nostrils, reminding her of that first day in his office when she had sensed the danger this man posed. She hadn't fully understood then, but she did tonight.

Leila had warned her: *Sam McQuaid would never be interested in a girl like Lucy.* A painful admission, but one she must never forget.

Looking taller, bigger, more masculine among the austere but feminine decor, Sam removed his hat and held it by its crown in one hand. Determination slanted his dark brows. His mouth was set into a grim, straight line of obstinance.

He pointed his hat at her. "Pack your bag."

Maggie stepped forward. "Marshal—"

"Sam, I—"

"Pack your bag, Lucy," he repeated. "You're moving to the hotel tonight and I don't want any arguments."

Stated like that, Lucy thought of several arguments. "I can't afford—"

"Taken care of," he said and, lowering his hat to his side, tapped the brim impatiently against his thigh.

Lucy took a moment to assimilate this sudden change from the argument she had expected. Perhaps this move to the hotel was some kind of diversionary maneuver to get her on that train Sam had mentioned this afternoon.

She pushed at her spectacles. "If this is some trick you have devised—"

Sam gave her an impatient look. "The trick, Lucy, is keeping you alive."

Lucy met his gaze and despaired at the weary resolve she encountered. He had always perceived her as a burden, a duty he must meet no matter how many times she had protested. Now the dangers were real, and so was his responsibility. How he must wish her gone and out of his life. Lucy didn't venture a reply.

Maggie stepped forward, her hands clasped tightly at her waist. "Let's get past the dramatics, shall we?" she said. "This move to the hotel would isolate Lucy and make her susceptible to any nefarious plans afoot to—" she cleared her throat "—to compromise her, which would influence the vote for Lucy's position for schoolmarm, thus achieving what that reprehensible bribe did not—Lucy's departure so she could no longer use her influence on the battle against demon rum."

"Exactly," Lucy said, though Maggie's suspicions weren't a perfect match to her own. They were close enough and could lead to the actions Maggie had described.

Sam scraped his hand through his hair, and on a long, deep sigh said, "Ladies, I have one plan and one plan only. I'm not giving Mendoza an easy target or," he turned his gaze to Maggie, "placing more citizens in danger." Sam pointed his hat at Lucy once more. "Pack up, Lucy."

Lucy glanced at Maggie, and the older woman held her thin lips tightly together, meeting her gaze with not a flicker of an eyelid or a movement of her clasped hands. Maggie was telling her to make up her own mind.

Lucy gathered her skirts. "I'll get my things together."

Packing her few belongings didn't take long. She returned to a silence so profound, Lucy slowed her step and guarded her breathing so as not to disturb its volatile stillness.

A temperance leader who counted on fair treatment from the law and a marshal who needed unbiased coverage in the paper stood with their backs in rigid compromise to each other. One wrong move, one unwary word might set off repercussions they all would regret.

Sam shoved on his hat. "You better carry your own bag."

Lucy understood why, and icy tingles started at her scalp and ended at her toes. Sam couldn't be distracted by polite gestures when he might be forced to draw the big Colt strapped at his hip. Lucy nodded and started for the door. Sam caught her arm, then brushed past her and opened the door carefully. He stepped out onto the small landing at the top of the stairs and scanned the night.

Lucy turned to Maggie. "Thank you," she said, though it struck her as slightly contradictory, considering Sam was searching for the murderer Maggie's article would bring to Starlight. But she meant it. Maggie had helped when no one else had dared, and without the older woman's belief in her, Lucy would be arriving in Boston about now, empty-handed and back where she had started.

Maggie nodded her head. "You'll do fine, Lucy Drummond."

Strangely bolstered by the woman's words, Lucy headed

out the door and into a night of damp wind and the fresh smell of rain.

Sam stepped back, indicating she was to precede him down the stairs, but Lucy hesitated. Without conscious thought, she turned her uncertainties to the night sky. Clouds drifted across the blackness like veils of spun moonlight. Peeking through the tatters, a scattering of stars shone through the gathering storm.

"It's beautiful, isn't it?" she said.

Sam completed his meticulous survey of the alley, then started over again at the other end. "What is?" he asked, giving special attention to a stack of wood piled next to the opposite building.

"The sky, Sam," she replied. "Just look at the sky."

Casting a brief, impatient glance at the sky, Sam renewed his visual search of their surroundings. "Looks like we're in for mud," he said.

"Mud?" she said in a flat tone. With a touch of sadness, she added, "Is that all you see?"

Tired, edgy, and frustrated with this headstrong woman who never listened, who insisted on making his life a misery of conflicting obligations and damnable indecision, Sam brought Lucy under his sharp inspection.

"I see rain clouds, Lucy." He took hold of the railing behind her and made a sweeping gesture toward the sky with the other. "Rain clouds," he repeated. "Rain clouds bring rain, rain brings mud, and mud—"

"Mud will slow down the rumsuckers who travel into Starlight every night," Maggie stated. She stood in the open doorway with her arms crossed. "His saloon will lose business."

Maggie's remark went through Sam like a shot of Taos Lightning, tearing the breath from his lungs and burning all the way down. He gripped the rail and managed a quick recovery.

"Speaking of business," he said, "I noticed an improvement in yours. You ran quite a few new ads from Hillsboro and Kingston in this issue."

Sam didn't say more and didn't need to. Maggie's thin mouth tightened and she shut the door, leaving him and Lucy in the dark.

"Whatever came over her?" Lucy asked.

Sam placed his hand at the small of Lucy's back and gave her a gentle reminder to start down the stairs. He glanced over the alley once more. "Maggie's an unpredictable woman."

He followed Lucy down the stairs after her mumbled agreement. This wasn't the time or the place to explain how the other towns hoped to pick up business Starlight lost because of the temperance trouble. A smile crept up on him as he contemplated the surprise the ladies would have when they realized they were marching bread right off their own tables.

The smile lasted as long as the fuse on his patience. Sam gave the rooftops a slow survey. Damnation to all interfering do-gooders and outsider lawmen. This temperance thing was building to some kind of showdown and Mendoza could ride in at any time.

His gaze drifted through the shadows and finally landed on Lucy making her way slowly down the stairs. Responsibility for her safety settled like a cold lead weight in his gut.

If the damn temperance ladies would leave the streets in peace, he could concentrate his efforts better, but he knew they would cause more disturbances. Mendoza would look for his time to strike, and Maggie's marchers would present a great opportunity. Damn the luck. But he had one blasted card left, and he was going to play it.

Lucy picked her way down the dark steps carefully, the heavy bag throwing her off balance and her skirts snagging on a nail or a splinter. She glanced down to the bottom of the stairs and saw a large shadow emerge from under the staircase.

Fear sliced through every nerve and a scream lodged in her throat, choking off all attempts to cry out. She dropped her bag and flung herself backward against Sam's solid body, as his arms closed around her.

"That's only Prescott come to make sure his prize witness makes it to the hotel," Sam said, a sharpness edging his soft voice.

Closing her eyes, Lucy grew still, absorbing his strength, the calming rhythm of his breathing, the heady sensation of his embrace. Then her eyes popped open and she freed herself from his protective arms.

"You might have told me Marshal Prescott was down there," she said, making a quick getaway and almost stumbling down the stairs in the process.

Sam grabbed her arm and pulled her around to face him. "Don't ever get between me and a target again," he said. "If that had been Mendoza, we'd both be dead."

Giving her spectacles a poke, she yanked her arm free. "I'll remember."

Her face burning with embarrassment, Lucy turned and began searching for her bag. A look at the bottom of the stairs revealed a large white puddle: her clothing.

Lucy made out Marshal Prescott kneeling by her things, a corset in his hand. Oh, heavens! Bunching her skirts in a fist, she took the steps as fast as possible, Sam's heavy footfalls thumping right behind her.

"Lucy!"

Maggie's call from above stopped her cold. Her shoulders taking on a decided droop, Lucy turned around and Sam stepped back so she could get a better look at the woman standing on the landing.

"Will you be coming to the meeting tomorrow night?" Maggie asked.

The tall, thin woman stood in a pool of light from the doorway, the expectant arch of her brow easily determined. Lucy hesitated, a part of her wishing she had never gotten involved with the temperance crusade; the part that hated the pounding of her conscience as much as the beat of Leila's drum. Nothing had changed. The schoolmarm's position depended on her continuing the front she had begun in Tildie's office. She couldn't hold back her efforts now.

Lucy whispered a quick vow to be a more enthusiastic member, then replied, "Yes, I'll be there."

"No, she won't," Sam stated with calm assurance.

After giving Sam an irritated frown, Lucy ducked a look over her shoulder in time to see the deputy marshal stuffing something that looked suspiciously like a pair of knickers into the bag. She decided not to argue the point. "I'll talk to you tomorrow, Maggie."

"I'll expect you here at nine o'clock to set up those broadsides," Maggie said.

Welcoming the chance to continue learning about the printing business, Lucy dared Sam to interfere. "I'll be here," she said.

Sam didn't argue. With a small sigh of relief, Lucy turned once more and made a speedy descent to rescue her unmentionables.

At the foot of the stairs, she discovered the frontier lawman needed rescuing more than her cotton drawers and petticoats. He stood abruptly as she stepped from the stairs. The deputy marshal gave his trousers a vigorous swatting, as if he were knocking dust from his pants. He wouldn't look at her. "I . . . I did what I could, ma'am."

The lawman resembled her twelve-year-old cousin Patrick when he had been made to take the girls' laundry down from the line. The comparison dissolved her own embarrassment.

"You were very kind to help, Marshal Prescott," she said, then knelt beside her bag and shoved in the last of her skirts. That's when she saw them—a jumbled fan of glossy covers glowing softly in the moonlight.

With a tiny gasp that slipped out before she ground her teeth together, Lucy gathered up her scattered collection of dime novels. Marshal Prescott had drifted several feet away toward Main Street, and Sam stepped down to take his place on the other side of the bag.

Lucy sped up her efforts, not caring that she was stuffing loose sand into the bag as well as bent-cornered dime novels. Sam knelt down and picked up one of the remaining books. Taking her cue from the deputy U.S. marshal's handling of sensitive situations, Lucy didn't look at Sam. At last, every book was hidden away except the one he held.

Taking a deep breath, she held out her hand and pretended she was arranging her things with the other. "My book, please," she said.

"*Marshal Earp Tames Tombstone*," Sam read, adding a liberal dash of sarcastic drama.

Lucy glared up at him. "Give me my book."

Sam looked down at Lucy, her features shadowed by the night, her eyeglasses capturing what moonlight the clouds let through. He studied the small face and understood at last this lunatic notion to stay in Starlight. Her world consisted of romantic notions and fanciful dreams, of good besting evil and happy endings. Such foolishness was likely to get her killed, and there might not be a damn thing he could do about it.

"This explains a lot, Lucy," he said, then tossed the book into her open bag.

"I have no idea what you're talking about," Lucy replied, and brought the sides of the bag together with a jerk and a yank.

"That's the trouble." Sam caught her chin in a firm grip and forced her to meet his gaze. "These books are mostly downright lies, and you've filled your head with heroic nonsense that's going to get you killed."

"Are you finished?"

Her words rushed at him on a whisper and Sam saw the glimmer of tears through the moonlight's reflection. How did a man reason with a woman like Lucy? He had asked himself that question all evening and still had no answer. With the little push he was providing, she had one more chance to see things right, but he wouldn't take bets on the outcome. Sam released that stubborn chin and experienced a grim satisfaction for not depending on Lucy Drummond's convoluted logic.

Lucy blinked at the tears stinging her eyes, cursing them, damning her vulnerability to Sam McQuaid. She grabbed her bag and stood up. Sam slowly rose to his feet. Giving her spectacles a push, Lucy looked him in the eye.

"No doubt, you think I'm a fool, Sam McQuaid, and . . . and maybe I am, but better a fool who sees possibilities than a cynic who sees nothing but doom and disaster." Turning her back to him, she marched away, her point made but satisfaction lost in his dire prediction and her own fears he might be right.

"Better alive than dead, Lucy."

Lucy lengthened her stride, rushing away from the soft, deep voice in the darkness. Heavy footfalls followed her, and she knew there was no escape from the man or his message.

"I knew you were up to something!"

Hands on her hips, Lucy glared at the opened entrance into the room connected to hers. She hadn't known the Grandview Hotel boasted a suite of rooms, but there Sam stood in the double doorway of a small parlor furnished as lavishly as the bedroom in which he had installed her. He looked as if his casual explanation of "this is the way things are going to be" was a comment on the weather, but they both knew such scandalous living arrangements would ruin her reputation and thus her chances to gain the school-marm's job.

"This isn't one of your backroom manipulations, Lucy," Sam replied. "I told you before, there wouldn't be any more of that going on, so believe it. This is survival. Your survival, which means Prescott across the hall and me in here."

"You can't stay there," she stated with a dismissing wave of her hand.

Sam tossed a key into the air, then caught it in his fist. "I'm staying in that room until you leave town or our friend is buried."

Determined to escape this trap, Lucy snatched up her bag. "Stay there, if you like, but I'm leaving." She turned with a whirl of skirts and marched toward the door leading to the hallway.

"Where will you go?"

The quietly spoken question stilled her hand on the doorknob. Where indeed? she thought. "There are other rooms in the hotel," she offered without much conviction.

"None that are paid for," he replied.

Returning to Maggie's was a consideration she quickly

dismissed. Doubtless, he had counted on that as well. "You're placing me in an impossible situation, Sam."

"The train leaves at nine in the morning," he said. "The saloon owners still stand by their offer."

Lucy detected the triumph in his voice, the certainty she wouldn't remain under these circumstances. Tapping the doorknob with an index finger, she tried to think.

"You know my reputation will be ruined," she said, speaking her thoughts without expecting a reply. "The school board won't hire me if you insist upon sharing this suite with me. Locked doors will have little significance."

"There're other school boards, Lucy . . . other towns," he replied. "A whole lifetime of towns ahead of you."

"A lifetime of towns," Lucy repeated. The phrase rang a doleful knell through her future, one she feared had already begun with a free ticket to Starlight. She allowed her hand to slip from the brass knob and her bag to drop to the floor. She turned and faced him.

"I'm not leaving, Sam."

Expecting a rush of questions she didn't want to answer, Lucy crossed her arms and lifted her chin. "I'm not leaving."

An arched brow and a long sigh were Sam's only reply. He pocketed the key and sauntered over the threshold, his black clothing a stark contrast to the red roses which twined through the carpet and over the wallpaper. One rose-adorned porcelain lamp had been lit on a bedside table, its glow casting his features into sharp planes and angles. His tall shadow followed him, looming over him, drifting over the roses as silently as he moved across the room.

A gust of wind splashed pounding rain against the windows and roof, breaking the silence, absorbing the street noise and merging with the rush of blood humming through Lucy's head. He had removed his hat and loosened his tie, lending an extra intimacy to the measuring perusal he gave her as he approached. Warmth flooded her face and she knew he must be aware of his effect on her. Not one clue to his conclusions appeared on his somber features.

He drew so close, Lucy had to look up to meet his gaze and uncross her arms lest they touch him. His eyes never left hers as he slowly raised his arm and planted his hand somewhere on the door behind her.

Roses and beeswax polish gave way to blue eyes, the spicy aroma of his cigars, and the memory of a wonderful kiss. Lucy stood so stiff she thought she might break should he touch her, then decided she would die of disappointment if he didn't.

The sharp sound of a lock shoved into place startled her and she jumped, causing her spectacles to slip down her nose. Adjusting them wasn't important at the moment.

"Keep this door locked at all times." He didn't move his arm from above her head.

Peering up at him over her lenses, Lucy nodded. "A reasonable request," she said. Another sigh and a decided twitch at one side of his mouth accompanied a brief glance heavenward.

"Don't stand in front of the windows," he continued. "A bathroom is down the hall. Let me or Prescott know when you're in there. In fact, don't go anywhere without telling one of us. I'm deputizing Dolf and Sarge. Between the five of us, you have a chance."

With a gentle nudge of his thumb, he pushed her eyeglasses into place. "And Lucy, I'm not Wyatt Earp."

Spurred by that awful complacency, that unshakable superiority, and with everything lost to her but pride, Lucy wrapped her hands in the black material of his lapels and gave them a yank. She stood on her tiptoes and kissed him hard, pressing her lips to his for what seemed a lifetime. Her heart pounding, Lucy released his coat, pleased indeed by the abject look of shock Sam couldn't hide.

Taking full advantage of his stunned immobility, Lucy patted the wrinkled lapels into place and gave him her own look of calm assurance, though her heart raced and a light-headed buzzing in her ears blocked out the sound of the rain.

"And Sam, I'm not a silly schoolgirl," she said, and tilting her chin with more than a tad of self-satisfaction, she made to move past him.

Sam caught her by the upper arms, stopping her before she had taken a step. Lucy looked up to protest, and her moment of glory slowly sank beneath the wicked reprisal promised in those smoky blue eyes.

"Is that right, Lucy?" he said, his voice silky smooth, challenging. "Then you had better learn to kiss like a woman."

His hands closing around her arms in a hold that wasn't gentle, Sam pulled her close. Her breasts brushed against his chest, an intimacy that forced her hands between them but closed her eyes to the scintillating sensation. He didn't give her time to exhale but captured her parted lips with his mouth opened and possessive. With one probing stroke, his tongue found hers, and a shivering excitement coursed through her, frightening in its intensity.

Lucy curled her fingers into the black fabric of his coat once more, holding onto Sam. She met his challenge, yielding to the demanding need for more of this madness, more of Sam McQuaid.

Suddenly, he released her mouth and Lucy looked up into wild, hungry eyes, dark with a passion as reckless and urgent as her own. She could only stare in a surprise and wonder that fueled a blaze already out of control. Acting on instinct alone, Lucy closed her eyes again and offered her parted lips to him.

He touched her face, her hair, then he slid his hands along the length of her arms until he reached her hands, which were placed on his chest. He took her tight little fists into his warm grasp, his knuckles pressing close to the fullness of her breasts. He hesitated, and Lucy waited, anticipating the demanding pressure of his mouth, yearning for that singular intimacy they had shared, that plunge into the dark world of abandon and promise.

Suddenly, he tightened his grip almost to the point of pain. Confused, she opened her eyes and saw the angry remorse that clouded Sam's eyes and cut at her heart. A coolness closed over his features as he retreated into his usual composure and pulled her hands from his coat. Lucy jerked her hands from his grasp. Words were lost to her.

Sam's mouth tightened into its set line. He turned and walked silently away. She wanted to call out to him, ask him how he removed himself from his feelings so easily, demand to know his secret because she hurt so badly. Pride sealed her lips, pride and the knowledge she had broken through those formidable barriers he erected around himself, if only for a moment. A moment she would savor forever.

Sam stopped at the connecting double doorway. He scraped his hand through his hair but didn't face her. "That won't happen again, Lucy," he said in his quiet way, then closed the doors.

"No, it won't," she whispered. Lucy didn't question her actions but found a likely chair and scooted it back against the doorknobs. She would keep all her doors locked from now on.

That task finished, a weariness took hold of her, and she

climbed onto the big feather bed's deep green counterpane. She curled her feet up beneath her, not caring that she hadn't removed her shoes. She touched one of the long crystal droplets hanging from the bedside lamp, setting the others into a swaying curtain of colorful sparkles. She would get a lamp like this for her parlor, and nice mahogany furniture too. But no roses, never any roses.

Sam stared at the oak panels of the connecting doors and downed another shot of aged Tennessee whiskey. The liquor hit his empty stomach and slammed into a system already overheated and out of control. He lifted a brow at the empty glass in his hand and decided he'd had enough.

Setting the glass on a nearby serving table, he shoved his hands through his hair and glanced about the room, attempting to pull his thoughts together. Good God, Lucy was under his protection. His behavior had been unacceptable. Sam looked at the connecting doors again.

"Damn," he muttered, turning away.

Giving in to the restless tension eating at him, Sam prowled around the room. He picked up one of the periodicals he never had time to read, then tossed it on the sofa, scowling at the rain's irritating chatter against his window. He gave a last sullen glance to the doors. How in the hell was he supposed to sleep now?

CHAPTER 12

"Your charge is not only ludicrous, Mayor Jones, but it is insulting," Tildie said, and slammed her hands on the long table. The six other members of the school board jerked to attention in their chairs.

Unable to contain her agitation Tildie rose to her feet. "Insulting! I tell you that this young woman has bravely placed herself in grave jeopardy to assist the law in catching a dangerous criminal, and you accuse her of engaging in an immoral liaison? Members of the board, look at her. Lucy Drummond is a moral woman."

Lucy blanched at the finger Tildie pointed at her but kept her gloved hands calmly folded in her lap. She remained composed under the stares and whispers directed her way by the board members. This was the largest turnout for a school board meeting in Starlight's short history.

Tildie folded her arms. "One laughs at the mere mention of a man like Marshal McQuaid having any interest of a carnal nature for a lady such as Miss Drummond."

Lucy frowned and shot Tildie a sharp look. The woman didn't have to go on and on about how impossible such an event would be, though the irony of this strategy had appealed to her during the four rainy days of meetings at the newspaper office. Lucy shifted on her chair with a little twist to her shoulders. Tildie had made her point, for heaven's sake.

The mayor shoved himself to his full, rotund height. "Ladies and gentlemen, we don't know what goes on up there when the doors are closed and the lights go out. We all know that where there's smoke there's fire, and it is my sacred duty as mayor of Starlight and a member of this board to see that our children are not touched by even a smudge of smoke."

Lucy thought of that first night in the hotel and grew warm at the memory of her secret—and Sam's. Smoke, indeed. Again, Tildie pointed in her direction and Lucy sat back, heat flushing her face with a guilty stain.

"See for yourselves, my friends," Tildie said. "Miss Drummond blushes at the thought of such a foolish and preposterous notion."

More stares and murmurs met this defense, one with which Lucy was growing increasingly annoyed, especially when so many heads nodded in agreement. She lifted her chin and straightened her back.

Mayor Jones turned to Tildie, his fists resting on the table. "The facts remain, Tildie Schindler. May I remind you and the board of Miss Drummond's questionable purpose for traveling to Starlight?"

"For the purpose of holy matrimony," Tildie replied.

"Questionable," the mayor said, shaking his head, setting his jowls aquiver. "Questionable, I say. And now she's as good as living with the marshal. No respectable woman would agree to such outrageous—"

"B.F., that's enough."

Lucy closed her eyes and waited for that deep, reasonable

voice to call Tildie a liar. She had truly believed he wouldn't come today. He would keep their secret no matter how much he didn't want her to live in Starlight. Her hands squeezed her reticule tighter with each bootstep down the middle aisle. They passed where she was seated and Lucy opened her eyes. She cast a quick glance at his back, then noticed the mayor's look of consternation. Apparently, Sam wasn't expected or welcomed. She breathed a little easier.

Sam took a seat on the front row next to Dolf Miller and sat back, crossing his arms. Lucy eased her hands open. She couldn't see his face, but considering the mayor's cherry-red pout and florid cheeks, Sam's expression couldn't be pleasant. He had come to defend her good name, and in that instant, Sam McQuaid won her trust.

"You were saying, Mayor?" Tildie prompted.

Mayor Jones cleared his throat and gave a jerk to the lapels of his tailored jacket. "I believe I have made my concerns known," he said, and sat down.

Tildie drew herself up, folding her arms around her ample waist, one hand clutching the other wrist. She briefly lifted her elbows, looking much like a mother hen settling in for a roost, and gave her audience a thorough survey. Lucy hoped the meeting would be over soon.

"Thank you all for coming and showing such interest in Starlight's educational matters," Tildie said. "As everyone knows, the board has received the application of a young woman of excellent education, high character, and unusual bravery."

Lucy smoothed her hands over her skirt, unable to look those around her in the eye. Tildie's high praise was as embarrassing as her earlier rebuttals to the mayor's rantings. Lucy wasn't brave; she was foolish.

"We have—" Tildie slanted a look of pure disdain at the mayor "—discussed Miss Drummond's qualifications, and

now it is time to vote. According to the bylaws, we vote by
a show of hands. Due to the volatile nature of this vote, I'm
asking that the town hall be cleared."

General agreement met this request, and several of the
assemblage rose to their feet with a scraping of chairs. One
man stood and held up his hand. Lucy recognized him as
Jack Shipley, owner of a billiard parlor and most likely a
contributor to her get-out-of-town fund.

Lucy dreaded whatever this man had to say. The temperance activities had been restricted by the rain and mud to
prayer vigils, and Jack's Billiard Parlor had received his
share. She prepared herself for another salvo.

Tildie frowned. "Discussions are closed, Mr. Shipley."

The mayor bounced to his feet again. "Now, wait a
minute. If someone has something to add, we should hear it.
Go ahead, Jack."

Jack took off his cap, revealing a headful of curly brown
hair the same color as his corduroy jacket. "There's something some of us saloon owners wanted said here today."

The mayor made hurrying motions with his hand. "Well,
get on with it, man."

Jack twisted the soft material of his cap. "We think Miss
Drummond's done a fine thing staying in town, facing up to
the threat of that outlaw and all. Many of us have kids, and
that's the kind of woman we want teaching them."

Lucy was numb to the applause that broke out. Deeply
touched by the simple speech, she blinked back the tears
stinging her eyes.

The mayor pounded his gavel, attempting to bring order
back to the town hall. "Clear the room," he said, raising his
voice above the uproar. "Clear the room, now."

People began to file out and Lucy rose to her feet. Leila
pushed through to her, catching her hands in a firm grasp.
"You're going to make it, Lucy. I just know it."

"I hope so, Leila." She squeezed the woman's big hands and couldn't restrain a broad smile. "I hope so."

Soon Etta Hamilton, Dolly, and Mary Pollett joined her, all offering their congratulations. Lucy nodded and smiled, accepted hugs, and heard about little Timmy's reading problem and Carol Sue's extraordinary intelligence. A wonderful warmth grew inside her, casting light into a future shadowed by doubts and uncertainties. She had arrived at last.

Lucy turned to greet another well-wisher, and the words drained away with her newly discovered peace of mind. Sam stood on the fringe of the little group, his black clothing a stark contrast to the brightly colored dresses and hats gathered around her. She noticed a tightness about his mouth and knew he hadn't come to offer congratulations.

"Come along, Miss Drummond," he said. "I've got time now for that shooting lesson."

The ladies' trillings trailed to silence, and those between herself and Sam moved aside. Lucy met his steady gaze with a frown. She didn't need his subtle reminder; she hadn't forgotten Raul Mendoza.

"Very well," she said. "I'll just be a minute or two longer," she said, perversely wanting to make him wait.

"I've got a buggy outside," he replied. "Cleve will be riding as guard and chaperon." Sam touched the brim of his hat. "Ladies."

A few titters followed his departure, but Lucy appreciated his consideration. Her reputation must remain spotless. Experiencing a pinch of guilt at keeping him waiting, she quickly finished her good-byes with hurried promises of later visits. With a quick glance given to the softly conferring school board members, she left the town hall.

Lucy's steps slowed as she got a better look at the red-wheeled buggy pulled up to the boardwalk behind Sam and Dolf. The top was folded back, and the view of the short seat she would share with Sam gave her plenty of reason to pause and reconsider this whole shooting lesson idea.

She wasn't eager to spend the afternoon with Sam's somber disapproval or his unpredictable effect on her sensibilities. She still couldn't believe that she actually had grabbed him and kissed him. What happened afterward didn't bear thinking about at all. Best forgotten. All of it.

Dolf nodded to Sam and started on his way with a wave to Lucy. She gave him a smile and a quick flutter of her fingers, then anxiously looked at Sam.

"Something wrong?" he asked.

"Is it safe to leave town?" she asked, offering up the only excuse she could think of.

"Probably not, but Starlight isn't safe, either," he replied. "You need to learn something about that little two-shot Remington I gave you. We won't be far from town."

"Then let's walk." She could control the distance between them that way.

"Too muddy." He gave his head a slight tilt and studied her. "Something else bothering you?"

Lucy was tempted to say that she wasn't feeling well and leave Sam standing on the muddy boardwalk, only he would probably know she was lying. Better to put on a cool, unaffected front and show him she was just as indifferent to him as he was to her. Besides, she wanted to learn to use the small pistol. Why deprive herself both opportunities?

"Of course not," she replied, and stepped briskly up to the buggy. "It's a lovely day for a drive in the country."

"With an armed guard to learn to shoot someone," Sam replied, and offered her his hand.

With an exasperated little sigh, Lucy refused his help and climbed onto the leather seat unassisted. Sam joined her, and she moved over as much as the seat would allow, which wasn't nearly enough. His long legs crowded her own and his arm brushed against hers as he took up the reins to start them on their way. Swinging her knees to the side, she turned her shoulder to him and said nothing.

As they approached the livery stables, she spotted Cleve leading out a saddled horse and gave him a wave. She hadn't seen him much lately. Sarge, Dolf, or Marshal Prescott were always nearby, yet she hadn't noticed Cleve. The young deputy lifted his hand to her when they passed, then swung into his saddle. She shrugged away her concerns. He must have other duties that kept him busy.

The fresh breeze felt good against her face after four days of rainy weather, stuffy meetings, sore knees, and the clang of the press by day and the sound of Sam's movements behind the thin hotel walls by night. She ventured a glance at the man seated too close to her and noted his dark scowl. The sunlight showed deeper lines around his mouth and shadows under his eyes, too.

"You should get more sleep," she said.

He gave her a brief glance. "So should you."

Lucy faced ahead to the new sights of the road leading out of town and didn't venture another attempt at conversation.

Main Street dwindled to a ragged assortment of miners' tents. Laundry flapped lazily on lines strung from tree to tent pole to tree. Lucy spotted two women working over a huge, steaming pot. Mud splattered their skirts and their difficult lives showed on their tired faces.

Sam touched his hat to the women and nodded. "They followed their dreams to Starlight, too."

"You don't know what kind of life they left behind," she replied.

"It couldn't have been much worse."

"At least here they have hope for something better. That's

what sent pioneers across the plains and immigrants across the seas and—"

"And Lucy Drummond into a pile of trouble," Sam said.

Lucy clamped her mouth closed and stared down the road, which narrowed between grassy banks of hillside. She admired the sprinkling of white and yellow wildflowers strewn carelessly over the land, caught a brief flash of a rabbit's white tail as it scampered off into the trees, and breathed in the clean scent of wet grass.

"I would much rather enjoy the countryside than go over old ground with you, Sam. You've made your opinions about my capabilities very clear in the past."

"You're plenty capable, Lucy." Sam ran a sharp eye over both roadsides, alert for glints of sunlight on steel, the sudden whirr of birds startled into flight, or an animal darting out of the trees. "It's your powers of observation I question."

"You mean my rose-colored spectacles." Lucy caught his brief, raspy chuckle. "What's wrong with a person seeing possibilities?" she asked.

"The consequences," he said.

"You make a poor example of your own argument."

He raised an eyebrow to her. "What makes you say that?"

"You came to Starlight," she said. "You bought a saloon. You took chances."

"I came to a boomtown with money in my pocket, not silver in my blood. I opened a saloon because I like to smoke cigars, play cards, and drink good whiskey, and I knew other men did, too."

Caught up in their debate, Lucy turned to him. "You didn't count on the temperance movement," she replied.

"The temperance leaguers will never shut me down," Sam stated. "The whole movement will die off in a few years. Which reminds me—"

"No, you don't," Lucy stated, not about to be side-tracked into an argument concerning her future temperance involvement. His marshal's star winked at her from under his coat and a smile curled at the tips of her mouth.

"And the marshal's job?" she said, knowing she had him. "How do you explain that? Consequences can be dire indeed for men who dare to pin on the star."

Sam sighed and shook his head. "I'm going to burn those dime novels," he muttered.

Lucy twisted around, her knees brushing his thigh. "You wouldn't."

"I will if I ever get my hands on them again."

"Well, you won't," Lucy replied, and shifted back onto her side of the seat. "Anyway, I made my point—you can't deny that you don't always consider the consequences."

"You didn't prove a thing, Lucy." Sam gave the bay's rump a gentle slap with the reins. "I make good money as marshal, and I didn't want my saloon shot up by wild cowboys every Saturday night. I weighed all the risks before I took on the job."

"There you see." Lucy smiled triumphantly. "I did the same with the schoolmarm's position."

Sam wasn't sure how it had happened, but he knew he had been cornered. He scowled his confusion. "That's not the same at all."

"You scowl too often, Sam McQuaid."

"What has that got to do with—oh, never mind." He gave up trying to make sense out of Lucy's powers of reasoning. A definite contrast in terms, he decided.

The turnoff to his practice range appeared around the next curve, and he turned the horse into the shaded lane. While handling the reins, his arm brushed against his coat pocket, and the crackle of paper reminded him of something he should have remembered earlier. Lucy's letter.

Sam dug the envelope out of his pocket and held it out to her without taking his eyes from the road. "This was waiting for you at the hotel."

Recognizing her mother's handwriting, Lucy eagerly accepted the letter. "Thank you, Sam."

She held the bent and wrinkled envelope, stroking her thumbs over the awkwardly formed letters. Her mother had been so proud of the penmanship her daughter had learned at school, but Lucy had never seen more endearing strokes of a pen. She hoped her mother would be with her soon and they could live in the little house outside of town. She thought of her scare at the meeting today and how one man could have made her stay impossible.

Lucy looked up and studied the fine cut of Sam's profile. A prominent brow and strong nose, his full lower lip no amount of sternness could hide, and that intriguingly cleft chin. So many contrasts, she thought.

"I owe you another thanks," she said.

"What for?"

She couldn't say it. She couldn't tell him how much his silence had meant to her. She couldn't reveal that much.

"For stopping the mayor today at the meeting," she replied.

Blue eyes rested on hazel ones, then looked ahead.

"Tildie was almost as bad," he replied.

Lucy looked down at her unopened letter. "You heard?"

"Ridiculous claptrap."

Lucy wasn't sure how to respond, so she changed the direction of the conversation. She looked at him once more. "Still, the mayor was especially insulting, and I appreciated your intervention."

"I was responsible and I met that responsibility. Forget it."

Lucy wasn't going to argue with him and returned her

attention to her letter. She opened the envelope and pulled out two sheets of paper. A whiff of her mother's favorite lavender sachet brought a lump to her throat. She took a deep breath and reminded herself she would see her mother soon, then focused on the familiar handwriting.

Sam heard the little sigh and slowed the horse's gait, giving Lucy time to read her letter. They were almost to the clearing. Hopefully, her mother had told her to come home. Maybe Lucy would listen to a parent's counsel.

He motioned for Cleve to ride on ahead, drawing a small circle with his finger pointed in the air, a signal to ride the perimeters of the meadow. Sam hated this damn waiting. Again, he considered riding out after the bastard, and like all the other times, he stopped short of committing to the idea. He couldn't leave Lucy alone in Starlight and refused to put her in anyone else's care. She was his responsibility. He gave a solemn-faced nod to Cleve as he rode by. And she was going to stay that way.

Sam glanced down at Lucy and the letter in her hands. Her studied expression didn't give any clues as to what the letter said. He thought of asking her outright, but that approach didn't work with Lucy. She'd tell him it wasn't any of his business. Normally, it wouldn't be, but he was dealing with Lucy. He didn't like to pry, but he would give it a whirl.

"Did your mother like your drawing?"

Lucy looked up and blinked at the bright sunlight, her thoughts still immersed in the goings-on at the crowded little house in Boston. "Drawing?"

"Of the house." He guided the horse toward the center of the meadow. "You know," he said, prompting her continued silence, "Lucy Drummond's vision of that old shack on the edge of town."

"It's not a shack," she replied.

Sam pulled back on the reins and the buggy rolled to a stop. He set the hand break, then picked out Cleve riding in and out of the trees surrounding the meadow's perimeter. Satisfied with his precautions, he sat back and directed his attention to Lucy.

Confronting the defiant pout that made him crazy, Sam almost regretted teasing her. Almost. "Looks like a shack to me."

"Well, it would to you," she replied. "And for your information, yes, she did like my drawing. She and Aunt Ada are going to make lace curtains for the house. She wrote that she was working hard on them so they would be ready in time."

"You told her you already had the schoolmarm's position?"

"I wouldn't lie to my mother, Sam. I told her the school board had to vote on my acceptance."

"And they started those curtains."

"Of course. Lace curtains take time."

Sam scraped his hand across his mouth and looked out over the meadow once more. "Of course," he repeated, and nodded his head as if understanding had finally come to him. "Lace curtains take time. That explains everything."

The whole family was loco, he thought.

"You've got to keep your eyes open."

Lucy eased open one eye and saw all five cans still sitting atop a fallen tree branch. Her arms dropped in disappointment. She thought for certain one of her two shots had hit them this time.

She turned to Sam, who had taken off his coat and looked thoroughly disgusted. "Let's move closer," she said. "You said this was a close-range weapon."

"If we were standing any closer, you could kick the damn things down."

"You needn't swear at me. I'm doing my best."

Once more, she suffered through one of his long sighs. Her ears rang and she was hot and her clothing smelled of gunpowder.

"Lucy, are you listening to me?"

She blinked and focused. "Yes, I'm listening, Sam."

"You aren't going to do your best until you keep your eyes open. You can't aim with the bead at the end of the barrel if your eyes are closed."

"Do you think aiming would do much good?" Cleve offered from where he lay stretched out under a nearby tree. "Those little guns aren't too accurate even in an expert's hands."

Sam took the Remington from Lucy, reloaded it, and shot off two cans in quick succession. "At this range, the Remington works fine. When was the last time you rode perimeter, Cleve?"

"About two minutes ago," he replied.

"Well, ride it again," Sam said.

Cleve gathered his long length up and, brushing his finger over his moustache, strode over to his horse. His spurs rang out in sharp annoyance. Lucy watched one man, then the other, sensing the tension between the two increasing with the heat of the afternoon.

"Maybe it's time we call it a day," she said, hoping Sam would agree. She wanted to get back to town to hear her official vote of acceptance.

"Not until you shoot this thing right," Sam replied, and reloaded the pistol. "It could save your life." He offered the pistol to her on his palm.

Lucy set her mouth as firmly as his and took the

miserable scrap of wood and iron from his hand. "Fine," she said. "We can stay out here all night."

"If we have to," he replied, and took his place behind her.

Lucy clasped the little gun between both hands and extended her arms toward the remaining cans. She pulled back the hammer and grimaced in anticipation of the loud report. Her arms wavered as she tried to hold the tiny metal bead steady on one of the cans. The bead swam before her eyes and she blinked to clear her vision.

"Oh, for . . . " Sam threw his hat to the ground. "Here, I'll show you."

Lucy stood stiffly as Sam's arms closed around hers and he moved in close behind her. His long legs crouched around hers, and her heart started its traitorous pounding. She swallowed and tried to concentrate on how he was aiming the gun, tried to ignore the brush of his whiskered jaw as he brought his eyes on level with hers.

"Are you ready?" he said softly against her ear.

She managed a nod.

"Keep your eyes open," he said.

"I'm trying to."

Sam caught the strained quality of her voice, the catch in her breathing. His own wasn't too steady, either. Never had he denied himself a woman who wanted him so plainly as Lucy Drummond. He'd never had to. He'd always been smart enough to avoid that particular trap—until now.

She fired one shot and missed again.

"Take your time, Lucy."

She thumbed back the hammer again, and Sam steadied her aim. If she could just hit one can, she could leave here with a little confidence and be more likely to use the gun. She better hit it this time or . . .

The little pistol popped again and the bullet nicked the

can. Immediately, he released his hold on her and stepped back.

She turned her beautiful smile to him. "I hit one, Sam. I finally hit one."

"Good enough," he announced. "Let's get back to town. It's about time for supper."

Dessert would be at Sweet Nell's tonight, he decided. "That's it for shooting lessons," he said. "Too dangerous to come out here again."

Sam turned toward the buggy, then motioned to Cleve. He paced back and forth, not bothering to offer Lucy a hand up. She wouldn't accept his help anyway, and Sam understood: touching her was painful—for both of them.

Striding out to meet Cleve, he grabbed the roan's bridle. "You drive back with Lucy. I'm riding guard."

"But, Sam I can—"

"Damnit, don't argue with me, Cleve. Lives are at stake here."

Cleve swung down from his saddle and threw the reins at him. "I don't know what's got into you lately, but whatever it is, you better get rid of it."

Sam's foot hardly touched the stirrup as he mounted Cleve's horse. Scraping his hand over his mouth, he glanced at Lucy's puzzled expression.

"I plan to, Cleve."

CHAPTER 13

"Attention everyone," Tildie called out, tapping her spoon on a glass of lemonade. "Attention."

Lucy stood by Tildie's side, smiling at the small crowd of well-wishers who had come to welcome her as Starlight's new schoolmarm. Most came from the increasing ranks of the temperance league, but several husbands had accompanied their wives, an encouraging sign of wider acceptance.

Tildie held up her glass. "I want to propose a toast to Miss Lucy Drummond, Starlight's new schoolmarm."

Glasses were raised and congratulations filled the hotel's restaurant, an endorsement strong enough, Lucy hoped, to reach the second floor.

"Thanks to all of you for choosing me as the new school teacher," she said, and drank in this exhilarating moment, this feeling of accomplishment, of success, of a promising future at last. She had persevered despite Mayor Jones's personal attacks, despite Marshal Sam McQuaid's determination to send her packing out of his town and out of his life. She savored this warm reception, a needed restorative to her lagging spirits after Sam's surly departure from the shooting range.

"I knew we would be victorious," Tildie exclaimed. "Didn't I say so?"

Everyone laughed, some offering a few joking comments suggesting Tildie should run for mayor, which brought on roars of laughter, especially from Tildie.

Lucy's eyes filled with all the noisy, smiling townspeople, some coming forward to offer their personal congratulations. Conspicuously missing were Mayor Jones and Sam. One she didn't expect to see, but the other . . .

Her gaze roamed through the milling people to the empty staircase. Disappointment vied with relief, leaving her as confused as she had been on the drive back to Starlight with Cleve. Blast the man, he was going to ruin her party whether he showed up or not. Refusing to let that happen, she gave herself another bolstering review of the people who wanted her to stay in Starlight.

Leila strode toward them, leaving Dolf at the door to talk to Whit Prescott, tonight's watchdog. "Tildie, you were splendid today," she said, and gave Tildie a hug.

"Yes, wasn't she?" Lucy replied, her smile slipping a little. Recovering it quickly, she added, "I thought Mr. Shipley's remarks were helpful and kind, too."

Maggie lifted a brow. "Don't be taken in so easily, Lucy."

"I think Mr. Shipley deserves credit for speaking up when he had every reason to remain quiet," Lucy said.

"I'm sure Jack Shipley had hopes we will avoid his billiard parlor with our prayer vigils in the future," Maggie replied.

"That beer he sloshes all over the boardwalk works for me," Leila said. "I'm not kneeling in that smelly stuff."

Picking up her cup, Lucy drowned her smile with a tart

dose of lemonade. She gave a silent toast of her own to Leila's sharp tongue.

"I've been thinking about that," Maggie replied, cutting a look at Leila that rivaled the punch. "Canvas sheeting will breach that unsavory defense."

Tildie wrinkled her nose. "But, the flies—"

"A little discomfort cannot deter us," Maggie said. She turned her argument to Lucy. "Right, Lucy? I'm sure you will agree with me that while we were able to overcome the obstacles in your way, the greater cause requires our utmost efforts."

Remembering her vow with sobering clarity, Lucy met those shrewd gray eyes and mustered all the enthusiasm she was able to for Maggie's "utmost efforts." "Of course," she replied.

Maggie's lips stretched into a brief smile. "As always, your expertise and guidance will lead the way."

Cornered by the stories she had told, the speeches she had given, Lucy dredged up more fervor for a cause she had never embraced but had used to her advantage. Taking a deep breath, Lucy smiled at Tildie and Leila.

"With so much inspiration, how could I do otherwise?"

Tildie and Leila gave each other pleased smiles, while Maggie measured out a satisfied nod. Lucy sipped at her lemonade and suddenly found it too sour. She set her glass on a nearby table.

"I think I'll try some coffee and cake," she said, needing a change of refreshment and company.

"Try my chocolate cake," Tildie recommended.

"I will, Tildie, and thank you for putting all of this together."

"My pleasure, *Liebchen*." Tildie regarded the room with a wide sweep of sparkling blue eyes. "What a lucky day for all of us when Davy McQuaid ran off with that Caroline Jones."

"Yes, how lucky," Lucy replied, hoping her luck held out. "Now, if you'll excuse me." Lucy stepped past Leila, who gave her a pat on the shoulder before pressing in closer to Maggie and Tildie's conversation.

Lucy circulated through the room, thanking people for coming, stopping now and then to discuss her curriculum for the fall. A few gave her well-meaning assurances not to worry about that outlaw, claiming that not many would come up against Sam McQuaid again. She tried to look confident, or at least comforted, and soon moved on.

Passing the entrance into the lobby, a detaining hand at her elbow turned her toward Etta Hamilton and her husband, Dirk, who were on their way out. Lucy accepted their handshakes and offer of a discount at their store. They left, and in the momentary lull, she caught Dolf's raspy voice speaking to Whit Prescott and decided to get the two men cups of coffee. She stepped toward the refreshment table.

"Sam upstairs?" Dolf asked.

Lucy paused, unable to resist overhearing the answer.

"Naw, said he'd be over at Nell's place if we needed him," Whit replied.

The smile Lucy had worn all evening slowly faded. Sam had gone to visit that Creole woman. No wonder he had been so impatient at their shooting practice then had rushed them back to town. No wonder . . .

"Figures," Dolf replied. "There's a beauty over there he sees pretty regular."

Lucy looked out upon the happiest night of her life while a darkness rose inside her, an anger that had no focus or reason, that fed on wishes and unanswered prayers, that forced her to listen to those voices.

"I tell you what, Dolf, McQuaid's got it nice here," Whit

continued. "Fancy women, fancy cigars, fancy clothes. I heard the saloons pay him ten percent of their take."

Lucy's eyes narrowed and she lifted her chin at that bit of news. Payoffs. Bribes. All of her suspicions about Sam McQuaid were justified after all.

"Starlight couldn't afford a marshal if they didn't," Dolf replied.

"Couldn't afford McQuaid," Whit said in his driest tone. "Most lawmen don't look to get rich from the job."

"We elected him. We think Sam's worth it."

Dolf's defense of his former commanding officer didn't surprise Lucy. He and Leila couldn't see what Sam had apparently become—a corrupt town boss who was as easily bought as the women he chose.

"I guess we'll find out how much he's worth," Whit replied. "How about we go outside and smoke one of Sam's good cigars?"

Suddenly flooded with memories of all the things Sam had done to get rid of her, Lucy curled her hands into fists and tucked them beneath her crossed arms. She stood in the midst of her success, counting up sins against Sam and rehashing all the times she had confused his cunning restraint for fairness. The scoundrel had to think of his voters, she reminded herself, just like the precinct bosses in Boston.

Through it all, razor-sharp visions of Sam kissing, holding, possessing a mysteriously beautiful woman cut in and out of her wandering thoughts until her head began to pound and all she wanted was to leave. Someone tapped on a glass, and Lucy picked out Maggie's signal for attention from the general hubbub.

"Ladies, ladies—and gentlemen, too," Maggie said, eliciting a ripple of laughter. "Lucy's acceptance by the school board has not only been a victory for her but a victory for our cause. The rains have stopped and the mud has dried. Let us join together tomorrow morning for a victory march down Main Street."

To Lucy's surprise, Maggie's announcement met with a low mumbling from the gathering and Tildie stepped forward. "Most of us don't think marches down the center of Main Street are safe with that outlaw lurking about ready to take shots at our new schoolmarm."

Recalling a certain fitting slogan she had set many times for broadsheets, Lucy spoke up. "I don't believe this Mendoza fellow will dare another daylight shooting, but for those who don't agree with me, precautions can be taken for everyone's safety."

"I don't know, Lucy," Tildie said, and nodded her head with others of the same opinion.

"Perhaps if you could explain," Maggie said.

"Of course," Lucy replied. "I'll carry our banner well in front of the marchers." She fixed her gaze on the woman who urged them on, who trumpeted the temperance call to arms at every opportunity, who never hesitated to use a weapon that came her way. "I'm sure Maggie will help me."

Maggie met the expectant looks passed to her with a proud tilt of her chin. "Tomorrow at ten o'clock, ladies."

A low, rolling boom rumbled through the usual street noise of a busy morning in Starlight. Sam tossed his mail in a desk drawer and frowned impatiently at Dolf. The blacksmith shrugged his shoulders and leaned back in his chair, folding his hands behind his head.

"That more thunder?" Whit asked.

"In a manner of speaking," Sam replied.

Whit switched his toothpick to the other corner of his mouth and ambled over to the opened door. Crossing his arms, he leaned a shoulder against the doorjamb. "What's going on out there?"

"Dolf's wife is giving demon rum his marching orders," Sam replied. He pushed away from his desk and, with a resigned sigh, joined Whit at the door. A runaway horse charged down Main Street, a warning the ore wagon drivers heeded by pulling up their teams. Sam leaned his forearm against the doorjamb. "That's Dolf's drum she's beating."

"Is that so?" Whit shook his head. He gestured toward the street. "The Drummond girl won't be fool enough to march down the middle of the road, will she?"

Sam gave the wooden door frame a tap with his fist. "Don't bet on it," he replied.

The faint voices of female fervor ebbed and flowed between resounding drum beats and shouted curses from the drivers, who hadn't been able to move ore for almost a week because of the mud. Sam didn't like the combination and stepped out onto the boardwalk. He peered down the road but couldn't see much beyond the line of heavily loaded wagons. "Onward Christian Soldiers" had never sounded so stirring.

"This is going to be a big one," he said.

Dolf moved up beside him. "Sounds that way."

Sam cut a glance at his friend of many years. "You could have warned me."

Dolf scraped his boot over a dried clod. "Leila didn't mention it. We aren't speaking much about this temperance thing. I told her they were hurtin' the town, and with that fella gunnin' after Miss Drummond, all this roamin' and prayin' around town was too dangerous."

Sam scanned the rooftops along the other side of Main Street, dropped his survey to the boardwalk, and gave a nod to Sarge O'Reilly who leaned against a post, his shotgun cradled in his arm. Cleve was out on the street.

Satisfied he had done what he could for now, he asked, "What'd Leila say?"

"Said if Lucy could face the dangers, she could do no less," Dolf replied.

Sam shook his head. Lucy wouldn't be able to pass on this one like she had the last march. "These women are the most stubborn, least cooperative females I've ever had to deal with."

"They aren't the paid-to-cooperate sort, and that's a fact." Dolf replied. "Heard Nell and that Laughton fella left town to check out rumors of a new strike. At least, you didn't have to listen to Nell complain last night."

"Hell, I never made it over there," Sam replied, and pulled at his collar. A glimpse of a wide white banner with red lettering caught his eye through a break in the wagons, but he couldn't make out much more.

"You must have sent that kid over from your saloon five times," Whit said. "Couldn't get away?"

"Meant to make a short stop to check over things with Sarge and got into a hot poker game that didn't let up till almost dawn." Sam tilted his head one way then another but still couldn't see past the restless teams and jeering drivers. "What makes these women so fired up about a man having a drink once in a while?" he asked, plainly perplexed.

"I can't say about the others, but Leila's pa hit the bottle pretty hard," Dolf said softly. "Lost his business. Things were pretty tough on her growing up."

"I'm sorry about that," Sam replied. "But, you and I both saw men like that in the Army. No matter what punishment they received, no matter how long they were restricted to quarters, they found liquor. I know of one man who died after drinking rubbing alcohol."

"Makes my heart bleed, too, McQuaid, but what are you going to do about those women?" Whit said. He raised his voice to be heard above the increasing clamor. "I didn't say anything about the boardwalk prayer meetings, but that parade is just the kind of distraction Mendoza could use."

Sam studied the toothpick-chewing deputy U.S. marshal. "I thought that's what you were looking for—a distraction."

Whit unfolded his arms and straightened to his full height. He tossed the toothpick to the boardwalk. "That girl won't get killed if we both do our jobs."

"Is that what you tell yourself so you can sleep at night, Prescott?"

Sam didn't expect a reply and didn't get one. He weighed his options, considered the consequences, then looked at Dolf. "Cleve should be nearby in case we need more help."

"Help to do what?" Dolf asked.

"Arrest those women for disturbing the peace," Sam said. He gave the big blond man a measuring look and noted his discomfort. "You can cover us from here."

Dolf swallowed hard and shot a deep frown at the glimpses of marchers seen past the wagons. He straightened his hat.

"No, Sam," he replied. "I'm going with you. Leila can be a handful."

Sam gave him a nod. "Then let's do it."

He walked to the edge of the boardwalk and paused, checking the street, he told himself. Dolf stepped to one side of him; Prescott took the other. He looked at Prescott, who gave him a nod, then at Dolf, who did the same. Sam stepped off the boardwalk, flanked by his deputies, and prepared to arrest the dangerous ladies of Starlight.

With sure, even strides he led his deputies to the middle of the road, where he turned and made his stand. He wasn't surprised to see Lucy and Maggie leading the way, but the banner they carried gave him a start: "THE TAX IS A CONTINU-

OUS BRIBE. 'Their right hand is full of bribes.' Psalms 26:10."

The banner was so new that red droplets of paint ran from some of the letters. Placards and brooms weaved and bobbed well behind the two leaders, a precaution Sam didn't miss. He looked at Lucy and expected to see an expression that matched the challenge written on the banner, but her features reflected none of the defiance she waved in his face. There was no fire in her eyes.

Sam held his hands at his sides, his feet planted slightly apart, his fingers curling then uncurling, the only outward sign of how much he dreaded arresting these women. He had led charges against mad-as-hell Comanches, but this was the worst. He spotted Dolly Hardesty, the pregnant Etta Hamilton, and even little Letty King. He had never thought it would come to this. Sam fixed his darkest scowl on Lucy and started down the road, Dolf and Prescott keeping pace beside him.

Lucy focused on Sam walking toward her and gripped the banner so hard that her hands grew numb. He looked ready to spit nails. She gave a nervous glance at the rooftops and windows and prayed that a tiny metal gun sight wasn't being centered on her at this moment, but right now, she was more worried about Sam. He was going to stop this march, and Lucy dreaded the confrontation that surely would result.

Each of Leila's whacks to the drum throbbed through Lucy's temples and banged at her conscience. She tried to tell herself that she was marching against graft, a marshal who accepted payoffs, but the arguments didn't ring as purely as they had last night. They hadn't since Dolly had appeared this morning full of temperance vinegar because Cleve had stayed out all night at the Outpost playing cards with the marshal. Sudden relief had been followed with sudden regrets. She had used the temperance league once more for personal reasons and now faced those consequences Sam liked to talk about. Hopefully, no one would be hurt.

Singing was impossible. All she could manage were long, steady strides leading her to Sam McQuaid, whose expression looked as ominous as the mood on the street. Quick glances revealed none of the usual laughter. The merchants stood in front of their stores looking angry or worried, the ore wagon drivers hurled curses at them that no lady ever expected to hear, and a few older boys were suspiciously hanging around the vegetable displays.

Checking out the other side of the road, Lucy saw Jack Shipley standing outside his billiard parlor with his hands on his hips, a disgusted look on his face. She marched passed him, unable to meet his eyes with any conviction.

As they drew closer to Sam and his deputies, the singing behind her grew fainter until only Dolly's off-key voice could be heard; then it, too, faded to silence. Leila's drum suddenly fell quiet, and one last jeer filled the air.

Lucy continued marching toward Sam to the rhythm of each breath drawing through her lungs, the rustle of petticoats kicked out of the way. He had never looked more like a cover on a *Beadle's Half-Dime Library*.

"Hold it right there," he called out.

Lucy hesitated, only to have the banner snap her along a few more steps. The rustle of skirts, whispers, and mumblings inched up behind her, but intense blue eyes held her gaze.

"What's the meaning of this?" Maggie said. "We have our rights."

Lucy stood stiffly under one of Sam's measuring glances, then his attention turned to Maggie.

"The rest of the town has rights, too," he said. "You ladies go on back to your homes, or I'm going to have to arrest you with a hefty fine for disturbing the peace."

Lucy gave the banner a tug to get Maggie moving in the right direction, but the newspaper woman twisted around to face her followers.

"Don't forget the law in this town owns a saloon, ladies."

Turning to face the women, Lucy bit her lip at the sight of brooms and placards bobbing their agreement. She tried to catch Tildie's eye, but the heavy set woman was glaring daggers at Sam. The other ladies' expressions varied from Tildie's outrage to Etta Hamilton's anxious glances at the growing disturbance along the boardwalk. The women clustered closer together and Leila took off her drum.

"The law in this town has always owned a saloon, ladies, as each of you well knows," Sam said. "Go home now or go to jail. It's up to you."

Lucy winced at Sam's ultimatum. A gauntlet thrown in the dust couldn't have been more of a challenge. As much as she hated this standoff, she was tempted to tell him to come and get her. Didn't the man know anything about diplomacy?

"You tell 'em, Marshal," a man's voice shouted. "Round up the old hens and put 'em up to roost for a while."

Laughter burst all around them, but Lucy found it an ugly sound. Maggie urged the ladies to stand their ground, but many turned worried faces toward Lucy. She ran her tongue over dry lips and tried to think.

Several men stepped out onto the street. Lucy recognized most as husbands she had met last night. The ore wagon drivers were climbing off their high seats, and Red Grady walked among the loungers in front of his place, spewing venom. Cleve was headed toward the Painted Pony.

Lucy clutched at the banner, its burden growing heavier and heavier. Something must be done to stop this. Now.

Sam looked at Dolf, then to Prescott, and the two men took their positions. Cleve was on his way to cover Red's group and Sarge was headed toward the back of the marchers' formation.

Suddenly a shot fired.

The ladies screamed and Sam's heart slammed in his chest. He drew his Colt on the run and rushed in Lucy's direction, scanning the crowd, shouting at his deputies to cover the women. Then he dared to look at the sight he had dreaded for days.

"Quiet," Lucy shouted, and fired the second shot of her little pistol into the air. The crowd silenced. She lowered her arm and chanced a look at Sam. She had never seen a more stunned expression on a man's face, but she hoped to see many more as she surveyed the crowd. She wasn't disappointed.

Another quick glance at Sam found him fully recovered, his revolver at the ready and studying the crowd, which had backed off. Shocked, wary, or merely cautious, Lucy didn't care. She had bought herself a few minutes, and Sam was going to let her use them.

She turned to the leaguers gathered behind them. "Go on home, like the marshal says." She disregarded Maggie's cold glare. "Nothing's worth this kind of trouble."

"Is that right, Dolly?" Maggie asked. "Are you ready to let demon rum out-wrestle you for your son's life? And you, Leila, do you want other families ruined by the mockery of wine and strong spirits? Tildie, are you ready to cave in to those who profit from—"

"Leave it alone, Maggie," Lucy said, not liking the woman's obvious manipulation.

A collected gasp rose from the marchers.

Lucy stepped over the fallen banner toward Maggie. "Can't you see the danger here?"

Maggie stood her ground. "Did you think the struggle would be easy, Lucy?" She turned to address the marchers. "Did any of you?" she asked.

"What did the ladies do in Boston, Lucy?" Tildie asked. "Did the police drag them off to jail for holding a peaceful march?"

"Yes, tell them what happened in Boston," Maggie said.

Lucy met those gray eyes, daring her to tell the truth, a truth Maggie must have known all along. She was an astute woman but over-confident. Lucy took a deep breath of the faint pine scent that was always present and faced the ladies once more.

"I never saw any temperance demonstrations. I had read about earlier crusades and used those examples." Lucy picked out Tildie's disbelieving face. "I'm sorry, Tildie, but I wanted the schoolmarm's position so badly. It . . . it truly was an answer to a prayer. I . . ."

She couldn't go on. She wanted to tell them so much more, but how did one explain needs so deep, so desired, one would do almost anything to fill them?

"I . . . I didn't mean any harm," she finished on a rush of breath.

"That's fine and good, Miss Drummond, but my business has been harmed plenty."

Recognizing Oscar Pollett's voice, Lucy remembered the day he wouldn't hire her, then remembered why. She turned to Sam and placed the responsibility for her predicament where it belonged—on those blue eyes that could see no other way but Sam McQuaid's.

One of Sam's roving searches rested on her briefly, but long enough for Lucy to know her memories were shared, if not with the same conclusion. Lifting her chin, she turned to face her medicine and found her bitter pill stomping toward them, knees locked and arms swinging stiffly at his sides. Pollett raised his hand and pointed at her.

"I haven't had a decent day's business since that newspaper spouting all of your temperance doings came out Monday."

Lucy swallowed hard, almost gagging on the accusations locked tight behind her guilt. She had done all those things glorified in Monday's *Starlight Observer*. Mr. Pollett hadn't made her make those speeches and hand out pledges. Caught between reproaches and apologies, she chose her only recourse: silence.

Maggie picked up the banner and started rolling it up. "Good heavens, man, it's rained buckets since then. You can't blame Lucy."

Oscar stopped mid-stride and planted his fists on his hips. "Don't you think I know that?" he said. "The rain keeps the men from working their claims. Rainy days are real doorbusters for me. I didn't have half my usual customers."

"Neither did I," the butcher shouted from the boardwalk.

Dirk Hamilton spoke up from where he stood by Etta's side. "My business was down, too."

Dolly lowered her placard. "I didn't sell nearly enough pies."

Lucy marked the number of brooms falling and placards wavering. Nods of agreement moved through the marchers, setting feathers aflutter and straw hats dipping. All of these ladies' livelihoods depended on the miners and cowboys who came to town and bought more than a night of hard drinking and good times. It seemed Lucy wasn't the only one who needed to do a little soul searching.

Oscar charged into the center of the controversy. "It's all this temperance talk," he said. "The men take their money to the other towns."

Casting her vexation at Lucy, Maggie rolled the banner

faster. "Profit is a powerful friend to demon rum," she said.

Sam saw his opportunity and decided it was time to step in. He shoved his Colt in his holster. "I'd guess profit was no stranger to you since the *Starlight Observer* started this temperance shindig."

"I don't have to listen to this," Maggie said, and rolled up the remaining few feet of banner.

Lucy remembered Sam's comment about the ads from the neighboring towns showing up in the paper. Many more requests had come in today's mail, a fact she was sure Starlight needed to know. She lifted her hand to speak, only to have it held down by Sam.

She turned to protest but instead followed the nod he gave. Leila had already maneuvered through the marchers to the front with definite plans on her mind. Lucy frowned up at Sam and jerked her hand back. Sam gave a slight shake of his head, and Lucy waited for Leila to speak.

"Maggie Thompson, I think you better listen," Leila said. "I saw all those ads from Hillsboro and Kingston in the last issue. More came in today. I saw them on your desk."

Maggie gathered the last of the banner into a tight tube. "What's wrong with that? I have a business to run, too."

"So do the rest of us," Oscar said.

"Businesses that have all taken a pounding as hard as Dolf's drum," Dirk Hamilton added.

Maggie swung the white tube in a sweeping arc that included her followers. "'Woe unto him that justify the wicked for a reward.' Isaiah 5:23."

"Lady, that's well and good, but a lot of us wouldn't agree with what you call wicked," Jack Shipley called out. A flood of widespread approval rushed down Main Street.

Maggie chopped the rolled banner down to her side and turned to Jack. "'Woe unto him that giveth his neighbor drink,'" she quoted. "Habakkuh 2:15, young man—a verse you should think about the next time you serve some poor, besotted wastrel."

Jack leaned against a post outside his establishment and crossed his arms, propping the toe of his boot in front of the opposite leg. "Lady, my ol' daddy was a preacher, a man who ministered to poor, sufferin' coal miners in Pennsylvania. He liked to quote Proverbs 31:6 and 7. Maybe you know it, too. 'Give strong drink unto him that is ready to perish, and wine unto those that be of heavy hearts. Give strong drink, and forget his poverty, and remember his misery no more.' I think of that verse when some busted up cowpoke comes into my place or a miner that's hit nothin' but clay for weeks and his heart's breakin' right along with his back."

Maggie turned to her marchers and slammed the banner into her palm. "We have only to look at our wasted youth and ruined homes to know we are in the right. Another meeting will be held tonight. Those of you who are not guided by the lust for mammon come to the newspaper office."

"You ladies might think of another verse my daddy liked to recite," Jack said. " 'Be not righteous over much; neither make thyself over wise; why shouldest thou destroy thyself?' "

Lucy joined the rest of the crowd in waiting for Maggie's rejoinder. The newspaper woman slapped the banner into her palm once more and, holding her head high, turned and walked toward her office in long measured strides, neither quickly nor slowly. She stopped before an ore driver blocking her path and stared up at the big, burly man. He stepped aside, and she disappeared behind his wagon.

A thick pall of silence hung over Main Street, then thinned as a low murmuring threaded through the crowd gathered along the boardwalks. The ore wagon drivers called to one another and climbed back up on their seats. A few shouts gave praise to Jack's daddy and Jack's fast thinking. Voices rose among the marchers, and Oscar Pollett strode back to his mercantile mumbling about another morning's business ruined. Lucy stood in the middle of it all, aware of little else but Sam McQuaid.

He tipped his hat back. "What is it I'm supposed to have done this time, Lucy?"

Lucy started walking. The direction didn't matter, just as long as she distanced herself from the question spoken to her in that quiet, measured voice.

She sped by Tildie and Leila, who were in deep conversation with the dwindling group of ladies still in the street. The ore wagon drivers paid her no mind as they called to their teams and cracked their whips. If she walked fast enough along the boardwalk, the sidelong glances, the whispers, the surly frowns hardly signified. She walked and walked until she saw nothing but the longings of her heart.

CHAPTER 14

The tall pine emerged into view from the grassy lane as Sam tramped up the long incline that led to the old house and Lucy. Layer after layer, short boughs of greenery flowed into outstretched sweeps of heavy limbs. Sam lengthened his steps, willing the lady with bright hair, neat white blouse and light-reflecting spectacles to be waiting at the end of his journey.

Lucy had to be there. Of course, she was there. He had searched everywhere else—the hotel, the train station, the whole damned town. Lucy must be at that blasted house.

He should have walked her back to the hotel, but he had assumed that's where she would go after that trouble on the street. Cleve had needed calming down; the ladies had needed to be told to take their discussion out of the middle of the road; Jack Shipley had needed thanking.

He had duties, responsibilities. He couldn't drop everything for one slip of a girl who had nearly started a riot—and had thrown her dreams away to stop it. He had intended to talk to her, find out what the devil had set her off again. Maybe approach her about leaving town now that she would lose the schoolmarm's job. The mayor hadn't wasted any time in calling another meeting after he had returned from Silver City.

Sam gauged the distance to the top of the hill with the length of pine tree revealed. A few more yards, that's all. A few more yards and he would find her.

She shouldn't have come out here alone. The woman never thought things through. Like traveling to Starlight to marry David, or getting all rolled up in that temperance thing, or saying that she would testify against Mendoza. Impulsive. That's what she was: impulsive, fanciful, too damned gullible. But gutsy.

Why in the hell hadn't Lucy taken that ticket money? None of this would have happened. She'd be safe back in Boston, the temperance leaguers would have met and held tea parties, and Raul Mendoza would be . . . somewhere blasting away at another victim.

"Damn," Sam muttered, and picked up his pace.

Mendoza needed catching, but he hated using Lucy to lure the tricky bastard out into the open, hated the constant worry of doing enough to keep her safe. And living next to her was driving him crazy—hearing her move about, hum soft little tunes, climb into bed. But most of all he didn't like walking out here, regretting he had let her leave Main Street alone, hoping she was sitting under that tree telling a cat her troubles.

Sam crested the hill and stopped in his tracks. The vacant spot at the base of the gnarled trunk set the whole scene off balance. He had pictured Lucy sitting there so strongly, that surely her absence was a distortion, an unacceptable flaw.

Sam set his mouth into a grim frown and started down the lane toward the house. Terrible images came to his mind, never forgotten nightmares of what hate, revenge, and savagery could do to a woman caught in lonely places by unmerciful hands. Mendoza was smart. He would bide his time, watching. One mistake, one hesitation, one glance in the wrong direction and the outlaw would strike.

As he drew closer, Sam combed the area, missing nothing. He immediately noticed the small footprint left in a sandy runoff, the yellow petals of a wildflower crushed into the muddy path leading to the house, the straw boater tangled in the weeds beneath the porch, its cluster of faded violets shivering in the breeze.

Sam drew his Colt. He focused on the house, every broken window, every overgrown bush, the darkness beyond the half-opened door. He broke into a trot, then a run, charging up the steps, crashing through the door, knocking it off its rusty hinges. The house swallowed him in silence. Deadly silence.

He stood in the middle of the parlor, searching, listening. Ragged strips of wallpaper scratched softly at walls, the fireplace moaned, a steady creak-creak sounded from the next room. He looked through the arched entrance toward a screened door, its fabric rusted and torn, which framed a view of the thick forest behind the house. Stepping over broken pottery, old newspapers, and shards of glass, Sam moved slowly forward and entered the kitchen.

The floor had been swept clean and the tile work around the stove gleamed in the dim light. Dirt and debris had been piled in a corner. A fine patina of dust covered Lucy's efforts to make this old, weather-beaten hovel into a home. She might have succeeded, too, if she hadn't spoken up today. He recalled the letter he had received from the Boston police this morning, an important piece in Lucy's puzzle.

A loud bang whirled Sam around, the heel of his hand fanning back the hammer on his revolver. His heart pounded out the seconds until he spotted a loose shutter over the kitchen sink.

Taking a deep, steadying breath, Sam continued his search. The two other rooms in the house revealed nothing more than cobwebs, dust, and torn, stained wallpaper. Unable to draw any conclusions or relief from the empty house, Sam took his search to the front yard.

He carefully examined the area around the porch and discovered a trail of small footprints that circled around to the side of the house. He followed them to the back and saw that they led into the woods that edged the clearing. No other tracks crossed her trail, and Sam took what comfort he could from that. Still, he didn't call out her name.

He listened to the wind move through the trees, a bird's song, the old house creaking and occasionally banging behind him. Lucy had gone into the woods, alone, and whatever had lured her into those shadowed depths made no disturbance. Immediately, he thought of the big cat and started for the trees.

A narrow footpath led him deeper into the woods. An occasional heel print or bit of thread assured him she was just ahead and thankfully alone. The forest closed in around him, shutting out all but brilliant streams of sunlight that pierced the dark green quiet.

Planning a good old-fashioned scolding, Sam expected Lucy around every twist of the path, but the sound of weeping caught him by surprise. He slowed his steps, the tearing sobs holding him at bay yet drawing him on. Louder, more distinct, the sound of a heartbroken woman pulled at his reluctant steps, tugged at emotions that slipped past his guard.

He found her at last, lying in a pile of leaves like a fragile flower crushed by a careless world. Her face was buried in the crook of her arms, and sobs jerked and shuddered through her small frame. He had seen a lot of misery in his time, but the sight of that proud, starry-eyed spirit broken and defeated hit him harder than he believed possible.

Easing his Colt into his holster, Sam moved closer. "Lucy," he called softly.

The sobbing caught on a gasp. Sam stepped off the path, closing the distance between them. "Lucy, what's . . ." Hell, he didn't need to ask that. Everything was wrong.

She didn't lift her head but gulped in air, hiccuping and trying to catch her breath. Sam eased in closer, as if moving too quickly might hurt her more. He knelt beside her and gently touched her shoulder.

"Lucy, everything is going to be fine," he said.

She rolled to her side and looked at him with great, watery eyes. "Oh, Sam . . . Sam, I've lost him."

Concealing his surprise, Sam pressed his palm into the soft curve of her shoulder. "Who, honey? Who have you lost?"

"Blackie," she replied with a hiccup.

Sam didn't try to mask his surprise this time. "You mean that cat?"

Closing her eyes, she nodded her head, then looked at him again. "I came out to see him, but I . . . I can't find him. He wasn't at the house. I've looked and looked, but he's gone." She shook her head. "Gone," she finished on a breath.

Sam brushed the tears from her face. "He's half-wild, Lucy. Probably took off some place. His kind take care of themselves."

She pushed herself to a sitting position. "No, Sam. He's just a poor old stray who needed me. He was only a little scared was all, and we had started to be friends." She grabbed his arm. "I think something bad has happened to him, Sam."

New tears rolled down her cheeks, and Sam brushed

those away, too. "I bet he's tom-cattin' around somewhere. Probably has a lady cat he visits."

She looked off into the distance. "Maybe, but there's so much out there to hurt him. I should have come and checked on him. He had started waiting for me, expecting me and I . . . I let him down."

Sam pulled a leaf from her hair. "You couldn't come out in the rain, and you shouldn't be out here now. It's dangerous. You know that."

She met his gaze once more, her eyes bottomless pools of heartache, their beauty ravaged by a storm of tears. "I shouldn't have let discomfort or threats keep me away." Her hand tightened on his arm. "He needed me, Sam."

Sam captured her other shoulder, and her hand dropped to her lap. He looked at her directly. "Lucy, you're being too hard on yourself. That old cat has taken care of himself for a long time. He likes his freedom."

"But, Sam, he was so lonely and . . ."

She looked deeply into his eyes, holding his gaze with her sorrow and tenderness. ". . . and weary. I had wanted to give him a place to rest—a warm, gentle place where he would feel safe and loved."

Sam explored the fragmented shades of autumn in her eyes and saw more than he expected or wanted to discover: the unfulfilled yearning, the willingness to give, the forlorn searching that had driven him to buy a train ticket the first time he had seen her, had forced him to make hasty, less than honorable decisions, and had chased him from her arms that night at the hotel. Lucy offered her heart too recklessly—to strangers, to stray cats, to him.

Sam slipped his hands from her shoulders. "That cat's too set in his ways, Lucy. It's his nature to roam. He's no hearth cat to be petted and milk-fed."

Lucy looked past Sam. "I didn't want to change him,

Sam . . . just love him." She blinked and focused, then her determined eyes challenged Sam. "I will find him. I won't quit looking until I find him."

Sam sat back and, resting his hand on his drawn up knee, looked anywhere but at Lucy's sad-eyed resolution to another losing proposition. She'd probably never see that cat again, but he didn't have the heart to break her spirit once more. Then he spotted her eyeglasses sitting on a fallen log lying next to her.

"You won't be able to find much of anything without your spectacles." Leaning over, he picked them up and handed them to her.

Scrubbing the tears from her eyes, Lucy accepted the delicate wire frames and round lenses, but she didn't put them on. She hooked her fingers through the earpieces and rested her clasped hands in her lap. Her gaze wandered over the high treetops.

"I didn't realize my search had led me so far into the woods," she said. Finally her attention settled on him. "I guess I got a little carried away again."

Her admission described Lucy's misadventures in Starlight from start to finish, and Sam suspected she knew it. He understood the kind of pride that allowed her to cry her eyes out over a lost cat but never over lost dreams, that offered explanations without excuses and spreading blame, though there was plenty of that to go around.

Sam directed his eyes to the sun-dappled forest rather than Lucy. "I've been known to do the same when I thought I was on the right path," he replied.

"That's the trouble, isn't it, Sam? Figuring out the right path."

"I never had any trouble before . . ."

"Before what?"

Before you came along.

Sam turned and wished he hadn't. Sitting in the middle of her nest, Lucy studied him with eyes red and puffy from crying over the cat. Twigs and leaves adorned her lopsided pile of hair. Her blouse and skirt bore brown and green smudges, and a ladybug crawled along the edge of a ruffle that spanned her bosom.

The little orange beetle held Sam's attention as it traveled over the folds of white material, oblivious to the rise and fall of each breath she drew. Her breathing quickened, and the polka-dotted bug scampered over the curved rise of her breast. Sam swallowed and found his mouth had gone dry.

"Before what, Sam?"

Ignoring her question, Sam reached over and held the back of his fingers against the thin white cloth, her warmth and softness a breath away from his touch. She held her breath, and the little bug climbed onto his hand. He lifted hand and beetle for her inspection.

"You're a mess, Lucy Drummond," he said, his voice low and rough.

Puckering her lips, Lucy blew a warm breath across his fingers and the ladybug took flight. "Ladybug, ladybug, fly away home," she chanted.

Sam curled his fingers closed and brushed his knuckles against her cheek. "Ladybug, you better fly away home, too."

She held his gaze with hers. "I don't have a home, Sam."

A man could drown in eyes like hers and never know he had stepped into deep water, Sam thought. He feared he was walking dangerously close to the waterline now and the river was rising; damned if he didn't want to take a swim. Sam shot to his feet.

He hooked his thumbs in his gunbelt and cleared his throat. "Lucy, I won't say I'm sorry about how things turned out today. You've known from the beginning I didn't think you should stay in Starlight. It's a dangerous place, as we . . . you discovered. You'll find another teaching job and—"

"Sam I don't need any reassurances, but I do need your help standing up."

Sam looked down and found her hand reaching up to him. Frowning his discomfort, he clasped her small hand in his and pulled. She rose to her feet and, slipping free of his grasp, gently caressed his cheek.

"You frown too much, Sam."

Sam caught her wrist. "Don't, Lucy."

Her fingers slowly curled inward. "What did I do?"

Sam held on to her wrist and gazed into those guileless eyes. She didn't know she was driving him crazy. For two heartbeats, he didn't care, then he released her.

"Let's get out of here."

With a puzzled look, Lucy stepped back and put her eyeglasses back on. She looked down at her skirt and shook it out. "You're right. I am a mess." Running her fingers through her hair, she began plucking leaves from the wreckage of dangling pins and slipping combs. "My goodness, how everyone will talk when I go back to town."

Sam didn't reply, too taken with the picture she presented fussing with her hair. An action so feminine in such primitive surroundings fascinated him.

"Not that the talk will matter anymore," she continued. "I guess there's a few bright spots in what happened today. I won't have every move I make examined and evaluated, and I'm certainly relieved to be done with Maggie's manipulations and Leila's drum." She rubbed her fingers through her hair and shook it out. "I do feel badly about . . . Sam, are you listening?"

Sam gazed at a shaft of sunlight that struck through her tossled mane of golden hair. The fine strands shimmered with all the colors of the rainbow. Sam's pulse quickened as he took a step toward Lucy.

She stared intently at Sam as he approached. "Sam," she said. "Sam?" She reached up and shook her hair. "Didn't I get all the leaves out?"

Colors shot through her hair like a prism and Sam couldn't resist touching it, grabbing handfuls of it, finding her hands in its silken tresses and holding them, holding her head still so that he could capture her mouth with his. If she resisted, he didn't notice; every sense was alive with the touch of Lucy's hair, her scent of earth and pine, the warm, wet sweetness of her surrender.

He tasted the corner of her mouth, kissed her jaw, the sensitive skin below her ear, her neck. Denial and restraint were lost to desire and possession. He wanted Lucy, burned for her, ached for her. The dam had broken, and rational thought rolled and tumbled out of control.

Taking possession of her mouth once more, he slipped his hands from her tangled loops of hair and found the first button at the back of her blouse, the closure for her high collar. Working it free, he moved to the next. As he trailed his fingers along her spine to the next button, Lucy pushed herself free.

She backed out of his reach, holding the back of her hand against her mouth, her eyes big and round, her breathing ragged and heavy, much like his own. Her blouse had slipped off her shoulder and her hair hung loose and wild around her face. Sam took in her disheveled appearance, and slowly, with each deep breath, reason returned and with it came total dismay at his loss of control.

He raised his hand to her. "Lucy, I don't . . . I can't ex—I'm—"

"Don't say you're sorry, Sam McQuaid." She grabbed her blouse and jerked it up. "Don't you dare say you're sorry."

Tossing her hair back, she marched past him and started down the trail.

Sam stared after her, trying to figure out what had happened in the last few minutes. As usual when dealing with Lucy, understanding escaped him, and he followed her fast pace through the woods.

Hurrying down the path, Lucy reached behind her and rebuttoned her blouse. Her shaking fingers had difficulty with the small buttons, a problem she recalled Sam had not encountered. He was probably an expert at such things. He certainly kissed as if he had had plenty of practice.

Properly buttoned, her flusters settled down to an odd apprehension that curled in the pit of her stomach. Sam frightened her with his extremes: cool disinterest, or a consuming heat that burned through her every resistance; conspiring against her, or offering her help when she needed it most; a lawman who faced flying lead without faltering, or a marshal who accepted payoffs from the saloons.

If not for all of those inconsistencies, she might be rolling around in those leaves right now. Even now, as she rushed ahead of Sam, the prospect was tantalizing. She quickly reminded herself that she would be leaving Starlight soon. Leaving with broken dreams was bad enough. She didn't want to leave with a broken heart, too.

The old house appeared through the trees just as Sam caught her arm. Pulling free, she turned a frown to him. "What are you doing?"

"Keeping you from rushing into a bullet," he replied in a soft voice.

"So what are we going to do? Stay in the woods all day?"

"No, I'm going to check around first."

"This is ridiculous," she said. "If Mendoza's waiting for me, he'll shoot you, then he'll shoot me anyway. In fact, this whole guarding thing is ridiculous. Mendoza's a snake, and he'll strike when he wants. Only God can decide the outcome."

"God and Samuel Colt's handiwork," Sam replied. He gave a nod toward the house. "You follow behind me."

Whispering a little prayer for them both, Lucy did as she was bid and followed Sam into the open. He muttered something, but she couldn't hear him. Despite her brave words, she gave a careful scrutiny to the area.

Lucy saw nothing alarming and everything appeared quiet. With his revolver drawn, Sam proceeded slowly toward the front yard and her heart slowed toward a normal beat.

As he rounded the corner of the house, he stopped and Lucy pressed close to him. "Sam?"

For a moment he didn't move, and Lucy thought immediately of Blackie. She couldn't make herself look around the tall man dressed in black. "Sam, it's not—"

He stepped aside and she saw her hat hanging on the front porch pillar. Puzzled and disturbed, she looked up at Sam, but he was engaged in a scowling survey of the outlying area. She took slow careful steps toward the porch and its odd adornment, a sense of dread in the pit of her stomach.

A closer look revealed a knife stuck through the crown of her hat with a note attached. Lucy folded her arms around herself and stared at her old straw hat, the knife an obscene reminder of dangers she had never truly accepted. She ventured closer, squinting to decipher the crude black markings on the paper. "Death came calling," she read.

"Mendoza?" she asked.

Sam jerked the broad blade from the post, freeing her hat and the note. With his back turned to her, he slipped the knife into his coat pocket and studied the note. "I don't think so," he replied.

"But, who else—"

He turned to her and slapped the paper against the hand that held her hat. "Mendoza wouldn't go in for theatrics like this. He would have found us, just like I found you, and killed us both. God knows I wasn't thinking straight."

Then Lucy realized where she'd seen the primitive scrawl before. "The note is like the one attached to the rock thrown through the newspaper's window."

"Exactly," Sam replied. "Similar lettering, same kind of grand gesture, but temperance didn't have anything to do with this one. Maggie's crusade to line her pockets is finished. The only connection between the two notes is you."

"What does a rock through a window to warn the leaguers have to do with this?"

Sam frowned at the hat, his thumb brushing the cluster of faded violets. "All I know for certain is that someone wants you to leave Starlight."

Lucy looked at Sam, the most assertive of those who wished her gone. "The only reason I'm staying is to identify Mendoza," she said, and hoped if she repeated those words often enough she might come to believe them.

"We never found out anything about Otis Tyler, the man who was killed," Sam replied. "Probably an alias." He looked at the hat and shook his head. "I think someone in town might have hired Mendoza, and whoever it is doesn't want him to stand trial. This little message was intended to be your last straw," he said, then added holding up her hat, "so to speak."

Unamused, Lucy reached a tentative hand to claim the straw hat, but Sam held on to the brim. Lucy looked up and found every grim line etched into his face, his solemn reserve once more commanding every feature. The kindness, the understanding, the passion might never have been there, except for the memory that lingered in her heart.

"There'll be no more idylls in the woods, Lucy."

She nodded.

"No more chasing after that cat."

Lucy dropped her gaze from those demanding blue eyes.

"Promise me, Lucy."

"I—"

"Damnit, Lucy, promise me."

Lucy swallowed back the painful knot in her throat. She stared at the tin star pinned to his vest. "I have to find him, Sam. I have to know what happened to him."

"He's not worth the risk, Lucy. None of this is. Go back to Boston to your mother. She needs you, too."

His reminder hit a sensitive area, a painful spot Lucy had avoided. She raised her gaze to his and looked at herself through Sam's uncompromising eyes, but nothing new was revealed.

"My mother doesn't need a daughter who runs away from hardship and trouble." Lucy turned away from him, looked at the house, and thought of all the plans she had made.

Sam was tempted to touch the shoulder she held so stiffly, but he dropped his hand to his side. "You've got nothing to prove to your mother or anyone else."

Lucy turned around and shoved her hat at Sam. "Maybe not, but I have plenty to prove to myself." She gathered up her loose hair and gave it several twists. "I'm not going to run out now simply because I've surely lost the school teacher's post and someone has a nasty little secret." She coiled her hair into a bun and fished pins from her pocket, stabbing them into place. "I'll go back to Boston, Sam, but only when I've done what I said I would do."

Lucy steadied her hands on her hips, ready to refute any argument he was bound to come up with. His long study ended with a decision that lifted one brow, in doubt or something else, she didn't know.

"All right." He gave the hat back to her. "I don't like it, but I understand. But you'll do as I say."

Lucy crammed the hat atop her head. "Let's get back to town. It's not safe out here, you know." She turned and started up the lane.

Sam watched her march away from him, her small hands fisted and her arms swinging with purpose. What was he going to do with the most stubborn person he knew—other than himself? As a man, Lucy Drummond would have made a damn fine trooper. As a woman, she made a damn fine millstone around his neck—and a distracting one.

He pulled at his tight collar and started down the lane after her, searching along the roadway and into the woods for a black-and-white ball of fur and more trouble.

CHAPTER 15

"What is it Mayor Jones has against me?"

Lucy slammed her hotel room's window closed on Main Street's noisy intrusion and turned to her morning callers, who had just delivered the surprising news that the school board had very nearly kept her on. "I don't understand why the mayor continually attacks me."

Tildie sent an inquiring look from her chair by the door to Leila, who sat in the middle of the bed's dark green counterpane with her legs crossed Indian-fashion. Leila lifted her cup of coffee and raised her brows as she sipped at the fresh brew they had brought up with them that morning.

Tildie set her plate of strudel on a nearby tray with the pot of coffee and turned to Lucy. "Mayor Jones *says* that Caroline won't come home until you leave, but . . ."

Lucy leaned into Tildie's pause. "But what?" she asked, going along with the woman's penchant for drama.

Tildie settled her arms over her ample middle, one hand catching the other wrist. "Leila and I have discussed this, and we could not fathom why Caroline would be so disagreeable. After all, she has David. What threat could you be to her?"

"My thoughts exactly," Lucy replied. She gave a slight shrug. "I suppose Caroline could be using my presence as an excuse not to return to Starlight."

Leila raised a finger toward the ceiling. "Or the mayor is making up this whole Caroline business," she said, pointing out each word.

Recalling her ruined hat and that awful note, Lucy voiced her doubts. "Then Mayor Jones would have to have something else against me, and I can't imagine what it could be." And she was trying, she thought. "Tildie, you said he was more hostile than ever at the school board meeting he called yesterday afternoon."

"I did my best for you, Lucy, but some of the members were swayed by the mayor's arguments concerning your character," Tildie replied. "I tried to explain your situation, that you were left stranded here, that I encouraged you to join us. I reminded them that no one would offer you a job but Maggie. My heavens, you would think that they were as pure as the driven snow, when I know for a fact that—"

"Tildie, you were most eloquent," Leila said.

Tildie's regal nod struck sunlight through her coronet of braids, and Lucy smiled at the image that suddenly popped into her head. "You've been an angel, Tildie," she said, then included Leila with a glance at the imposing brunette. "I want to thank you both for your understanding. I felt so badly about everything. I thought no one would speak to me again."

"Some of the ladies were a bit disenchanted," Tildie said, drawing her mouth into a disapproving bow, "but most of us agreed that we admired your daring and loyalty."

"Daring and loyalty," Lucy repeated. She walked over to the vanity and tossed, one by one, the crumpled attempts to write her mother into a waste basket. "Thank you, Tildie," she said softly.

"People are still talking about how you snapped Red Grady's suspenders and stood up for Dolly," Leila said. "And that was pretty good shooting in the street yesterday."

Lucy faced the two ladies. "About yesterday's march. I owe you all—"

"No one twisted our arms, Lucy," Leila said.

"Certainly not," Tildie added. "We should have spoken more strongly against it after we saw your banner. You don't understand . . . well, Leila, you tell her."

"After I returned home yesterday, Dolf and I had a long talk about my temperance efforts, and yesterday's march, especially. Did you overhear Dolf discussing the captain with the deputy marshal at your party?"

Lucy's cheeks flushed with embarrassment. "Yes, I happened to be standing by the door and—"

"We thought so," Leila replied. "He mentioned you might have heard him discussing the captain's arrangements with the saloon owners."

"I shouldn't have eavesdropped, but—"

"Anyone would have, my dear," Tildie said.

Lucy offered Tildie a faint smile. "I heard Dolf tell Deputy Prescott that Sam received ten percent of the saloon's profits, which sounded like payoffs to me."

"You misunderstood," Leila said.

"He doesn't receive the money?"

"Oh, yes, he does," Tildie said, "but that's the offer the town made Sam. We figure the trouble starts in the saloons, and they should be the ones to pay for the lawman to keep the peace. The owners like it because they don't suffer as much damage to their premises, and the citizens are satisfied with the arrangement because they get good law enforcement at a low cost to them."

Giving in to a sudden sinking sensation, Lucy sat down on the small bench seat in front of the vanity. "The arrangement does seem fair," she said.

"Of course, it's fair," Leila said. "But, considering your background—"

"My background?" Lucy squared her shoulders.

"Yes, I'm afraid the town knows about your father's untimely death and the scandal—"

Lucy shot to her feet. "How does—"

"The mayor, Lucy," Tildie said. "The mayor read a report about you at yesterday's meeting. I'm afraid it was the final blow to your chances at the schoolmarm's position. Now, don't be embarrassed. We know about your father's political troubles and how he was under investigation by the authorities. Many people come to the West to escape such family problems. It's certainly no mark against you, even if the mayor tried to make it one. Which brings us back to the mayor's animosity."

Stunned by Tildie's revelation, Lucy could only listen in silence.

"We believe the mayor doesn't want you in Starlight because of your strong sentiments against dishonest politics. He may have started out being concerned about Caroline, but his continued hostility against you makes us believe something else might be going on. We suspect the mayor may be up to some kind of skulduggery. A woman with your background and experience could pose problems the mayor hopes to avoid. You would certainly know the signs of wrongdoing."

"We thought of something else, too," Tildie continued. "You would be invaluable as help to another candidate's campaign, growing up as you did watching Boston's politics unfold in your parlor."

Lucy had listened to all she could take. She had to stop

this. They were doing it again, embroiling her in their causes with the mayor's fabrications and their own misunderstandings. But she wasn't sure where to begin.

Lucy took a step toward Tildie. "That so-called report and scandal is—"

"Don't say another word about it," Tildie said. "You needn't make excuses for something your father did."

"Ladies, I—"

"Let's change the subject," Leila said. "The temperance league decided to take a more moderate approach to the problems caused by the over-indulgence of spirits. We are opening a mission for those in need of a place to stay, whether it's some poor lost soul too gone from drink to make it home, to wives and children who might suffer because their breadwinner is incapacitated by liquor's vile hold."

"That's fine news, but—"

Tildie rose from her chair. "Well, I must be going. I've got laundry to see to and preparations for lunch to check on." She picked up the coffee tray and turned to Leila. "Are you coming?"

"I'll be along in a minute," the tall woman replied from her perch on Lucy's bed.

Tildie nodded. "You are going to the suffrage meeting tonight?"

"At Etta Hamilton's house?" Leila asked.

"Yes. At seven o'clock. Lucy, do you know anything about the suffrage movement?"

Lucy quickly disowned her extensive studies of women's struggle for the vote and shook her head. She had enough of a mess to straighten out. "No, I don't, Tildie," she said, and walked to the door, blocking its access. "But I do know about my father. I don't know what lies the mayor is spreading, but my father was an honest man. He had discovered corruption in the precinct elections and was killed by unscrupulous men who needed to silence him. I'm certain all this trouble with the mayor stems from his concern over Caroline's continued absence."

Tildie crossed the room and petted her arm. "Now, now dear. Forget this upsetting business. You come along with me tonight. A new project and companionship is the best remedy for a troubled mind."

Lucy saw that explanations were impossible until the mayor's report was repudiated. Tonight's meeting would be the ideal opportunity to lay all this scandalous business to rest. She stepped away from the door and opened it.

"I'll be happy to come with you this evening, Tildie."

"My pleasure," Tildie replied, and she stepped into the hall. "Meet me in the lobby at six-thirty."

"I'll be there," Lucy said, and shut the door. Now to see what Leila wanted, then she could begin searching out these lies about her father.

Lucy turned and discovered Leila's concentrated regard held an intriguing touch of humor. Curious, Lucy pulled up a chair and sat down to hear what else this surprising morning would deliver.

"You're in love with Sam McQuaid," Leila announced.

Lucy gave her spectacles a sharp poke that almost dislodged them. "Leila Miller," she exclaimed, and fumbled with her glasses, "you've gone completely around the bend."

Leila laughed. "I thought so."

"Don't be ridiculous," Lucy replied, and forced her fluttering hands to her lap. "Whatever brought you to that absurd notion?"

"I've suspected more than the schoolmarm's position has held you in Starlight, but after Dolf told me the rest of his conversation with Whit Prescott, I knew," Leila replied. "You thought Sam was spending the night with one of Nell's soiled doves, which I imagine added a good deal of pepper to your stew over Sam's agreement with the saloon owners."

Lucy studied Leila's handsome features but found nothing more than friendly interest. "You aren't angry?"

"About the march?"

Lucy nodded.

"That march was the best thing that could have happened for this town. Cleared the air," she said with a wave of her hand. "Like you, each one of us had our own personal reason for lining up behind Maggie. Every time I hit that drum, I got rid of a little more frustration." Leila fussed with the hem of her skirt. "Frustration I had been holding on to since I was a little girl and my pa drank up all of our possibilities," she said in a soft voice. Raising her head, she continued. "You brought us all together, and you gave up a great deal to keep us from tearing each other apart. No, Lucy, I'm not angry—especially considering we have so much in common."

"You hardly seem the foolhardy type, Leila." Lucy rose from her chair and returned to the window, her gaze lingering on every man who wore a black hat. "What could we possibly have in common?"

"Papas who disappointed us . . . falling in love with men who are the biggest jackasses when it comes to knowing what will make them happy."

Lucy let the first comparison go by. She didn't want to hurt Leila's feelings, but curiosity about the second drew her attention back to the woman.

"Dolf loves you deeply," Lucy said. "Anyone can see that."

"Everybody did see it except him—the big, stubborn ox,"

Leila replied. "I almost gave up on him, but I finally convinced Dolf that I could make him happier than the bachelor's life he thought he couldn't give up."

Lucy couldn't suppress an enthusiastic, "How?"

Leila held her answer behind a mysterious little smile and a faraway look. Finally, she said, "Sometimes a two-by-four upside the head is the only way to get a jackass's attention— figuratively speaking, of course. And that's all I'm saying."

Lucy turned to the window once more. "A real two-by-four wouldn't help my situation. You said yourself that Sam would never be interested in a girl like me."

Behind her, the bedsprings squeaked and petticoats rustled, then Lucy heard Leila's determined footsteps approach the window. Soon Leila's bright yellow dress appeared in the glass's reflection next to her own faint image.

"Can you make out those posters nailed up on every corner?" Leila asked.

An odd question, but Lucy gave special attention to each intersection. "Yes, I hadn't noticed them before, but—"

"Dolf said Sam was beside himself after he got back to town yesterday. Ranting and raving about you getting lost and how he searched all afternoon for you. Anyway, he had those wanted posters printed up with a twenty-dollar reward for anyone with information leading to the capture of that cat you were looking for."

"Twenty dollars," Lucy said, touched and surprised by Sam's endeavors to find Blackie. Leila surely didn't think . . .

Lucy looked up at the tall brunette. "What are you saying, Leila?"

"I'm saying Sam McQuaid has hardly walked into that saloon of his except the night he was supposed to go to Nell's. He hasn't visited that Creole woman since you arrived. He's put up his own money and most likely himself for ridicule so you won't go traipsing through the woods anymore. I'm saying use those spectacles of yours and see that the man is interested in you."

Recalling Sam's opinion of her spectacles, Lucy refused to be whisked along by another of Leila's wild theories. "Sam has made his interest more than clear to me on too many occasions," she said. "He wants me to leave Starlight."

"Of course he does," Leila replied. "You pose a threat to everything he holds dear. That saloon of his, all-night poker games, paid-to-please women, even that tin star. Keeping the law isn't a job for a family man."

"I wouldn't want him to change, Leila," Lucy replied. "Except for the women, of course."

A smile flitted across Leila's generous mouth. "Don't convince me. Convince him." She gathered up her reticule and started for the door.

Lucy followed her. "You wouldn't happen to have a handy two-by-four?"

With one hand on the doorknob, Leila turned a significant glance to the double doors that led into Sam's room. "You'll think of something," she said, and opened the door. "And do it quickly," she added. "No woman likes her husband's best friend to be a bachelor."

Lucy pulled her surprised expression from the doors to Sam's room and all the images Leila's glance had implied and addressed the realities of her situation. "I could never . . . you know . . ." She slid another glance toward the doors.

"You've always impressed me as a woman who was willing to take chances," Leila replied. "You'll have to decide what chances are worth taking." Leila squeezed her hand, then swept into the gloomy hallway.

Lucy closed the door and turned to the rose-bedecked

room. Her gaze wandered over the wardrobe, the windows, the big bed, and finally landed on those double doors.

Leila and her wild ideas. She expected her to open those doors and boldly advance into Sam's territory, to offer him all the love she had to give. The thought frightened her more than meeting up with Raul Mendoza.

Something wild and unexplainable had slipped past Sam's guard yesterday in the woods, something she knew he regretted and would never let happen again. She couldn't open those doors and face that cold reserve, that distant, measuring regard.

She was through taking chances that only led to disappointments and failure. Surely Mendoza would be caught soon now that two more federal deputies were on his trail, then she could testify and leave, and use her education to open the doors her parents had intended.

Leila's speculations were crazier than the conspiracy she and Tildie had thought up to explain the mayor's unflagging efforts to force her to leave Starlight. Mayor Jones simply wanted his daughter home . . . unless he had hired Mendoza. An interesting possibility, considering the mayor's trumped up report. Maybe she should discuss it with Sam.

Lucy took up her reticule from the nearby vanity, its lightness a reminder to retrieve her little pistol from the bedside table. She checked to make sure the Remington was loaded, then dropped it into her bag. Mayor Jones's report needed attending to, but another task must be seen to first. Sam's generous campaign to find Blackie deserved her thanks, and she supposed she might add a small apology for that banner.

The ringing steps behind her told Lucy who her escort was today. She turned and smiled at Cleve. "So you have the boring duty of following me about town today?"

A dimple appeared above Cleve's thick moustache. "I don't think I could ever find your company boring, Lucy."

Saddened by the warm interest in Cleve's brandy-colored eyes, Lucy quickly directed her attention to the busy boardwalk ahead. "You're very kind, Cleve," she said, and continued on her way to the marshal's office.

"I was hoping—" Cleve stepped aside for a scolding mother with a petulant-faced son attached to each hand to pass between them. He stepped closer. "I was hoping I could talk with you alone this morning."

Lucy allowed herself several steps before replying. She didn't want to embarrass Cleve or herself, and his request portended both possibilities. "I'm pretty busy this morning, Cleve."

"I see," he said.

Lucy slowed her steps. She searched for words to explain, though his resigned tone made explanations unnecessary.

Time to move on and let Cleve do the same. A change of subject was badly needed. "How's your mother?" Lucy asked.

"Not too well, I'm afraid," Cleve replied.

"She's not ill, I hope," Lucy said, and returned the nod from a passing woman whose name always slipped her mind, a miner's wife who had joined the temperance league later on. Most of the people she passed were civil, if not overly cordial. Lucy accepted the first and understood the latter, a balance she found comfortable.

Cleve tipped his hat to the woman. "No, nothing like that," he replied. "She's worried about her pie sales."

"Oh," Lucy said, a sharp stab of guilt cutting off any other reply. She cleared her throat and tried harder. "Tildie and Leila mentioned that the league was moderating their efforts. I imagine word will spread and business will pick up."

"No doubts about that," Cleve replied, "but I don't know if Ma can hold on that long."

Lucy stepped down from the boardwalk to an intersecting roadway. She turned as Cleve joined her in his loose-limbed jingling way. "I'm truly sorry, Cleve. I feel a great deal of the blame is mine."

"There's plenty of blame to pass around," Cleve said. "That whole temperance thing got away from all of us." He leaned against the building and propped his boot on the wall behind him. "I tried to warn Sam on this very corner, but he thought the ladies would get bored with it all and eventually give it up."

Lucy recalled the sparse attendance at the temperance meetings and all the dithering and bickering before Maggie had given the ladies something to rally around: the brave and dedicated Lucy Drummond.

"Sam shouldn't have underestimated Maggie Thompson," she said. *None of them should have*, she thought.

Cleve looked out over Main Street. "I guess all of us thought the marchin' and Leila's drum were kinda' comical, but no one's laughin' now."

Following Cleve's gaze, Lucy remembered her first sight of Main Street, how determined she had been to make this journey to Starlight a success. Instead, she had been instrumental in bringing hardship to people she had grown to care about. She spotted one of Sam's posters tacked up on a telegraph pole across the road, but she couldn't make out exactly what was printed on it.

She crossed over to get a better look, Cleve's ringing footsteps trailing behind. In bold black letters, the reward was printed at the top of the poster. A description of Blackie was included below with instructions to bring information to the marshal's office.

"Sam's wanted poster for that cat has liven'd things up a

bit," Cleve said. "He's taking a pretty good ribbin' about the whole thing."

Lucy heard Cleve's comments, but her thoughts were occupied with the formation of a plan to set things right. "I suppose Maggie printed these up for Sam," she said.

"I took Sam's order over there last night," Cleve replied. "She said they were her last job."

Lucy spun around to face Cleve. "She's leaving?"

"Said she had a sick aunt that needed her . . . something like that. I say good riddance."

"When was she leaving?"

"Didn't say," Cleve replied. "Probably as soon as possible. She isn't too welcome . . . hey, what's got you in such a—"

"Come on, Cleve," Lucy said, already on her way down the boardwalk. "We've got to stop her. She's got to get out one more edition of the *Starlight Observer.*"

Lucy hurried past the shops and businesses with Cleve close behind her. She side-stepped Mr. Pollard's busy broom and surly looks, gave a distracted wave to Lettie King, and peeked inside the marshal's office. Sam sat at his desk, his usual scowl deepening as she passed, and the mayor gave her one of his sour cherry frowns.

She slowed her pace as she approached the boarded-over front of the *Starlight Observer.* The newspaper office held a deserted air and Lucy lengthened her stride. She noted the closed door with a sense of dread. Maggie usually opened that door at eight o'clock every morning and it didn't close until eight each night.

Lucy peered through the dusty glass pane in the door and found the interior dark, the press and printing equipment standing silent.

Grabbing Cleve's sleeve, Lucy pulled him toward the end of the building. "Maybe she's upstairs," she said.

A train's lonesome whistle brought her to an abrupt halt. "What time is it?" she asked.

"That'll be the nine o'clock eastbound coming in," Cleve replied, consulting his pocket watch. "Running late this morning," he added, and closed the cover with a snap. "It's nine-thirty now."

Lucy glanced at the still, silent newspaper office, then set out for the train depot at the opposite end of town. "We've got to catch her, Cleve."

Cleve trotted up beside her. "It's too late, Lucy."

"You don't know that until you've tried," she replied. "Come on." Lucy stepped off the boardwalk and onto the road. "We'll make better time down here."

"What's that girl up to now?" Mayor Jones asked.

Sam watched Lucy rush past his window, her skirts lifted to show slim ankles and a brisk pace. His deputy followed after her, his long, rangy legs taking wide steps to keep up with her. Sam shook his head.

"I have no idea," he replied, and didn't think he wanted to know. A dangerous frame of mind.

"Probably something to bring more trouble to the town," the mayor muttered. "She should be on that train with Maggie this morning."

Sam didn't offer any arguments to that statement. He couldn't agree more. "I hadn't heard Maggie was leaving."

"Saw her on the way to the depot with her bags packed," the mayor replied. He leaned forward in his chair. "Isn't there some way we can speed the Drummond girl's departure? I want my Caroline home."

"Caroline hasn't changed her mind?" Sam asked. He hadn't heard from David in over a week, and he didn't know if that was a good sign or bad.

"Of course she wants to come home," the mayor replied,

and sat back. "I had to wire her Monday to stay where she was until this risky Mendoza matter is settled. Sent her some money, too," he added with a flourish of his hand.

Sam drew his mouth into a tight frown. He still didn't know what to make of David's silence. He had hoped . . . hell, he had his own problems. Like who hired Mendoza and a townful of suspects with no apparent motive.

He gave the corpulent mayor a long study. "You ever hear any talk about Otis Tyler?" he asked, and took careful note of the mayor's reaction.

"Who?" B.F. asked.

"The man Mendoza's partner killed at the Painted Pony."

Knitting his brows, the mayor tilted his head to the side and scratched his neck, his lower lip drooping. He shook his head. "Can't say that I have, except right after the killing." He looked at Sam. "And no one claimed to know him back then. You heard anything else?"

Satisfied with the mayor's reaction, Sam rose from his chair and walked over to the window. He hated suspecting people he had known for years, but someone had written that note yesterday, and that someone had hired Mendoza.

"Not a thing," he replied.

"Wouldn't it be safer for the Drummond girl to go home?" B.F. asked. "The whole town would be relieved."

One person out there would be especially relieved, Sam thought. He searched down the road but could no longer spot Cleve or Lucy.

"She's bound and determined to identify Mendoza and testify at his trial," he said.

"I thought she would leave after losing the schoolmarm's position."

Sam turned around and faced the mayor. "That was nice work yesterday, B.F., telling the whole town about that report of yours."

The mayor drew himself up. "I had the town's best interests in mind, as you should, Sam," he replied.

"You had Caroline's interests in mind," Sam said, but he was beginning to wonder.

"I see no difference," B.F. replied. "That federal deputy is only guessing that Mendoza is heading this way, and there're no guarantees he'll be caught. This waiting could last for weeks."

"One of the other deputies sent word this morning that Mendoza was seen over at Kingston," Sam replied. "Whit rode out not ten minutes ago. The three of them will track him down for sure," he added, trying to sound confident.

Mayor Jones pursed his lips and his brow wrinkled.

"Something wrong?" Sam asked.

The mayor's anxious expression quickly cleared to his usual bluster. "No, no. That's good news. The sooner this business is cleared up, the better off Starlight will be. I was just thinking about Miss Drummond and hoping the marshals don't miss Mendoza."

Sam took another long look at the mayor. "This sudden concern for Lucy surprises me, B.F."

"I know I've been hard on the girl, but I had to think of my Caroline's welfare. You'll have to agree, Sam, that David is hardly the best husband material."

Sam raised a brow. "I can understand why you're worried, but David has potential. Marriage might be just the thing he needs."

"I'd feel better if they were here," B.F. replied. He rose from his chair and walked to the door. "Keep me informed on the Mendoza situation. Caroline's waiting to hear."

"I'll do that, B.F.," Sam replied.

He waited until the mayor had left, then returned to his desk. Tapping a pencil on his unopened mail, Sam recalled that note waiting for Lucy yesterday. A threat had been implied, but he was certain the writer had only wanted to scare her.

B.F. could have done it, but despite the mayor's odd reactions, Sam had a difficult time picturing him writing notes, throwing rocks, and stabbing hats. Throwing insults and stabbing people in the back were more the mayor's style. Still, he would keep a close watch on him. Whoever had hired Mendoza would be getting mighty desperate now.

Sam rose from his desk and started for the door; he better find out what Lucy was up to. He reached for his hat hanging on the rack by the door and turned to find Dolf entering the office.

"Trouble?" Dolf asked.

Sam settled his hat on his head with a tug in front and back. "Why do you ask?"

"You look like you're on your way to a fight," Dolf replied.

"Did you see Lucy and Cleve just now?"

"I saw them headed for the depot. She looked pretty determined about something."

"That's where I'll be," Sam replied. "I've got to tell her to stay at the hotel until we hear from Whit."

Dolf crossed his arms and nodded his head. "Don't envy you, my friend. No, sir. Know just how you feel."

Sam pushed Dolf aside with a deep scowl. "Very funny," he said, and started down the boardwalk.

"I'll let you know if anyone comes in with information about Lucy's cat," Dolf called after him.

Sam increased his pace and soon couldn't hear Dolf's soft, raspy chuckles. He jerked at his collar. Dolf didn't understand. This was business and wasn't the same as Leila using his drum. Not the same at all.

"Damn," he muttered, and hurried toward the depot.

CHAPTER 16

"You can't leave now," Lucy said.

Maggie picked up her bags and walked around Lucy. "My aunt needs me," she said, and pushed open the train station's door.

Lucy followed her out onto the platform. The train's whistle called in the distance and she gave a worried glance down the tracks. Thin streamers of smoke floated above the treetops, and the rails rumbled and sang. She didn't have much time.

Maggie hadn't appeared pleased to see her at all and had given Mr. Jenkins a tongue lashing for the late train, as if the stationmaster had control over the vagaries of steam locomotives and washed-out tracks. Turning to Maggie's tight-lipped profile, Lucy sympathized with him. Predicting train arrivals must be like dealing with steamed newspaper publishers and washed-out causes—one had to be prepared to deal with tough customers.

Lucy gave her spectacles a shove. "The town needs one more issue of the *Starlight Observer*," she said. "Leave on

Monday's train. I'll help finish up the printing and distribution."

Maggie sliced those sharp gray eyes over her, then turned to look for her train. "My aunt needs me as soon as possible."

Lucy moved to block her view. "You're running out on Dolly and the rest of the women who trusted you."

"Don't lecture me about trust, Lucy Drummond. I gave you a job when no one else would, took you into my home, but you made a fool of both of us over that no-good marshal."

"Sam had nothing to do with yesterday," Lucy said, then took a deep breath. The locomotive had nosed around the last bend. "All I'm asking is for one more issue," Lucy shouted over the shrill call of the train whistle. "We owe these ladies—"

"*I* owe them nothing." Maggie picked up her bags as the train rolled into the station, bell ringing and spewing steam. The engine hissed and screeched past them, making conversation impossible, followed by the rattling, clacking passenger cars. Gradually, the train slowed to a sighing, clanking stop.

Lucy leapt into the momentary lull. "But, Maggie—"

"I thought you were a smart girl, Lucy," Maggie replied, and handed her bags up to a waiting porter. She climbed aboard but turned at the top step. "Forget Sam McQuaid and pack your bags. Run, Lucy. Run back to Boston. Starlight's no place for you."

Clenching her hands into frustrated fists, Lucy watched Maggie disappear inside the train. Getting out another issue would be up to her now, and she wasn't sure she knew enough about the printing process. She might not even have a press; Maggie could have sold it. Anything was possible.

She spotted Maggie taking a seat by an open window in

a car farther down the platform. Rushing to a spot below it, she called up to the woman. "What about all of your equipment?"

Maggie gave Lucy one of her assessing inspections, then thinned her mouth with decision. "A banker in Kingston will be coming by as soon as he hears there's no issue on Monday," she said, and slammed the window closed.

"All aboard," the conductor called, and the train cranked and wheezed out of the station.

"So that's the way it is," Cleve said.

Lucy turned a disgusted frown to the tall young deputy. "Can you imagine?" she said. "A bank in Kingston had backed the *Starlight Observer*."

Cleve looked down at her with an odd mixture of pity and disappointment. "That's not what I meant," he said. He gave a nod and glanced past her shoulder.

Puzzled by Cleve's odd behavior, Lucy looked behind her. Sam McQuaid waited on the other side of the platform. He wore an expression as grim and forbidding as the first time she had seen him, and like that time, a disturbing rush flowed through her. Only today, that restlessness, that confusion of mind and body had a name: desire.

She recalled those notices posted all over town for Blackie and remembered Leila's crazy assumptions. One had only to look at Sam's controlled reserve to know that he allowed little to pass beyond that commanding exterior. Sam McQuaid wanted no one, needed no one, least of all her.

"Cleve, it occurs to me that our hearts and our brains should be connected in some way," she said.

"Life would be a lot simpler," he replied. "Happier, too."

She glanced back into his warm brandy eyes, eyes that comforted and clung to merriment despite the edge that sharpened them. "I'm sorry, Cleve."

Cleve looked down, passed a finger over his moustache, then gave a squinting look at Sam. "I am, too, Lucy. For both of us."

With no reply for Cleve, Lucy left him standing by the empty tracks and started for the other side of the platform and Sam. She had only traveled a few steps when she heard Cleve's spurred tread following her across the platform. Each ringing stride made hers that much more difficult, but she never hesitated.

On closer inspection, she noted Sam's uneasiness and her thoughts turned immediately to Blackie. "Did you hear something about the cat?" she asked.

"Nothing like that," Sam replied. He looked past her to his deputy. "Go over to the Outpost and tell Sarge that Mendoza was seen over at Kingston. Whit rode out to meet up with those other deputies, and they're scouring the countryside. I'll want to see both you and Sarge at the office in thirty minutes."

Cleve nodded and gave Lucy a look she couldn't decipher, then he left without a word to either of them.

Sam watched the young man stride down Main Street toward the Outpost, then turned a pointed expression to her. "I'll be glad when all of this is over," he said.

"No more than I," Lucy replied, and stepped down from the platform. She started down the road, and Sam fell in beside her.

Glancing over the busy thoroughfare, Lucy had difficulty imagining that quiet afternoon torn apart by gunfire, but Mendoza's cold-blooded intent to shoot her remained sharply etched in every darkened window, around every shadowed corner.

"They'll probably catch Mendoza this time," she said, fishing for reassurance. "I mean, he doesn't know the federal marshals are on his trail."

Sam gave a noncommittal, "Maybe."

Lucy passed him an irritated frown, then looked ahead. "He wouldn't actually come into town looking for me."

"He's seen that last *Observer* if he's been through Kingston," Sam replied. "Whit thinks he'll take the chance. Don't forget, witnesses have disappeared before."

Lucy picked up her skirts and dragged her feet up the two steps to the boardwalk. "I'm not likely to forget that, Sam."

Sam caught her arm and gestured toward a shade tree with a bench built around it. "That's what I wanted to talk to you about."

She sighed, thinking of all the work waiting for her, work she couldn't allow her fears to delay, but she complied with Sam's request. She stepped back down to the road and, walking quickly to the tree, took a seat on the bench. Sam joined her but remained standing, resting a booted foot next to her skirt.

He crossed his forearms on his thigh and leaned toward her. "You've got to stay put in your hotel room until we get Mendoza locked up."

Lucy held her hands in her lap. "But, Maggie left."

"And you were trying to catch her," he replied, then frowned at being lured off course. "What has that got to do with anything?"

"Starlight needs one more issue of the newspaper," she replied. "You know, to spread the word that Starlight's temperance troubles are over. That last issue had such an impact. I thought another might undo some of the damage, but Maggie wouldn't stay until Monday."

"I'm not surprised, but . . . don't tell me. You're planning to publish the next issue yourself."

"I have to, Sam. I'm the only one who knows enough to pull it all together, and if it's not out Monday, some banker in Kingston is going to come and take away all of the equipment."

Sam pushed back his hat. "Kingston. I should have checked Maggie out, but someone was always distracting me, turning those spectacles of hers to stars and shacks and old stray cats and making trouble."

Not particularly interested in hearing another list of her transgressions, Lucy rose abruptly to her feet. "I have work to do and—" she looked into his smoky-blue eyes, so guarded and hardened "—and none of that matters now."

With a none-to-gentle push on her shoulder, Sam convinced her to sit back down. "It matters plenty, Lucy. The truth is that you distract me, and I can't be distracted now. Someone could get hurt, even killed. That day in the street, you stepped right into my line of fire. Don't ever do that again. I've got to know where you are. I've got to know that you're safe."

Sam's declaration took Lucy by surprise. She took a moment to respond. "Sam, I appreciate your concern, but this is important. Dolly's pie business is in trouble, and I imagine many others are, too. I can fix—"

"What can you fix if you're dead, Lucy?"

"Sam, we don't know—"

"That's right," Sam said. "We don't know. We don't know who hired Mendoza. We don't know if whoever it is won't try to take care of Mendoza's witness so there can't be a trial. We don't know anything except that you're in grave danger." He paused then continued in a softer voice. "That puts me in danger, too, Lucy. And Cleve and Sarge and Dolf."

Biting her lip, Lucy turned her anxious expression toward Main Street. Sam's statement made sense. She didn't want to cause more trouble, but she needed to do something to help the townspeople recover. A compromise must be reached.

Lucy thought of the mayor's fraudulent charges against her father. "If we knew who had hired Mendoza, much of the danger would be lessened."

"But we don't know and aren't likely to," Sam replied.

She looked intently at Sam. "I think I might know who hired Mendoza to kill that man."

Sam studied her imploring eyes, her determined little chin. "I'm listening," he said.

Lucy looked around them to make sure no one was near enough to hear. "Who has worked hardest to make sure I left town?" she said in a lowered voice. "Benjamin Franklin Jones, that's who."

"The mayor?" Sam recalled the mayor's earlier visit and his own conjectures about the mayor's possible guilt, but he didn't want Lucy interfering. "B.F. has plenty of reasons why he wants you to leave Starlight, but I can't think of one reason he would want Otis Tyler killed."

"Well, that doesn't mean there isn't one," she countered. "There's something strange about the mayor's desperation. Why has the man resorted to repeating this pack of lies about my father? Leila and Tildie told me about yesterday's meeting, and they believe—"

"Hold it right there," Sam said. He slid his foot to the ground. "I have something back at the hotel you'd better see."

Lucy noted the lines deepening around his mouth. He must be planning some unpleasantness. "What is it?" she asked.

"You'll have to see for yourself," he replied.

Frowning slightly, Lucy rose from the bench. "All right," she said. "But, I'm telling you. The mayor—"

Sam touched her elbow to prod her along. "We'll talk about it up in your room."

"This isn't a trick?"

"I wish it were, Lucy."

Sam had never appeared so disturbed. Worried, Lucy started for the hotel.

Lucy opened her door to late morning sunlight beaming in through the window. A tall vase filled with blood-red roses had been left on the bedside table, and their heavy aroma closed around her as she entered the room. She walked immediately to a window and opened it to a fresh pine-scented breeze.

Pacing the carpet, she listened to Sam rummaging around inside his room. Like always, each step he took filtered through the wall between them, a sound she anticipated and dreaded each night.

Today, she didn't hear the clink of glass on glass or catch a faint, spicy whiff of cigar smoke. Today, she waited for those doors to open and reveal the cause of Sam's silent, troubled escort back to the hotel.

Each heartbeat increased her apprehension. Holding her hands close to her, rubbing them together as if warming the coldness from her heart, Lucy passed by the mirrored doors to the wardrobe and stopped. There, behind her pale, pinched expression, she saw the dark mahogany doors surrounded by rose-trellised wallpaper. She couldn't look away.

The doors swung open and Sam emerged from between them. He walked toward her as if he were coming to her from another place, another world, then she noticed the large brown envelope in his hands. A whisper, a sigh through her thoughts, told her that Sam held her own

Pandora's box. She met his sober gaze in the mirror. "Do I really need to see this, Sam?"

"I think you do, Lucy."

She looked at herself in the mirror and didn't like the doubts she saw behind the round glass lenses, her rose-colored spectacles. She turned to Sam and accepted the envelope without comment or hesitation.

One corner held the imprint of the Boston Police Department, and the envelope was addressed to Sam McQuaid, Town Marshal, Starlight, New Mexico. Lucy looked up at Sam.

"You sent for this?" she asked.

He nodded and his mouth tightened. "Not long after you arrived."

"But why?"

"I . . ." His frown deepened, then eased into a crooked half-smile. "You're a curiosity, Lucy Drummond."

Unsure what to make of that statement, but affected more than was wise by that engaging twist to his mouth, Lucy returned her attention to the envelope.

"This has something to do with my father's murder," she said, preferring the obvious to the inevitable. "I really don't want to know all the details." Lucy met his blue eyes once more.

The little smile had vanished. He held his hand out to her. "Then don't open the envelope, Lucy. Give it back to me and don't read the report, but don't publish a rebuttal of the mayor's Pinkerton report."

"Pinkerton report?" Lucy said, surprised to learn that the mayor's accusations stemmed from the famed detective service. "I didn't know. . . ."

She looked at the envelope once more and slid her fingers along the rough, dry paper toward the string-tied closure.

She suspected there was much she didn't know and the time had come to lift the lid of mystery at last.

Fighting her reluctance, Lucy unwrapped the string and slipped out a sheaf of papers. She walked over to the window and adjusted the shade. Taking a deep breath, she studied the first page.

Sam watched the blood drain from her face. The defiant pout he found so irresistible trembled then disappeared as she pulled her lower lip between her teeth. Her hands shook as she shifted the first page to the back and began the second, but she kept on reading. Her shoulders drooped slowly as she read the third and last page. Damn, he was forever giving her bad news.

Until today, he had thought she had known the truth, perhaps had been running from it. Instead, she had been trying to change her world into the truth she wanted to see. Like that house and that old cat.

Sam joined her by the window and took the report from her lifeless fingers. "I'm sorry, Lucy."

She lifted her watery eyes to look at him through the round glass lenses. "So much is clear to me now," she said. "The whispers I endured at school, the sudden silences when I approached. And so many lies, Sam. My mother's, my family's. No one told me about my father's dirty deals, his . . ."

Lucy closed her eyes, held them closed tightly, and raised her trembling fingers to her pale, hard-pressed lips. She took a deep breath.

"No one told me about his suicide," she whispered, and opened her bewildered eyes. "I had made my father into a hero, an honest man I measured all others by." She blinked and focused on Sam. "I . . . I must apologize for all those accusations . . . for misjudging you."

"We both made mistakes," Sam replied. He searched for

something to say, anything to lift the pall of disillusionment that dimmed her autumn eyes. "That's all in the past . . . your father, all of it."

Lucy shook her head. "He deserted her, Sam. Ran away and left my mother to face all the hardship alone. Just like I did."

"That's not the way I see it," Sam said. He shoved the report into the envelope and placed it on a nearby table. "Your father took the coward's way and you're no coward. It took guts to come out here to marry a man you didn't know, to stay against all the odds. You didn't abandon your mother. You were scouting new territory."

"You don't understand," she replied. "I hated Boston, I hated attending a school where no one spoke to the Irish girl. I hated the thought of spending my days working in a factory like my cousins. I didn't belong anywhere. Boarding that train wasn't difficult and staying was . . ."

She turned to the window. "I had to stay," she finished.

He stepped closer to her, wanting to comfort her, but didn't know how and hated feeling so helpless. Instead, he took on the mantle he was most comfortable wearing: command, responsibility, protection.

"Lucy, move away from the window," he said.

She folded her arms around herself and wandered over to the vanity where she sat on the bench, her eyes fixed on the carpet. Sam reached for his watch but didn't pull it from his pocket. His deputies could wait for a while. He found a chair and pulled it up beside her. He wasn't leaving her alone like this.

Sam lifted her chin with the crook of a finger. "Maybe I understand more than you think," he said.

She brushed his hand away. "Oh, Sam. I can't imagine—"

"Now that would be a first," he replied, and was rewarded with a tremulous smile that didn't last long.

"Those days are finished," she stated. "I must see things as they are."

Strange how her statement didn't bring him the pleasure he had thought it would. "All right," he said. "Hear me out, then look at yourself the way you are."

She brushed away a tear under her spectacles. "I'm listening."

"I was raised on a hard-rock farm in Kansas by a father who was as ungiving and as stubborn as the land. The droughts, the grasshoppers, the blizzards—he survived them all, but my mother didn't. She died right after David was born. I held her hand and watched the life bleed out of her. I was nine years old."

"Oh, Sam," she said, her voice as hushed as the quiet hotel. "How . . . how terrible."

Sam dropped his gaze from her sad, soft eyes. He leaned forward, resting his elbows on his knees, and clasped his hands. "Pa left David's raising to me, along with all my chores and helping in the fields. It's a wonder the boy didn't die, but he thrived—more than the farm."

He looked down at hands that once had been dirty, cut, and calloused but were smooth and clean now. "The years went by and Pa got meaner with each failed crop. Finally, I had enough and at sixteen took Davy to our grandparents in St. Louis. I joined the Army and let them raise him."

"But you had no choice."

He looked up at Lucy. "Not then, but later . . ." Sam frowned at the memories but plunged ahead. "Later, when I went to visit David on leave, I could see what was happening to him. My grandmother spoiled him, smothered him, gave him everything he wanted. I should have mustered out sooner, Lucy, finished raising him. I made men out of kids just like him. I could have made a difference, but I didn't. I stayed in the Army, telling myself he was safe in the East and my regiment needed me."

Sam shook his head, found his hands easier to study than Lucy's sympathy and remembered all the years that had sped by as he educated himself and rose from the ranks. "I guess I needed the Army, too."

He grimaced and faced her again. "Finally, when our grandparents died and David had gone through the money they had left him, he came out here and I bailed him out of one fix after another, thinking, hoping that he had learned his lesson after each mistake, until he did something I couldn't forgive. He sent for a bride and left her standing on that train platform all alone."

Lucy lifted her hand and hesitated, then brushed a feather's touch to the corner of his eye. Sam held his breath.

"You aren't responsible for the way David turned out," she said, then lowered her hand to her lap. "You thought you were doing what was best."

Sam took her hands in his. "And so did you, Lucy."

She squeezed his fingers. "I almost made it, didn't I?"

Sam had to swallow back the tightness in his throat. "One of these days, you're going to win big, Lucy. You're going to make one of your wishes come true."

She looked deeply into his eyes, blue and gray, crisp and clear. "I know just the one it will be, too."

Sam swallowed again and withdrew his hands. He sat back and slapped his palms on his thighs. "My deputies are waiting for me. I better be—"

"You better listen, Sam McQuaid," she said, and lifted her chin. "I'm going to print and distribute the last issue of the *Starlight Observer*."

Sam's relief lasted an instant too long. He missed his

chance to stop her before she had risen from the bench but
caught her arm before she turned toward the door.

"I can't let you leave the hotel," he said, and rose to his
feet, circling his fingers around the small bones of her wrist.

"Sam, you aren't being reasonable."

"And I suppose you are," he replied.

Lucy pulled free of his loose grasp. "You needn't sound
as if the prospect were impossible," she said, and planted
her hands on her hips.

"All I'm saying is that staying here in the hotel makes
better sense than having you down on the street."

"Until?"

"Like I told you," Sam replied. "Until we get Mendoza
locked up."

"What about who hired him?" Lucy asked. "Do you plan
to keep me locked up until after Mendoza's trial?"

"If I have to," he replied. "I'm going to make sure you get
back safely to Boston."

Lucy dropped her hands and turned away from him.
"Can't you ever stop seeing me as another of David's
mistakes?"

"You are my responsibility, Lucy."

She sat down on the bench once more and looked up at
him. "I have responsibilities, too, Sam. The town needs that
last issue of the paper."

Sam retrieved his report from the table and walked to the
door. "Then you better start wishing Mendoza is brought in
soon and he tells us who hired him." He left without looking
back.

CHAPTER 17

"Are you sure you want to do this?" Lucy asked, and fixed her uneasiness on her two companions.

"I wouldn't miss it," Leila replied.

Tildie crossed her arms. "Just try to leave me out."

Lucy paced the rose-garden carpet before her two friends, who had returned to their positions of the morning meeting. "I really don't like involving you two, but I can't get the paper ready by Monday without your help."

"I don't see how anything could go wrong," Leila said from the center of the bed. "Dolf is on duty out front. I'll talk to him while you sneak out the back. You're wearing different clothing and a shawl over your hair. Anyone watching will think you're one of the staff. We'll tell our husbands we're going to the suffrage meeting, then we'll join you at the newspaper office. Once you let us in, we'll barricade the doors and not leave until the last issue of the *Starlight Observer* is ready for distribution."

Tildie gave her a gracious bow of her head. "An excellent plan, Lucy."

Lucy found her seat on the small bench. "Thank you,

Tildie," she said. "I tried to think of every precaution. I don't want to endanger anyone."

"Everyone in town knows you're up here," Tildie said. "You'll probably be safer over at the newspaper office."

Leila nodded her agreement. "Dolf is certain the deputies will bring in Mendoza," she said. "There are only so many trails between here and Kingston."

"From what you've told us about the note attached to your hat, I am sure one of those saloon owners must have hired those gunmen to kill that poor man," Tildie said. "That Englishman hasn't been seen for a couple of days. Most likely he's the one and has cleared out of town."

"I wish . . ." Lucy stopped and cleared her throat. "I'll be glad when all of us can go back to our regular lives."

"You're still planning to go back?" Leila asked, her voice softened by the merest touch of sadness.

Lucy glanced out the window to the dark wreath of worn-down peaks revealed through gentle waves of lace curtains. She had hoped to view those peaks through her own window and her own lace curtains, but her scouting trip was over.

She couldn't hold back a little sigh but managed a smile for Leila. "My mother needs me, but I'll keep in touch with both of you."

Tildie rose from her chair and came to stand beside her. She placed a hand on her shoulder. "You'll find another teaching job," she snapped her fingers, "like that, then some fine young man will come along and you'll be sending us letters filled with baby news. All of this unpleasantness and your father's scandals will be behind you."

Lucy patted her hand. "Thank you, Tildie." Telling the ladies about her discovery that day had been difficult, but talking about her father had lightened the heaviness from her heart. Sam had helped her through the worst. He was capable of giving so much, but he always withdrew behind an aura of authority and command that kept everyone at a distance. But she couldn't think of Sam now. She needed all of her wits and strength to pull this off.

Lucy rose to her feet. "Let's get to it," she said. "I've written several articles to get us started. You'll have to help me with headlines."

Leila scrambled off the bed in an unladylike show of stockings and petticoats. "How about 'Starlight Shines Again'?" she said, sweeping her hand in front of her.

"Keep that thought, Leila," Lucy said.

"Yes, keep it to yourself," Tildie added.

The ladies gravitated toward the door and Lucy followed them, smiling broadly at the raised brows and an exchange of huffs. She had a feeling that the next twenty-four hours were going to be interesting.

Leila was first to reach the door. She rested her hand on the doorknob. "Let's hear you come up with something better, Tildie Schindler."

"I'll be thinking on it," Tildie replied.

"That was just off the top of my head," Leila said, demonstrating her point with a wave of her hand.

Lucy placed a hand on each arm. "Ladies, don't forget— not a word past this door."

Both nodded and chorused, "Of course not."

"Just a reminder," Lucy said. "Talk over what you plan to bring for supplies but be careful. If Sam learns of this before we get started . . ." Lucy didn't want to think of those consequences Sam was always talking about.

"Don't you worry," Leila said. "We'll eat like queens. Dolf will be here and Gus will think Tildie's taking refreshments to the meeting."

Lucy shook her head. "All of this trouble because Sam McQuaid is—"

"Trying to take care of you," Leila said.

Lucy sighed. "Yes, but does he have to be so overprotective?"

"Yes," Leila replied. "Now, I'll be downstairs talking with Dolf. Will fifteen minutes give you time to dress and get out the back way? I don't want him to suspect anything."

"Fifteen minutes should give me plenty of time," Lucy replied. "I'll see you ladies in an hour or so."

Leila opened the door and led the way into the hallway. Lucy closed it to their soft but quiet conversation. She hoped they would be careful.

Lucy quickly changed into the plain dress Tildie had brought her and draped a white shawl around her hair, which she had fashioned in a plain knot atop her head. As an afterthought, Lucy removed her spectacles and put them in her skirt pocket. She could see well enough to make it to the newspaper office.

Spreading a skirt on the bed, she tossed in the things she thought she might need and the stack of articles she had worked on all afternoon. She would show Sam McQuaid once and for all that she wasn't a silly schoolgirl who sat about wishing on stars and worrying about cats.

Thinking of Blackie pulled her brows into a frown. Surely, someone would find him. She had asked Cleve to take some food out to the old house, and he had promised to check it later. That's all she could do for now.

Lucy tied her bundle together, then inspected herself in the wardrobe mirrors. She did look somewhat different, and if she kept her face lowered, no one would be the wiser. She thought over each step of her plan once more, and the only thing that could go wrong was if Whit rode in with Mendoza and someone came to fetch her, but that wasn't likely to happen.

The only thing she needed to worry about was when Sam found her down at the newspaper office. She could weather that storm. She had to get that paper out.

Grabbing her reticule, Lucy opened her door and peeked both ways. The hallway was deserted. Holding the bundle next to her chest, she moved swiftly down the hall to the back stairs. The door was locked, but Tildie had given her a key. It was longer than the one that opened the upstairs entrance to Maggie's apartment and was easy to find in her skirt pocket. Soon she was out the door and down the stairs to freedom.

Walking quickly behind the buildings, she made good progress down the alley. At every intersection, she stopped and looked toward Main Street, then hurried across the open space. Her plan was working perfectly.

Behind the jailhouse, she detected Sam's voice through the barred windows just above her head. She stopped to listen. Her heart gave a flutter at hearing the conversation revolved around a black and white cat, then plummetted to her toes when she caught Sam's denial that the cat was Blackie. She had to believe the big cat was all right, that she would see him again, even if she couldn't keep him. The alternative was too sad to ponder.

She moved on, keeping to the tall shadows of late afternoon and saw no one else. Squinting her eyes, she could make out the back steps to the newspaper office in the next block. Her luck was holding out for once, she thought.

The intersection brought her to a stop, and she gave Main Street a quick glance, then looked again at the horse-man riding slowly by: the canvas duster, the star, that old, beat-up gray hat. The rider had to be Whit Prescott riding past.

Peering around the edge of the loosely woven shawl, Lucy's eyes lingered on his hat. Whit had pulled the brim down low and he was slouched in his saddle. The poor man was exhausted and returning empty-handed and down-hearted. She didn't feel much better.

Well, she might as well go ahead with her plan. She just hoped Sam wouldn't be eager to bring her the bad news Whit was so obviously carrying. She rushed past the opening between the buildings and made for the stairway that led to Maggie's back door, more determined than ever to reach the newspaper office.

With her goal so close, Lucy didn't slow her pace, spurred on by a growing excitement. She counted off all the tasks waiting for her: editing stories to fit pages, setting type, looking up past ads for Starlight's businesses. They deserved some free advertising. She wouldn't run any ads that had come in from Kingston.

With a sense of relief, Lucy grasped the banister and started up the first step when someone called out to her. Her heart thudded against her ribs and she glanced over her shoulder. Whit Prescott had dismounted next to the wood-pile stacked against a deserted mining office and was walking towards the *Starlight Observer* building. He must have seen her with those sharp eyes of his.

Lucy gathered a handful of skirt and started up the stairs again. She would keep him talking long enough for Leila and Tildie to make it down here. Maybe a story for the paper could be pulled out of him. Something about Mendoza, or perhaps a piece about his adventures as a deputy U.S. federal marshal. Thinking of all the questions she could put to the federal lawman, Lucy fished around in her pocket for the key to the door.

Whit's progress rang out with each step he took. Lucy paused as she was about to place the key into the lock. She didn't recall Whit wearing spurs. She shrugged. Most likely he did when he was riding, she thought, and worked the key into the lock. To her disgruntlement, she discovered she had chosen the wrong key.

Whit's steps grew closer. She made a quick exchange of keys, and just as she felt a hard jab in her back, she remembered Whit hadn't worn spurs in Sam's office that day and he had come right off the trail. He had worn a white duster just like . . .

"Newspaper lady, you owe me," an accented voice hissed against her ear. "You said that town marshal would be at supper when we got rid of your little problem."

"Thought I'd find Whit over here," Dolf said.

Sam passed a black-and-white cat to Dolly and gave Dolf a questioning look. "Thanks for taking her in, Dolly," he said, and brushed at the cat hair on his coat.

Dolly hugged the purring feline to her. "I'm sure we'll be fast friends," she said. "I'll mention you have some more that need adopting at the suffrage meeting tonight," she added.

"I'd appreciate that," Sam replied.

He waited until Cleve's mother had left the office then turned to address Dolf.

"Whit hasn't made it in yet," Sam said.

Dolf ducked a look through the door that led into the jail cells. "I saw him riding in not fifteen minutes ago," he said. "How many cats you planning on taking in?"

Sam joined Dolf at the door and gave a shake of his head to the four cats sporting various blotches of black and white penned into one of the jail cells. Each one had staked out a corner and was calmly napping or grooming.

"How many black-and-white cats can there be in the county?" Sam asked.

"I guess you'll find out," Dolf replied with a slow grin.

Sam leaned his shoulder against the doorjamb and crossed his arms. "What was I supposed to do, Dolf? Let them run all over town?" He jerked his head toward the cell. "Better pick out the one you want before Leila picks one out."

"We aren't taking one of those damn cats," Dolf stated.

"She told me she would be by tomorrow."

Dolf gave him a look he hadn't seen since the big blacksmith had used it on ten-thumbed recruit trainees, but Dolf ambled into the cell room and scowled down at the scraggly collection of homeless cats.

"I don't know what Whit will think when he sees this," Dolf said, and squatted down for a better look.

Sam had deliberately avoided asking about Whit. If the deputy hadn't come directly to the office, that meant he didn't have good news. "He better be worried about what I'm going to think when he comes in here empty-handed. He shouldn't have talked Lucy into this idea."

Dolf looked back at him. "He didn't talk Lucy into staying. She had other reasons. I'm glad Whit showed up and brought along his friends."

"If she hadn't made that promise to stay and testify, she would have boarded the first train out of here after losing the schoolmarm's position."

Dolf stood and pointed to the scarred head of a veteran glaring at him from under the bunk. "I'll take that one," he said. He wrapped his hand around one of the bars and turned to Sam. "You gonna let her leave when this is over?"

Sam pulled out his pocket watch and checked the time. "Of course I am."

"You're lettin' a fine woman get away. I think you need some of those spectacles of hers."

Sam snapped his watch closed and walked back into his office. He shuffled through papers on his desk. "When did you say you saw Whit? We might as well hear what he didn't find."

Dolf studied his old friend a moment, then shrugged and walked across the office to the window. "He should be coming along. I know I saw him coming this way when I was saying good-bye to Leila. Cleve came along to take my place, and when I looked back, I didn't see him on the street."

"Probably stopped to stable his horse," Sam said. "He'll be along."

"You expectin' Gus?"

Sam tossed down the newest wanted posters, Mendoza's among them, and joined Dolf by the door. "He's supposed to be keeping an eye on Lucy," he said. "She had some crazy notion about printing another issue of the paper to help out the businesses."

Dolf glanced back at him. "That Lucy's a strong woman. And a fighter, too. She even stands up to bullies like you."

Sam gave him a scowl as he stepped out on the boardwalk to meet Gus. The little man scampered along, looking over his shoulder and mopping his brow with his handkerchief.

Gus stepped up onto the boardwalk. "Marshal, I couldn't get away sooner." He looked over his shoulder. "Tildie will make sauerbraten out of me if she finds out I've come down here, but I had to let you know."

Sam exchanged a worried glance with Dolf. "Come on in the office, Gus," he said.

Dolf stepped aside, and Sam led the way into the cool interior of the adobe building. "What's happened?"

"Tildie and Leila were upstairs visiting Lucy and I listened from inside your room. They're planning on barricading themselves inside the newspaper office and printing another issue of the paper. Lucy disguised herself and slipped out the back way. I couldn't get away from Tildie until now."

Gus turned to Dolf. "That was part of Lucy's plan. Tildie and Leila were to make sure you and I were occupied while she slipped away."

"Pretty good plan," Dolf said.

Sam grabbed his hat and reserved his comments; they weren't worth repeating. "Dolf, go find Leila and stop her. Gus . . ."

Gus stared at him and made a face as if he had just swallowed a mouthful of cod liver oil.

Sam put on his hat. "Gus, you tell Cleve to come back to the office and wait for Whit."

The little man nodded and mopped his face. "I'll do that, Marshal."

Sam stalked out the door and headed for the newspaper office. Any man who got mixed up with Lucy Drummond had no idea of the trouble he was in for.

"Find that key, *gringa*."

Lucy tightened her mouth at the gun poked in her ribs and ran her trembling hands through the weeds and sand below the stairway, purposely ignoring her fingertips as they brushed against the key she had dropped from the landing.

"Find it quick, or I will lose my patience," Mendoza said.

Lucy swallowed back the sour taste of fear. "I'm doing the best I can."

She was convinced he wouldn't shoot her. Even this dolt would know the sound of gunfire would bring people back here. For a man purported to be so cunning, Mendoza had proven himself easily duped into believing she was Maggie's assistant and knew the combination to her safe.

When they got inside, he would soon learn Maggie didn't have a safe. She hoped to put that eventuality off as long as possible—long enough to get a chance at her Remington.

A sharp snick, a hard yank on her hair, and a knife at her throat persuaded her to locate the key. She held it up. "Found it."

He leaned close to her ear and held the knife just below her eye. "If you lose it again, I will cut you," he said, his words smelling as foul as their message.

Lucy blinked her agreement, not daring to move her head.

Mendoza jerked the key from her hand. *"Bueno."* He stepped back and gestured with his knife. "Back up the stairs, *gringa,* and no tricks." He grinned, showing the gap between his teeth. "It would be a shame to carve up a pretty face like yours."

Thanking God she hadn't worn her spectacles, the first and usually last feature men noticed about her, Lucy clutched her reticule to her and ducked under the stairway.

"Faster," Mendoza said.

A hard shove sent her sprawling across the stairs, and her bag knocked loudly against the wooden steps. Lucy ignored an array of painful scrapes and scrambled to her feet, hoping Mendoza hadn't noticed the sharp sound of the Remington hitting the wood. She made quick work of the first few steps, his ringing footfalls following slowly behind her.

"Very good, *gringa*. You learn quickly," he said. "Now tell me where to find Lucy Drummond."

Lucy jerked at her skirts and held the reticule close to her body. She slowly pried her fingers inside. "Word got around that you were in Kingston and she left on the morning train." Her hand closed around the little pistol's smooth grip. "She was going back to Boston."

"You are lying, *gringa*," he replied. "I know she's still here."

Taking another step, Lucy held on to her gun and fought the fear rising to her throat, clutching at her breath. On the next step, she would turn and fire. She couldn't miss.

Lucy raised her foot and lifted the little pistol slowly from her bag. She stepped, hesitated, then turned halfway around.

"Whit, stop her."

Sam's voice stunned her as much as Mendoza's arm whipping around her and jerking her to his chest. He yanked her around to face Sam, the knife blade tickling her throat. She couldn't see Sam, only the sky above and a faint glimmer of the evening star. She closed her eyes, said a prayer, and held on to her Remington.

"I'll kill her, lawman," Mendoza said. "I'll slit her throat. Now drop your gun."

Lucy heard the dull thump of Sam's revolver hitting the ground. Waves of panic washed over her and rolled through her stomach. She grew numb and hardly felt the steps beneath her feet as Mendoza pushed her ahead of him down the stairs.

"Don't move, Lucy," Sam said.

Mendoza's arm tightened around her. "*Lucy*, you are a very tricky girl." He laughed. "My devil's luck never fails. Step back, lawman."

Lucy's foot touched the ground, and she caught her first sight of Sam. She was close enough to make out his expression: his face was a stone mask of hatred and his eyes held the promise of death, never once wavering from the man holding her.

Lucy gripped her little gun. Sam had told her on these very steps to never get in his line of fire again and here she was. But Mendoza couldn't go for his gun, either. Only she was armed with a pistol. And she must use it. Reversing her little gun into an awkward upside-down position that pointed the barrel backwards, Lucy's stiff fingers fumbled with the hammers.

Mendoza edged them toward his horse. "Lawman, stay in front of me where I can see you."

As the blade stung her neck, Lucy hooked the hammer and fired. Mendoza dropped the blade in a flurry of sputtered Spanish. With a hard jab of her elbow, Lucy twisted out of his slackened grip and dove to the ground.

Two sharp blasts sounded from the direction of the stairway. Lucy rolled to her side in time to see Sam fire another round from his prone position. Then silence.

Sam shifted position and looked at her, though without her spectacles, Lucy couldn't make out his expression through the haze of dust. In a heartbeat, he was on his feet and Lucy pushed herself to a seating position.

"You all right?" he asked on his way over to Mendoza.

Not trusting her voice, Lucy nodded. She dug her spectacles out from her pocket and attempted to straighten the bent wires. Her hands shook so badly, the task was nearly impossible and took her most concerted efforts. Thankfully so, because she couldn't look at the man sprawled no more than five feet from her.

She cleared her throat. "Is he . . . ?"

Sam came over and knelt in front of her, taking the eyeglasses from her hands. "Yes," he replied. He pulled a handkerchief from his pocket and touched it to her throat. "Hold this, Lucy. You're bleeding."

Lucy pressed her hand over his and looked into the smoky swirls of his blue eyes. He didn't move, just looked at her, his concentration intense and mesmerizing.

Shouts and trampling feet gradually made their way into the stillness. Sam slipped his hand from beneath hers and began working on her spectacles.

Lucy watched his deft fingers reform the fragile wires. "Maggie hired Mendoza," she said. "He came to ask her for more money because she had told him you would be at supper when he and his partner killed Otis Tyler."

Sam slipped the earpieces over her ears, his fingers brushing sensitive skin that sent tingles up and down her body. He tipped the lenses higher on her nose, then folded his hands and simply looked at her.

"If not for you, I would have been," he replied.

Lucy dropped her gaze and shook her head. "You've been right all along. I don't belong in Starlight."

Sam tipped her chin up. "I have to say that every time you've caused me trouble, it was because I pushed and you shoved back. You're a fighter, Lucy. You've got enough sand to live wherever you want."

A crowd of people flowed into the alley and Sam rose to his feet. He helped her to stand, and she found her legs to be as shaky as her hands. She leaned on Sam for support as he led them away from the body.

Sam made quick explanations to all the questions, telling about her fancy pistol work. Lucy watched him take control of the situation with a few words and gestures, while gently stroking her stiffened shoulders before Tildie and Leila arrived and swept her aside with generous hugs.

"Cleve, saddle up the Colonel and collect a posse," Sam shouted. "We've got to try to find Whit." He turned to her. "Tildie, you take Lucy on back to the hotel. She's had quite a scare."

Lucy pulled his handkerchief from her neck and stepped forward. "I still have a newspaper to publish," she said in a strong, steady voice. She looked at Sam for arguments, but he only gave her a crooked smile and walked away.

She turned to Tildie and Leila. "Time's running out, ladies. Let's get to work."

CHAPTER 18

Sunday night was quiet in Starlight.

Lucy stood on the boardwalk in front of the *Starlight Observer* and breathed in the pine-scented air she would miss so much. Tildie and Leila's footsteps faded into the soft strains of a Spanish guitar and Lucy knew she would miss so much more. She tucked the last issue of the *Starlight Observer* under her arm, and without a backward glance at the dark and silent newspaper office, she started for the hotel.

Across the road, the saloons were open but not nearly so boisterous as they had been last night. She smiled at the memory of the miners and cowboys who had come by to see the lady who had gotten the drop on Raul Mendoza.

No one seemed to care how she had done it. That item in the paper describing her less than fantastic upside-down, backward shot to the man's thigh should set the record straight. Not that it mattered anymore. Her smile faded at the thought of tomorrow, and she walked on toward the marshal's office.

With each step, she recalled the people she had met in

Starlight. Many of them had stopped by, even a grumpy Mr. Pollett, who had wanted to take advantage of the free ads. Most simply wanted to chat, Maggie's devious plots a favorite topic. Starlight had harbored a big secret after all. Sam had discovered that Otis Tyler was a bank teller from Kingston.

Murdering the man had been an extreme measure, but then, Maggie had carried things to their extremes.

Tildie and Leila had spent considerable time trying to figure out how Maggie had managed that rock through the window. A paid child was most likely the culprit, they thought. No one had confessed, and Lucy doubted anyone would. Possibly Starlight had other secrets only Maggie knew, and she had used a little blackmail. Lucy liked to think Tildie didn't know everyone's sins, but the matter certainly had given her friend fits.

The marshal's office loomed just ahead and Lucy slowed her steps. She was about to end the circle of her journey to Starlight and she wasn't eager to close the last link. Passing the window, she peered through the dusty glass. Sam sat at his desk. He appeared to be writing a letter, or perhaps a report. A quick inspection revealed no one else. He was alone.

She stepped through the door and heard a cat meowing from the back room. Well, almost alone, she thought, and smiled.

Sam tossed his pencil to the desk when he heard her come in and sat back. His blue eyes moved over her, only his reserve no longer made her uneasy. She understood the mannerism for what it was, a distancing tactic to keep others at bay and uninvolved.

"You look pleased tonight," he said. "Finish up the newspaper?"

"Enough so that Pete Cassidy can print tomorrow," she replied. Dreading to move on to the purpose for this visit, Lucy ventured into more comfortable territory. "I was thinking of Starlight's newest citizenry of black-and-white cats," she said.

The corners of Sam's mouth tightened. "I'm sorry we didn't find Blackie."

Lucy examined her ink-stained hands. "Me too," she replied. She sighed and gave him another small smile. "At least your search has helped some of his friends and saved Whit Prescott's life."

Sam shook his head. "Doc says he'll make it."

"That's good news." Lucy ran her hands over the top rail of a chair, the question she needed to ask glaring at her, but she couldn't face it. Not yet. "Have your telegrams helped track down Maggie?" she asked.

"She's disappeared, but I'll find her," he replied, his tone calm, flat, and lethally determined. "She ran out, leaving you to face the consequences of her deal with Mendoza."

"She tried to frighten me away, and I think she tried to warn me the day she left, but I—"

"Didn't listen," he said.

Lucy frowned, his comment skirting too close to the question she still must ask, though it stuck in her throat like a rock. She glanced up at him. "Do you have many cats left?"

"Only two," he replied. "Sarge is going to take one over to the Outpost. Named him Dice. I think the girls over at Nell's will take in the other one."

Lucy gripped the chair. "How nice," she said, and decided the time had come to close the circle. She cleared her throat and gave her spectacles a push. "Sam, I'll be leaving on tomorrow's train. I . . ." She took a deep breath.

"I'll . . . I'll need that ticket money," she finished in a rush.

His sudden scowl surprised her. "I'm sorry," she said. "I don't have quite enough saved from sewing."

"No, no, Lucy." Leaning forward, he crossed his hands on his desk. "I just . . ." He swiped a hand over his mouth and threw his shoulders back. "I'll get your money."

Sam pulled open a drawer and took out an envelope. He set it on the edge of his desk. Lucy saw that her name had been written across the front. Sam had expected her to come back for it and here she stood. All of her vows and hopes and wishes had come to nothing, just as he had predicted.

Stepping around the chair, Lucy retrieved the thick envelope without a look or a word to Sam and started for the door. She couldn't bring herself to say thank you.

"Lucy."

She stopped but didn't turn. "Yes, Sam." She closed her eyes, embarrassed at the eagerness that had slipped past her guard. His chair scraped back, and she listened for the sound of boots crossing the wooden floor. The Regulator on the wall ticked off the seconds, and gradually her heart slowed to the clock's rhythm.

"I hope your journey home is a safe one."

Lucy held back the sigh rising from somewhere deep inside and held her shoulders straight. "I hope so, too, Sam." She walked out the door and into the night.

Sam moved away from his desk and ambled over to the doorway. Leaning against the doorjamb, he took out a cigar and lit it, his eyes never leaving the woman with the crown of golden hair and gently swinging skirts. He couldn't look at her enough, not after seeing her with Mendoza's knife at her throat. He took a puff of his cigar but couldn't rid his mouth of a sudden metallic taste.

What would become of a woman like Lucy? Probably settle down with some town man who'd give her a passel of kids. Best thing for her—a nice young man with a good, safe job and possibilities.

Sam leaned farther out. What in the hell was she doing? He saw her pull one of Blackie's wanted posters down from a telegraph pole and slide it into the newspaper under her arm, then she walked on toward the hotel on the corner. Sam settled back against the doorjamb. Hell, he wished someone had found that cat.

A scowl fell over Sam's features. Lucy didn't stop at the hotel but walked right past it and turned at the corner. The woman was going off looking for that cat!

Sam clamped the cigar between his teeth and started after her. His long strides and a shortcut through several back lots brought him up behind Lucy before she had ventured too far down the moonlit lane that led to the old house. Sam tossed his cigar to the dirt and crushed it beneath his heel.

"Hold up there, Lucy," he called out.

She stopped abruptly and turned around. "Must you always sneak up on people?"

Sam closed the gap between them at an easier pace, enjoying the play of moonlight on her hair, her defiant pout charmingly displayed. "Comes in handy on occasion," he said.

"Not this one," she replied. "There's no use arguing with me. I'm going out to the house. I have to see if—"

"I know, Lucy," he said. Sam lifted his hand and gestured down the lane. "Let's go."

She gave him a long considering look, then shrugged. "I'm glad you see it my way," she said, and started down the narrow dirt road again.

Sam shook his head and walked along beside her, enjoying the warmth of the night air.

Lucy walked along in silence, Sam's dark presence both a comfort and a torment. Midnight strolls along deserted country roads weren't her favorite activities, but she couldn't leave tomorrow without one more search for Blackie.

"I want you to know that I realize finding Blackie out here is only vaguely possible," she said.

"That's never stopped you before," Sam replied.

Lucy cut him a quick glance and discovered that moonlight and Sam's crooked smile did odd things to her stomach. She stared at the shadowed roadway ahead and picked up her pace. She wanted this torture to end as soon as possible. Being with Sam, knowing this was all she would have of him, played havoc with her resolve to remain reserved and controlled.

"It's not impossible." She frowned, realizing she'd spoken out loud. "About finding Blackie, I mean. Cleve has been leaving food out here. Blackie might have been lured back."

Sam didn't mention the other possibility, the most likely possibility. Something must have happened to the old son-of-a-gun. His nine lives had most likely run out. But he'd hate to see Lucy throw the dice one more time and lose, so he gave her the encouragement she needed.

"Who knows, Lucy? Maybe he'll be sitting on that front porch."

Lucy gave him an odd look. "No gloom and doom, no lectures on my waste of time—my rose-colored spectacles?"

Sam pulled at his tight collar. "I was simply offering a little hope."

Lucy took a step in front of him and turned, forcing him to stop. She stared at his bothersome collar, then jerked at the end of his tie.

"Take this off, for pity's sake." She busied her fingers untying it. "You do nothing but pull and tear at it."

She slid the tie from his neck and stuffed it into her pocket, then unfastened his collar and threw the stiff thing into the bushes. She looked up at him and smiled.

"Now, isn't that better?"

The evening breeze cooled the warmth from her touch. "Yes." He rubbed at his neck. "I suppose it is."

"I thought so." She started up the long incline that ended with a view of the house. Sam followed her, keeping his thoughts to himself.

She stopped just before they reached the top of the small hill. Being taller, he could see over the rise to the clearing below. The tall pine cast a shadow over most of the yard and the house, but the moonlight brightened the porch. He pulled his mouth into a stiff line. No cat.

He looked down at Lucy and found her staring up at the star-filled sky. "Making wishes?"

She gave him a winsome half-smile. "Wishes can't hurt," she replied. "That's what they're for. Giving a little extra nudge to the possibilities."

Sam nodded, preferring a loaded Peacemaker and two aces showing, but he didn't say so. "You ready?" he asked, eager to end her heartache.

Looking ahead, she held her smile for a moment longer. "I'm ready," she replied.

Sam took her arm, and together they topped the rise. He felt her hesitation and knew she had seen the empty porch, but not saying a word, she forged on and he stepped along with her, offering his arm around her shoulders for comfort and support.

Lucy stared at the empty porch and accepted the warmth Sam provided. "I had wanted Blackie to be here so badly," she said.

"I know, Lucy," Sam replied quietly.

She didn't say more but continued to walk, continued to hope. "I have to make certain," she said.

Lucy appreciated the firm squeeze to her shoulder. The gesture said more than any words. Maybe he understood her at last—understood she couldn't give up until she knew all hope was gone. The packet of money in her deep skirt pocket brushed against her thigh with each step she took, reminding her she had given up on Sam.

Sam McQuaid knew nothing of love, the enduring power that held two people together through every storm. No one had ever given him love. He couldn't know how to return it.

Yet, Sam had shown her patience, when clearly he was a man who had little. He had wiped away her tears when no one had ever shown him how. He had strengthened her spirit when she knew his was so weary. Tonight, he followed her wishes and hopes when she knew he believed them to be a waste of time. Perhaps if she had given him enough of her love, maybe that day in the woods, he would have lowered his guard and taken a chance.

Lucy frowned at the empty porch. She had missed her own chance. She had been too frightened, too unsure, too careful. The one time since beginning this journey to Starlight, when she had used caution and had thought things through, she had made the biggest mistake of her life. Tomorrow she would probably make the next one, but she didn't know what else to do.

They stepped into the deep, moon-dappled shadows under the pine and Lucy stopped. She looked over the old house. Under the kinder moonlight, she imagined once more how it might have looked.

"My mother's curtains would have looked nice in the windows," she said, her thoughts rolling off her tongue.

"They'll look nice in another house," Sam replied.

Lucy glanced up at him and noted the hard line of his mouth, a sure sign of his displeasure. He didn't say more, nor did he look at her. She looked back at the house, and a seedling possibility took root in the fertile ground of unanswered prayers.

"Perhaps." She slipped from beneath his arm and walked to the house, up the steps to the porch.

"Watch out for the loose boards up there."

"I'm looking for them." Lucy set her newspaper down and proceeded carefully over the broken boards, and remembering Leila's suggestion wondered if they were two-by-fours.

She peered into the dark house. "Kitty, kitty, kitty," she called.

"That cat's no kitty," Sam said. He gave a sharp, shrill whistle.

Lucy turned and propped her hands on her hips. "You whistle for dogs."

Sam hooked his thumbs in his gunbelt and whistled again. "You black sinner, come on out," he called.

To Sam's utter amazement, a shadow separated itself from the darkness beneath the porch. A white crest shown in the moonlight and a cat's gold eyes glimmered at him. With a deep, rolling meow, the cat trotted out to him and rubbed against his leg.

"Sam, look!" Lucy cried as she stepped down on the first board. "Sam, I can't believe it!" She took another step down. "You found him."

Sam bent down and scratched the old reprobate's rough fur atop his head. The cat lifted his head into Sam's hand, obviously enjoying himself. Sam knelt to one knee and gave the cat a rub under his chin. Blackie stretched his neck back, and Sam could have sworn the blasted cat gave him a furry smile.

"*You* found him, Lucy," he said. "You believed and you found him."

Lucy dropped to her knees beside him. "Do you think he'll let me pet him?"

"He'd better." Sam gave her a quick smile.

"He never would before." Lucy sat back on her heels. "I wonder what made him come to you like that?"

"You just have to know how to talk to tough characters like him," Sam said. He lifted his hand to her knee and the cat rubbed against Lucy's skirts, his tail twitching for more attention. "I think he missed you."

Lucy ventured a finger behind the cat's ear. He dipped his chin and she rubbed his head, then gave him a full body rub. Soon a rough, loud purring rivaled the wind slicing through the pine.

Lucy looked up at Sam. "I dreamed it would be like this." She dropped her gaze to the cat and gave him another long stroke. "Well, almost like this."

Blackie gave a lick to his front leg, then trotted away, bringing an end to the petting session. Lucy watched him collapse to the ground in a boneless heap not far away and give them a blinking perusal.

Sam tipped back his hat. "Arrogant fellow, isn't he?"

Lucy glanced up at Sam's sharp profile. "Yes, his kind usually is."

He turned an odd expression to her; something about his eyes—perhaps the moonlight—was disturbing and tantalizing at once. Those blue eyes held her attention as they always had, and she knew she didn't want to make any more mistakes.

Sam gave her spectacles a nudge. "I'd say you're partial to his kind," he said.

Lucy rose up on her knees, fitting herself against Sam's thigh. She tossed his hat to the side. "I'd say you're right."

His large hands grasped her waist and he pulled her closer, close enough to feel the hard evidence of her effect on him press into her abdomen. With a boldness he inspired, Lucy inched in closer still, rubbing his hardness against the heat building in her.

"You must be crazy," he said, his voice low, rough, little more than a growl.

Lucy brushed her fingertips over his full lower lip, then along the square angle of his jaw and, remembering her reaction to his touch, to the soft skin below his ear.

"I must be," she whispered.

She swept her fingers into his hair, pulling his head toward her. He wrapped his arms around her and captured her mouth in a long, hungry kiss, her tongue meeting, stroking each thrust of his.

Heat spilled into her breasts, flushing her nipples into rosy sensitivity, demanding appeasement. She curled her arms around his neck and moved closer to the solid warmth of his chest.

Sam groaned and lifted his mouth, ending the kiss with a flick of his tongue to the corner of her lips. "Lucy, this is—"

"Magic, Sam." She splayed her fingers against his beloved face, holding him still, keeping him near. "One night, one wonderful night of magic."

He turned his lips to her thumb and brushed his lips against the pad. "I can stop now, but not later."

Lucy touched his dark brow so often drawn into a scowl. "Don't stop the magic."

"Lucy, the cons—"

Lucy kissed him, hard and sure, giving him all her love,

her hopes, her desires. Sam took over, bending her against his thigh, one arm supporting her shoulders, while his hand reached between them and closed over one breast, gently squeezing its soft fullness. Her heart raced, flooding her body with a tingling sensation that pooled between her legs, and Lucy discovered the full, opulent world of desire.

Sam released her mouth and pulled them both upright. Breathing heavily, his eyes never leaving hers, he unbuckled his gunbelt and set it aside, then his hands went to the front of her blouse and started to work on her buttons.

Her own breath coming in ragged, uneven gasps, she gave his fingers trembling assistance. Her blouse floated to the soft bed of pine needles. His jacket followed, then other items of clothing found their way to the accumulating pile. His vest and shirt, her skirt, petticoats, corset and stockings. Her shoes and his boots were thrown aside. All accomplished in feverish haste, one helping the other, never speaking.

Down to her chemise and knickers, Lucy laid back on the soft jumble of clothing and propped herself on an elbow. Sam stood over her, clothed in only his drawers. Moonlight and shadows drew shifting patterns over his muscled physique, revealing a welted scar running across his rib cage. She saw other scars, too, white and stark in the brief flashes of moonlight. He had endured a rough, dangerous life, and she understood why his eyes had seen too much pain.

He ran his hand down her arm. "This is your last chance, Lucy."

Lucy lay back and lifted her arms to him. "I know, Sam."

He hesitated and Lucy was glad she couldn't see his eyes, afraid she might see cold reserve stealing over the smoky blue. Still, she held her arms out to him, offering him all she had to give.

Sam had never wanted a woman more than he wanted the woman lying among her petticoats. Black lace and red satin had nothing on prim white cotton.

Sam lay down within the circle of her arms, holding himself above her on his elbows. Lucy's luscious mouth spread in a smile and she slid her hands down his back to his waist, then trailed her fingertips over his skin, tracing his lance scar and a dozen others he had forgotten.

She planted a soft, butterfly's kiss to his chin and a quick stab of desire stole his breath, urged him past his last doubts. Moving in closer, he straddled her thigh, taking pleasure in the firm, warm caress to his arousal.

"See what you do to me," he said.

She kissed his chin again, this time her tongue tracing its cleft. "Yes."

She shifted beneath him and rubbed her thigh against his swollen flesh. He caught his breath, not knowing if the slight movement was planned or accidental.

He wanted to see her eyes. Propping himself up on an elbow, he took off her eyeglasses and set them carefully out of harm's way. She blinked up at him with round apprehension, but the lovely medley of colors held a fiery eagerness, too. He'd have to go slowly, gently.

"You have beautiful eyes and," he started pulling pins and combs from her hair, "the prettiest hair. I've wanted to tell you that for a long time."

"Why didn't you?"

Sam tugged the last pin free and ran his fingers through her hair, watching moonlight flash streaks of gold through it. "I don't know."

He kissed her again, tasting her tongue, her teeth, every delicious part of her mouth. Her breathing quickened, and he remembered how she had rubbed her breasts against him.

His hand slipped beneath her chemise and explored her soft, flat stomach, caressing her ribs, inching up to the fullness of her breasts. She shuddered with reaction and he deepened his kiss.

Gently kneading one breast, then the other, his thumb found each pointed crest and teased it to the hard little nub he had felt through her chemise. Sam trailed kisses to her earlobe, gently grazed it between his teeth, then helped her to sit up. He wanted to see all of her bathed in moonlight.

Leaning back on her stiffened arms, she watched him with eyes filled with sultry heat, her mouth swollen and wet from his kisses. His gaze strayed to the dark circles puckered against their cotton covering. He slowly unbuttoned the top, then reached up and drew her chemise slowly off one shoulder, then lower until the thin material dropped from her rosy nipple.

He touched the tight nub, squeezed it, heard her low moan, then kissed it, swirling his tongue around the swollen peak, suckling the sensitive flesh, drawing pleasure from her soft little cries.

Lucy could no longer hold herself up. She caught hold of Sam's muscled arms, and reveled in the hot, wet pulling at her breast. He lifted his head at last and kissed her mouth, lowering her to their nest of clothing, where he trailed more kisses over her throat, telling her how beautiful she was, how much he wanted her.

He pushed her chemise to her waist and kissed her quivering stomach, trailed his tongue along her ribs, licked the underside of her breast, then caught her nipple once more in a hard, suckling caress. Fire shot to her core and she rubbed herself against his thigh, her hands roaming over the hard muscles of his back.

He rolled away from her and pulled down her knickers and chemise. She kicked her underclothing from her ankles, then hugged him to her, pressing her breasts to the hot skin of his chest. His hand smoothed over her back, her bottom, her thighs.

Breathing in the smell of him, she kissed his chest, tasted the salty skin, twined her leg around his and pushed her need against his hardness. "Sam," she breathed. "Sam, I . . ."

She didn't know what she wanted. Something urgent and powerful, something to fill the empty longing burning inside her, something to relieve this aching need.

Sam tilted her lips up to his and kissed her long and deep. She pushed against him again, telling him in the only way she knew of her longing.

He released her and rolled away. Opening her eyes, she saw that he was unbuttoning his drawers and quickly averted her eyes. She lay back and looked at the stars sparkling through the pine's branches, knowing what was about to happen but not knowing, and the mystery intrigued and frightened her at once. She wanted the mystery to end, wanted the fulfillment to come from Sam.

He moved over her, shutting out the stars and the pine, shutting out everything but Sam McQuaid's smoky blue eyes and the feel of his warm, hard body. Brushing his hair back, she closed her eyes and trailed her fingers over his ears, down his neck and shoulders, memorizing his scent, the contours, the textures of his body. Her memories might have to last a lifetime.

"I . . ." She bit back the words she was about to say. Sam must know she loved him. She would put no conditions or burdens on him.

"Lucy, look at me."

She opened her eyes to the intensity of his.

· "I can give you the release you need and you can do the same for me without—"

"No, Sam." She drew her arms around his neck. "I want all you've got to give."

He kissed her and the magic started again. He caressed every sensitive part of her body, and some she didn't know existed until the touch of his fingers or tongue sent shivers of heat coursing through her, swirling in ever tightening circles to a center point of hot, burning need that demanded completion.

Finally he touched her where she needed him most, his fingers exploring gently, stroking her to a frenzy of wild desire. She clung to him, calling his name in a hoarse, raspy voice she hardly recognized. He nudged her thighs apart with his knee and she gladly welcomed his weight, accepting the tentative touch of his manhood to her melting core.

Slowly he entered her, stretching the tightness within her until a slight stinging caused her to stiffen. He hesitated, whispered something she didn't catch, then plunged through the thin barrier.

Lucy opened her eyes and gasped at the tearing pain. He didn't move but held her close, kissing her temple, her cheek, her lips.

"I'm—"

"Don't you dare say you're sorry," she whispered.

He looked down at her. "You're an amazing woman, Lucy Drummond."

She looked into his eyes, no longer distant and weary but sparked with admiration and passion. She wrapped her legs around his hips, allowing him in deeper still, the pain slowly ebbing with the renewal of her own desires.

"Hardly amazing, Sam."

"Is that so?" He gave her a long kiss, then began to move

within her. "I'd say you're the most amazing woman I've ever met."

Lucy closed her eyes and picked up his slow, even rhythm. He rotated his hips, giving her an added burst of pleasure deep inside. Lucy planted her heels beside him, setting a faster, harder pace, answering the need growing stronger with each pounding stroke. She rode the wind through the night to the stars above, hanging there for a brief, impossible moment, then falling into shuddering, gripping climax. Sam tumbled with her, calling out her name with his last frenzied thrust.

Sam rolled to his side, pulling her with him, holding her against his warmth, their bodies still entwined. Gradually, her breathing slowed with his, and she snuggled against his damp skin, breathing in his scent, knowing this was where she belonged. To this man. She waited, wondering if two-by-fours truly worked on mulish men as Leila had suggested. If not, she had no regrets. One night of magic was better than none at all.

Sam pulled what cover he could around them, mostly her skirt and petticoats, then settled back and she rested her head against his shoulder, her palm cupping the puckered scar along his ribs.

"Dolf Miller was right," Sam said.

"About what?"

"This and that," he replied.

She sensed he wasn't going to be more forthcoming so remained quiet. He didn't speak for a long while, and again she wondered what he was thinking. She wanted to ask but contented herself with his nearness, his caressing hand on her hip. After her long hours of work with only snatched catnaps, she grew sleepy. Her eyes drifted closed.

"Lucy."

"Hmmm?"

"You're not taking that train tomorrow."

Her eyes blinked open. "What about my mother?"

She caught the barest sigh.

"We'll bring her out here."

She lifted herself so that she could see his face. "What are you saying?"

"I'm saying . . ." Sam drew a big breath. "I'm saying you're going to marry me."

She raised her brows. "I am?"

"Yes."

"Why, Sam? Not because of this, not because of what happened tonight." If he mentioned one thing about his duty, his responsibility, she was going to put on her clothes and walk back to town.

He turned to her and took her chin between his finger and thumb. "Because I can't let you leave me. I can't face each day not knowing where you are, what you're doing, trusting another man to share his life with you. I need you, Lucy. I need someone to show me the possibilities and the magic." His thumb caressed her jaw and his mouth hooked into a smile. "Lots of magic. What it comes down to is I . . . I love you, Lucy Drummond. Will you take a chance on a stubborn, set-in-his-ways, saloon-owning marshal? Will you marry me?"

Lucy closed her eyes, absorbing the words into her very soul—words she had longed to hear from him for so long. She wanted to savor them before answering.

"Yes, I'll marry you."

He gathered her into a tight embrace, crushing her to him. Finally, he released her and she lay back once more, her head cradled between his shoulder and arm. Above her, the pine limbs creaked and sighed with the wind and the stars winked at her.

Sam combed his fingers through her hair. "I never had a chance, did I?"

Lucy looked past pine boughs, past the stars, and remembered her desperate prayer the day she had stepped off the train. "No, Sam. I don't think you did."

EPILOGUE

July 15, 1888

Dear Mother,

We received your curtains yesterday and Sam and I hung them in the parlor last evening. They fit the windows perfectly. You'll soon see how beautiful the mountains and our old pine tree look through the delicate pattern. I didn't like the way Blackie eyed them, so I'll be keeping a close watch on the blasted cat as Sam calls him.

Did I tell you in my last letter that Blackie now follows Sam and I into town every morning and presides over the marshal's office from Sam's desk? I wonder if the big bowl of milk Sam gives him makes the walk worth his efforts.

I know I told you David was coming to see us. The visit went better than I expected. He was a bit uncomfortable at first, but I asked so many questions about Army life, he soon got over his embarrassment and felt at ease. He's stationed at El Paso, Texas, which isn't far from here and I expect we'll see him as often as the Army allows. Army life appears to agree with David. He looked fit and self-assured, if a little sad.

Mayor Jones, you remember I've mentioned him before, hasn't heard from his daughter. All we know is Caroline boarded a train for California soon after her father sent her money. David never mentioned his wife during his stay and neither did we. I think he must have loved her very much.

Speaking of love, we may have a new romance blooming in Starlight. The schoolmarm we hired is a pretty red-head and she has led Sam's young deputy on a merry chase. I have a feeling Starlight will be looking for another schoolmarm soon, something Mary Elizabeth should think about.

I'm so relieved Aunt Ada is sending her with you. Not only is she my favorite cousin, but she had sense enough to stay in school. Both of you be especially careful in the larger cities. I haven't mentioned it before because I didn't want you to worry, but while waiting for my train in St. Louis, a young woman was robbed right in the station. I had just met her and another young lady when this dirty looking man ran by and snatched one of her bags.

She left for Denver quickly after the incident, then my train was called. I wonder about those two women from time to time. Our paths crossed so briefly, yet we shared something difficult to explain. Though very different in appearances, I suspect we were very much alike. We were striking out on our own, each seeking her fortune at her journey's end. I hope Lady Luck rode the rails with them as she did with me.

With love,

"Time to close shop," a deep voice called.

Lucy looked up and smiled at the man dressed in black filling the doorway. "I'll be just a minute longer."

Sam stepped into the room. "This isn't one of those two more pages minutes?"

"No." She signed her letter and placed it in a desk drawer atop a stack of dime novels. "This is one of those I can't wait to get home minutes." She closed the drawer and watched the tall, solemn-faced man approach her. A restless longing stirred through her, an excitement at once familiar and new, expected yet always surprising.

Sam took hold of her wrist and pulled her into his embrace. "Those are the minutes I like best."

Lucy curled her arms around his neck and explored the mysteries and promises in his smoky blue eyes. "Regretting your investment in the *Starlight Observer*?"

Sam gave her a soft, brief kiss. "Never," he whispered against her lips.

Lucy teased his mouth open with the tip of her tongue and kissed him long and deeply, then gave him a peck on his beard-roughened chin. "Promise?"

Sam tucked her head into his shoulder and held her tight. "Promise."

His reply rumbled comfortingly into her ear. Monday's editorial championing women's suffrage shouldn't cause too much of a disturbance.